The Desert Flowers - Rose

Judith Keim

BOOKS BY JUDITH KEIM

THE HARTWELL WOMEN SERIES:
> The Talking Tree – 1
> Sweet Talk – 2
> Straight Talk – 3
> Baby Talk – 4
> The Hartwell Women – Boxed Set

THE BEACH HOUSE HOTEL SERIES:
> Breakfast at The Beach House Hotel – 1
> Lunch at The Beach House Hotel – 2
> Dinner at The Beach House Hotel – 3
> Christmas at The Beach House Hotel – 4
> Margaritas at The Beach House Hotel – 5
> Dessert at The Beach House Hotel – 6
> Coffee at The Beach House Hotel – 7 (2023)
> High Tea at The Beach House Hotel – 8 (2024)

THE FAT FRIDAYS GROUP:
> Fat Fridays – 1
> Sassy Saturdays – 2
> Secret Sundays – 3

THE SALTY KEY INN SERIES:
> Finding Me – 1
> Finding My Way – 2
> Finding Love – 3
> Finding Family – 4
> The Salty Key Inn Series . Boxed Set

THE CHANDLER HILL INN SERIES:
> Going Home – 1
> Coming Home – 2
> Home at Last – 3
> The Chandler Hill Inn Series – Boxed Set

SEASHELL COTTAGE BOOKS:

A Christmas Star
Change of Heart
A Summer of Surprises
A Road Trip to Remember
The Beach Babes

THE DESERT SAGE INN SERIES:

The Desert Flowers – Rose – 1
The Desert Flowers – Lily – 2
The Desert Flowers – Willow – 3
The Desert Flowers – Mistletoe and Holly – 4

SOUL SISTERS AT CEDAR MOUNTAIN LODGE:

Christmas Sisters – Anthology
Christmas Kisses
Christmas Castles
Christmas Stories – Soul Sisters Anthology
Christmas Joy

THE SANDERLING COVE INN SERIES:

Waves of Hope – 1
Sandy Wishes – 2 (2023)
Salty Kisses – 3 (2023)

THE LILAC LAKE INN SERIES

Love by Design – (2023)
Love Between the Lines – (2023)
Love Under the Stars – (2024)

OTHER BOOKS:

The ABC's of Living With a Dachshund
Once Upon a Friendship – Anthology
Winning BIG – a little love story for all ages
Holiday Hopes
The Winning Tickets (2023)

PRAISE FOR JUDITH KEIM'S NOVELS

THE BEACH HOUSE HOTEL SERIES

"Love the characters in this series. This series was my first introduction to Judith Keim. She is now one of my favorites. Looking forward to reading more of her books."

BREAKFAST AT THE BEACH HOUSE HOTEL is an easy, delightful read that offers romance, family relationships, and strong women learning to be stronger. Real life situations filter through the pages. Enjoy!"

LUNCH AT THE BEACH HOUSE HOTEL – "This series is such a joy to read. You feel you are actually living with them. Can't wait to read the latest one."

DINNER AT THE BEACH HOUSE HOTEL – "A Terrific Read! As usual, Judith Keim did it again. Enjoyed immensely. Continue writing such pleasantly reading books for all of us readers."

CHRISTMAS AT THE BEACH HOUSE HOTEL – "Not Just Another Christmas Novel. This is book number four in the series and my introduction to Judith Keim's writing. I wasn't disappointed. The characters are dimensional and engaging. The plot is well crafted and advances at a pleasing pace. The Florida location is interesting and warming. It was a delight to read a romance novel with mature female protagonists. Ann and Rhoda have life experiences that enrich the story. It's a clever book about friends and extended family. Buy copies for your book group pals and enjoy this seasonal read."

MARGARITAS AT THE BEACH HOUSE HOTEL – "What a wonderful series. I absolutely loved this book and can't wait for the next book to come out. There was even suspense in it. Thanks Judith for the great stories."

"Overall, Margaritas at the Beach House Hotel is another wonderful addition to the series. Judith Keim takes the reader on a journey told through the voices of these amazing characters we have all come to love through the years! I truly cannot stress enough how good this book is, and I hope you enjoy it as much as I have!"

THE HARTWELL WOMEN SERIES:

"This was an EXCELLENT series. When I discovered Judith Keim, I read all of her books back to back. I thoroughly enjoyed the women Keim has written about. They are believable and you want to just jump into their lives and be their friends! I can't wait for any upcoming books!"

"I fell into Judith Keim's Hartwell Women series and have read & enjoyed all of her books in every series. Each centers around a strong & interesting woman character and their family interaction. Good reads that leave you wanting more."

THE FAT FRIDAYS GROUP :

"Excellent story line for each character, and an insightful representation of situations which deal with some of the contemporary issues women are faced with today."

"I love this author's books. Her characters and their lives are realistic. The power of women's friendships is a common and beautiful theme that is threaded throughout this story."

THE SALTY KEY INN SERIES

<u>FINDING ME</u> – *"I thoroughly enjoyed the first book in this series and cannot wait for the others! The characters are endearing with the same struggles we all encounter. The setting makes me feel like I am a guest at The Salty Key Inn...relaxed, happy & light-hearted! The men are yummy and the women strong. You can't get better than that!"*

FINDING MY WAY- _"Loved the family dynamics as well as uncertain emotions of dating and falling in love. Appreciated the morals and strength of parenting throughout. Just couldn't put this book down."_

FINDING LOVE – _"I waited for this book because the first two was such good reads. This one didn't disappoint.... Judith Keim always puts substance into her books. This book was no different, I learned about PTSD, accepting oneself, there is always going to be problems but stick it out and make it work. Just the way life is. In some ways a lot like my life. Judith is right, it needs another book and I will definitely be reading it. Hope you choose to read this series, you will get so much out of it."_

FINDING FAMILY – _"Completing this series is like eating the last chip. Love Judith's writing, and her female characters are always smart, strong, vulnerable to life and love experiences."_

"This was a refreshing book. Bringing the heart and soul of the family to us."

THE CHANDLER HILL INN SERIES

GOING HOME – _"I absolutely could not put this book down. Started at night and read late into the middle of the night. As a child of the '60s, the Vietnam war was front and center so this resonated with me. All the characters in the book were so well developed that the reader felt like they were friends of the family."_

"I was completely immersed in this book, with the beautiful descriptive writing, and the authors' way of bringing her characters to life. I felt like I was right inside her story."

COMING HOME – _"Coming Home is a winner. The_

characters are well-developed, nuanced and likable. Enjoyed the vineyard setting, learning about wine growing and seeing the challenges Cami faces in running and growing a business. I look forward to the next book in this series!"

"Coming Home was such a wonderful story. The author has a gift for getting the reader right to the heart of things."

HOME AT LAST – "In this wonderful conclusion, to a heartfelt and emotional trilogy set in Oregon's stunning wine country, Judith Keim has tied up the Chandler Hill series with the perfect bow."

"Overall, this is truly a wonderful addition to the Chandler Hill Inn series. Judith Keim definitely knows how to perfectly weave together a beautiful and heartfelt story."

"The storyline has some beautiful scenes along with family drama. Judith Keim has created characters with interactions that are believable and some of the subjects the story deals with are poignant."

SEASHELL COTTAGE BOOKS

A CHRISTMAS STAR – "Love, laughter, sadness, great food, and hope for the future, all in one book. It doesn't get any better than this stunning read."

"A Christmas Star is a heartwarming Christmas story featuring endearing characters. So many Christmas books are set in snowbound places...it was a nice change to read a Christmas story that takes place on a warm sandy beach!" Susan Peterson

CHANGE OF HEART – "CHANGE OF HEART is the summer read we've all been waiting for. Judith Keim is a master at creating fascinating characters that are simply irresistible. Her stories leave you with a big smile on your *face and a heart bursting with love."*

Kellie Coates Gilbert, author of the popular Sun Valley Series

A SUMMER OF SURPRISES – "The story is filled with a roller coaster of emotions and self-discovery. Finding love again and rebuilding family relationships."

"Ms. Keim uses this book as an amazing platform to show that with hard emotional work, belief in yourself and love, the scars of abuse can be conquered. It in no way preaches, it's a lovely story with a happy ending."

"The character development was excellent. I felt I knew these people my whole life. The story development was very well thought out I was drawn [in] from the beginning."

THE DESERT SAGE INN SERIES:

THE DESERT FLOWERS – ROSE – "The Desert Flowers - Rose, is the first book in the new series by Judith Keim. I always look forward to new books by Judith Keim, and this one is definitely a wonderful way to begin The Desert Sage Inn Series!"

"In this first of a series, we see each woman come into her own and view new beginnings even as they must take this tearful journey as they slowly lose a dear friend. This is a very well written book with well-developed and likable main characters. It was interesting and enlightening as the first portion of this saga unfolded. I very much enjoyed this book and I do recommend it"

"Judith Keim is one of those authors that you can always depend on to give you a great story with fantastic characters. I'm excited to know that she is writing a new series and after reading book 1 in the series, I can't wait to read the rest of the books."!

THE DESERT FLOWERS – LILY – "The second book in

the Desert Flowers series is just as wonderful as the first. Judith Keim is a brilliant storyteller. Her characters are truly lovely and people that you want to be friends with as soon as you start reading. Judith Keim is not afraid to weave real life conflict and loss into her stories. I loved reading Lily's story and can't wait for Willow's!

"The Desert Flowers-Lily is the second book in The Desert Sage Inn Series by author Judith Keim. When I read the first book in the series, The Desert Flowers-Rose, I knew this series would exceed all of my expectations and then some. Judith Keim is an amazing author, and this series is a testament to her writing skills and her ability to completely draw a reader into the world of her characters."

THE DESERT FLOWERS – WILLOW – "The feelings of love, joy, happiness, friendship, family and the pain of loss are deeply felt by Willow Sanchez and her two cohorts Rose and Lily. The Desert Flowers met because of their deep feelings for Alec Thurston, a man who touched their lives in different ways.

Once again, Judith Keim has written the story of a strong, competent, confident and independent woman. Willow, like Rose and Lily can handle tough situations. All the characters are written so that the reader gets to know them but not all the characters will give the reader warm and fuzzy feelings.

The story is well written and from the start you will be pulled in. There is enough backstory that a reader can start here but I assure you, you'll want to learn more. There is an ocean of emotions that will make you smile, cringe, tear up or outright cry. I loved this book as I loved books one and two. I am thrilled that the Desert Flowers story will continue. I highly recommend this book to anyone who enjoys books with strong women."

The Desert Flowers – Rose

A Desert Sage Inn Book - 1

Judith Keim

Wild Quail Publishing

The Desert Flowers - Rose is a work of fiction. Names, characters, places, public or private institutions, corporations, towns, and incidents are the product of the author's imagination or are used fictitiously. Any resemblance to actual events, locales, or persons, living or dead, is coincidental.

No part of *The Desert Flowers - Rose* may be reproduced or transmitted in any form or by any electronic or mechanical means, including information storage and retrieval systems, without permission in writing from the author, except by a reviewer who may quote brief passages in a review. This book may not be resold or uploaded for distribution to others. For permissions contact the author directly via electronic mail:

wildquail.pub@gmail.com
www.judithkeim.com

Published in the United States of America by:

Wild Quail Publishing
PO Box 171332
Boise, ID 83717-1332

ISBN# 978-0-9999009-1-8

Dedication

For all my readers ... without your love and support,
the beginning of another series would not be possible.
You are my desert flowers!

PROLOGUE

R ose Macklin stared at the letter in her hand and felt awash in memories. Alec Thurston was the one man she'd truly loved, and now he was dying and wanted to see her. She grasped the letter tightly in her fingers and walked over to the sliding glass door leading to the deck off her great room and stared out at Black Mountain from her condo in Henderson, Nevada.

Once she and Alec had liked hiking together in the Coachella Valley desert around Palm Springs. For six years, they'd laughed and teased and made love before he gently told her it was over. She'd been devastated, but she couldn't yell or scream at him. He'd been honest with her from the beginning of their relationship, two years after he'd hired her as the social director of his hotel, the Desert Sage Inn. She'd always known it wasn't a permanent thing. Not because he was promiscuous or a jerk, but because he couldn't get over the guilt of losing his wife and unborn child in a fire when he wasn't there to save them. That's why he couldn't stay long-term in any happy relationship. Twisted, but true.

She stared at the writing on the page:

> **"My dear Rose, I've been following your career and am pleased to know you're doing well. I hope you will consider coming to Palm Desert to see me. It seems I'm dying and need to make plans for the future."**

Rose closed her eyes to hold back tears. *Dying? He was only sixty-two. How could this be? He'd always been such a strong, vital man.*

She'd kept up with his activities too and knew about the woman he'd dated for a couple of years following their breakup. After that, he'd apparently had no other romantic relationships worth noting.

On this late January day, the air outside was cool. It might be a little warmer in Palm Desert, but even there, winter was chilling the air and clouding the sun.

She studied the letter again:

"If you're willing to come, please let me know your arrival plans, and I'll make sure to have someone meet you. You're welcome to stay at my house on the property. I have plenty of room. Things haven't changed that much around here in the last fourteen years."

She couldn't hold in a chuckle. Only someone like Alec would think of the last fourteen years as nothing. But then he was the kind of person who, if he made a friend, would keep that friendship regardless of how much time had passed between visits.

Yes, she would go to see him as soon as possible. The thought of Alec dying without her seeing him again was too painful to consider. He'd been the person who'd made her believe she was loveable.

Lily Weaver came home from work, threw the mail on the table in the entry hall, hung up her winter coat, and headed into the kitchen for a cup of hot tea. A glass of wine would come later when she got the energy to cook herself some dinner. As the office manager and only legal secretary in the law office of Bakeley & Dibble in upstate Ellenton, New York, she felt overcome some evenings from the workload of running the office, acting as personal assistant to both law partners, making sure they were following through on all their commitments, and scheduling more. In addition, she took care of her three-year-old niece three nights a week while her sister worked for a telecommunications company.

Sighing, she looked out at the snow and ice and wondered how she'd ever gotten herself into this horrible pattern of constant work and little else. She'd talked to the law partners about getting more help, but they were in no hurry to do so. Why would they? She did it all without anyone helping her.

She took a sip of the hot tea and, feeling better, went to pick up the mail in the hallway. She couldn't let things get behind at home, too.

When she saw the return address on a letter, her breath caught. It had been eleven years since she'd worked at the Desert Sage Inn and had enjoyed the warmth of both the desert and the environment at the hotel. Eleven years since she'd packed her bags and left the hotel heartbroken that Alec Thurston had kept his earlier vow to end their relationship if it got too serious. She knew from the beginning a relationship with him wasn't permanent, but she'd hoped she could change his mind.

With trembling fingers, she opened the envelope and read:

"My dear Lily, It is with great sadness that I tell you that I've been given a short time to live. I'm wondering if I might prevail upon you to come and see me. It's time for me to make plans for the future. If you're willing, please let me know your plans and

I'll arrange for you to be met."

Tears sprang to Lily's eyes. At almost forty-two, she was no closer to having the life she'd always dreamed of. Spending two years at the Desert Sage Inn during her early thirties was the closest she'd ever come to it. That time had provided an oasis of loving calm amid what had always been chaos for her. The thought of going back there was enticing. She continued reading the letter and decided that, like it or not, the law firm would have to find extra help, because she was going to be gone for a while. Her sister would have to understand her need to go, especially if Lily helped pay for a babysitter.

Willow Sanchez sat at her desk at Boston University grading papers for the Business Writing course she was teaching in the School of Hospitality Administration. It was appalling to realize how few students were fully prepared for her class. Misspelled words, poor punctuation, and difficulty in making clear statements were problems for too many students. She knew social media had adversely affected the correct way to communicate at a high level, but still, it was irritating. At thirty-one, though, she understood the pull of social media, the need to use as few words as possible to make your wishes known.

She put the last graded paper in a folder and sat back, wondering if this was the life she wanted. She sorted through the stack of mail on her desk and stopped with surprise when she saw the letter from the Desert Sage Inn. Frowning, she picked it up. It was from Alec Thurston, a family member by marriage and her mentor, the principal reason why she had gotten into hospitality management. It was he who'd believed in her and her dreams from the time she was a little girl.

She ripped open the envelope and stared with dismay at his words:

> "My dear Willow, it's been a while since we've spoken, but I need to ask a favor of you. Will you come and visit me at the Inn? I've been given some bad news about my health and need to see you in order to make plans for the future. Please let me know if and when you'll arrive and I'll make plans for you to be met."

Her vision blurred as she read through the rest of the letter. Of course, she'd go to see him. He was like a father to her.

CHAPTER ONE
ROSE

Rose told all her readers on her blog she would be traveling for the next couple of days but would add to her post whenever possible. In addition to acting as a virtual assistant to small businesses wanting to grow an online presence, Rose had successfully established a blog relating to unusual items she'd discovered for decorating, interesting places to visit, and easy-to-prepare foods to enjoy. She titled her blog "You Deserve This." Her followers, mostly professionals who were too busy to discover these things on their own, kept growing exponentially.

Some of her friends thought she was crazy to do this, but the blog ads had begun paying her bills, and she didn't want to give it up. Besides, she was a social person and liked the idea of having so many friends online. It sometimes made up for the fact that she was alone. Friends told her that fifty-two was far too early for her to give up hope of finding a man as exceptional as Alec. Heaven knew she'd tried and then decided not to worry about it. If or when the right time and right man came along, she'd enjoy it. Otherwise, she wasn't focusing on it.

As for her condo, she kept it sparsely furnished so she could easily pick up and take off anytime. After her brief marriage to a man who lived in a large house full of "stuff," she'd been more than happy to downsize. At her age, the last thing she wanted to do was fill her home with things she'd have to take care of. She'd thought of getting a cat, but even that idea was too much for her.

She kept only one framed picture on display. It was of Alec and her a long time ago. Picking it up now, she saw the light in her eyes when she smiled at the photographer with Alec's arm draped around her shoulder. He'd always made her feel so alive.

She set the photograph down on the table and let out a sigh. It hardly seemed possible that if what he'd said was true, he would soon be gone.

Her heart heavy, Rose packed her clothes in a suitcase, checked the condo for anything that might be amiss, and then headed out the door. She'd decided to drive to Palm Desert so she'd have access to a car if she needed it.

The trip to Palm Desert passed quickly as Rose listened to one of her favorite author's audiobooks. But when she reached the I-10 near San Bernardino in California, she grew tense.

After fighting her way through the dense, fast-moving traffic, she finally saw the exit for Palm Desert and Monterey Ave and made her way down the hill to turn left onto Highway 111. After traveling a short distance past Portola, she turned right and entered the driveway to the Desert Sage Inn.

Funny, after being away for so long, she felt as if she were coming home. From the time she and Alec had broken up, she hadn't allowed herself to return. Now, she was glad she had.

Tall, straight palm trees topped by green swaying fronds lined the long entrance into the property. As she drove up to the front of the main hotel building, she realized it hadn't changed that much since she last saw it 14 years ago.

Four two-story buildings, each holding 30 guest rooms, 15 per floor, bordered two free-form swimming pools connected by a lazy river and a small, burbling waterfall. Rose liked how the brown, stacked-stone exteriors of the buildings seemed to melt into the desert landscaping around them, allowing the shapes and textures of palm trees, cacti, and flowering plants to attract her attention. The patios or balconies of the rooms overlooked either the lushly landscaped pools or the stately mountains in the distance.

Trying to delay the moment when she'd come face to face with Alec and knowing she was early, she pulled up under the porte cochere, climbed out of the car, and stood a moment to study the entrance to the hotel. To one side of the wide, brown-brick walkway leading inside, a large waterscape shimmered in the sunlight, set in motion by the spray of a fountain in the middle. Small, green water plants nestled in the cracks of the upper layers of the stone walls of the pond, adding a touch of color.

A uniformed bellman approached her with a smile. "Welcome to the Desert Sage Inn. May I help you with your luggage?"

"No, thanks. I'm staying at Mr. Thurston's house. I just wanted to take a look at the hotel for a moment. Okay, if I step inside?"

"Sure. I'll keep an eye on your car," the bellman said agreeably.

"I'll only be a moment. I promise," said Rose. Now that she was at the hotel, she couldn't resist taking a peek inside.

She climbed four wide stone steps into a central courtyard where a multicolored stone statue of a Native-American woman stood holding her arms out as if to greet each guest. Gently waving grasses planted around the statue enhanced the welcoming atmosphere. Rose bypassed the figure and walked through a wide entrance into the lobby, whose stone floors shone from care.

A short, low wall separated the front entrance courtyard from the lobby. Pushed up against it, a long, narrow wooden table held a large turquoise vase filled with a stunning arrangement of a mix of peach blooms, white lilies, and succulents. On either side of the table, large, potted green palms added a softness to the area.

The décor had changed from what she remembered, of course, but the same open space welcomed her with a view through the sliding glass doors and paned windows above them of the mountains outside. A pergola above the extended patio protected the lobby from the sun to some extent and served as shade for some of the outdoor seating.

Lobby seating areas consisted of conversational groups of couches and comfortable chairs covered in bold-colored patterns of sand, purple, gray, and green. The furniture sat on custom-designed rugs swirled in complementary colors giving the room a burst of refined color from the duller, desert colors outside. Dark-brown tables were interspersed among the rest of the furniture, making each grouping a convenient place to enjoy cocktails or coffee or as a place simply to read or relax.

Rose sighed with satisfaction. It was as tasteful as it always had been. She knew the Desert Sage Inn had begun as a small inn before the large, international hotel chains began to show their interest in the area in the late 1970s and 1980s. In 1988, Alec bought the undeveloped property with money he'd made in the film industry directing a string of successful movies. At the time, plans had already been drawn to develop it into a resort, but the former owner, Bruce Williams, had run out of money before the process could begin. However, he was willing to sell a half-interest to Alec so he could continue with his dream. Alec bought it with the understanding that, upon the death of one of them, the half-interest would revert to the other. That's how at age 32, with Bruce's unexpected death,

Alec ended up owning the entire resort.

For the next eight years, he struggled to oversee the creation of the present-day hotel and to get it operating profitably. It was during this time that he married and lost Conchita Perez and their unborn child. He'd never forgiven himself for not being there when a fire took their lives as it destroyed their small home.

Rose returned to the hotel's front entrance, her emotions battered by the history of Alec's tragic loss. A valet helped her into her car, and after thanking him, she drove away full of questions about the future. She and Alec had talked on the phone, but she hadn't seen him since she'd left her position at the hotel. Lung cancer, he'd told her. It was ironic because, after his wife and child had been killed in the fire, Alec had ceased smoking. He didn't even like to light up a grill.

Rose traveled on a paved road beside the golf course and drove to the far corner of the property, where Alec's large, luxurious home sat in an area far removed from the original house on the property.

The large, one-story, contemporary home spread across the desert landscape like a lazy lizard. Wings of the house extended on either side of the small courtyard that led to the dramatic, large, wooden double doors that were the main entrance to the house. Tall windows of varying widths lined the front of the house, indicating one room after another. Inside, Rose knew, every convenience made living comfortable and yet private for those who resided there. Alec stayed in one area at the end of one wing of the house where he had a small, private kitchen, living room, and master suite separate from the rest of the house. Being a social man, he liked opening the rest of the house to guests who might never suspect he had his own private quarters.

She pulled into the circular drive in front of the house.

Later, she'd park her car in the four-car garage. For now, she couldn't wait to see Alec, to assure herself that though he'd received bad news about his health, it wasn't as bad as he thought. After climbing out of the car, Rose breathed in the air, enjoying how much clearer it was than in the Vegas area. Then, summoning up her nerve, she headed to the front door.

As she approached, the door opened, and Alec stood there smiling at her.

When she saw how fragile he was, tears blurred her vision. He looked awful. She forced a smile and kept moving forward, though a part of her wanted to collapse on the ground.

"As beautiful as ever," he said, his gaze remaining on her.

She smiled. He'd always loved her long, auburn hair and green eyes. Though it was a bit faded and cut shorter, with a little help from her hairdresser, her hair still was a striking feature.

"Thank you for coming, Rose," he said, holding out his arms to embrace her.

She hurried into them, careful to be gentle.

As his arms wrapped around her, she couldn't hold back a shuddering sob. "Oh, Alec. I hoped you were wrong."

He hugged her tighter. "You know me better than that. I'm honest to a fault."

She stepped away and looked up at him. His full head of gray hair was still there. He'd opted out of chemotherapy treatments. As he'd told her, by the time he decided to see the doctor, the cancer was too pervasive, too aggressive for him to consider it. Even though he'd become horribly thin, he was still a tall, handsome man with craggy features and light-blue eyes that missed nothing. Some compared him to the movie actor Sam Elliott. She understood why. They shared not only rugged good looks but a sense of unspoken authority about them.

"Do you have luggage?" he asked. "I can ask Pedro to carry it in for you."

She shook her head. "Not necessary. I can get it. I didn't know how long I'd be staying, so I didn't bring too much. Just two suitcases."

He nodded. "Sensible. I'll help."

Rose hurried back to her car and unloaded the bags from the trunk. Alec took hold of one of the handles she'd extended, and she took the other.

"You're in the west wing and may choose whichever suite you want. The other two aren't here yet. In the meantime, you can get settled. And by all means, feel free to use the garage."

"Other two?" Rose said, surprised. "What's going on?"

"It'll all become clear this evening," he said cryptically.

She studied him. "Are you sure you want me here?"

He nodded. "Oh, yes. It's all part of my plan. You'll see."

"You know I don't like secrets. Tell me."

He shook his head. "Not until everyone is here. It wouldn't be fair."

She followed him into the house and into the west wing, where she found three guest suites, each decorated in a different color scheme. She chose the suite decorated in soft green colors.

Alec left her suitcase by the king-size bed and said, "Juanita is in the kitchen. Please have her bring you whatever refreshments you'd like. The other two will be here before six o'clock. My apologies. I'm going to lie down for a while. I'll catch up with you later."

He bent down and kissed her on one cheek, then the other, French style. "You've always been such a lovely woman. I'm counting on you to understand what it is I want to do."

Before she could respond, he left the room.

She lifted a suitcase onto the bed and opened it, wondering

what was going on with Alec. Two others were to join them. People she likely didn't know.

She took her things out of the suitcase, hung some clothes in the large closet, and put other items in bureau drawers. Like the rest of the house, the guest room was beautifully furnished. She particularly loved this suite with its soft green walls and green Oriental rug, offset by dark, walnut furniture. The white duvet on the bed was accented by green, white, and rose-colored pillows that complemented the large oil painting of desert flowers that hung above the bed.

Juanita knocked at the door of the room. "Hello, Ms. Rose. I'm Juanita Sanchez. Mr. Alec asked me to see if there's anything I can do for you. Are you hungry? Thirsty?"

Rose smiled at the stocky lady whose bright, dark eyes sparkled with an openness Rose found charming. "Thanks. I remember you. After I walk around outside for a bit to stretch my legs, then, maybe, I'll have some ice-cold water."

"Very well. I'll be in the kitchen." Juanita turned to go.

"Wait!" said Rose, approaching her. "How long have you been with Alec here at the house?"

"For about ten years. Several years before that at the hotel. He was married to my cousin, Conchita. Why?"

"Long enough to see the changes in him. When did he start to feel sick? Didn't he know he needed to see a doctor? He told me it was too late to even start chemotherapy."

Juanita gazed at her sadly. "I tried to talk to him about it when he began losing weight, but he wanted no part of any such conversation." She sighed. "Sometimes people don't want to know."

Rose felt the sting of hot tears. "I wish he'd asked me to come here earlier. Maybe that would've changed things."

Juanita patted her arm. "I don't think that would've helped. He's a stubborn man, Rose."

She turned and walked away.

This time, Rose let her go. Juanita was right. Once Alec made up his mind about something, he wasn't about to change it. That was the main reason why they'd broken up years ago.

Rose headed outside, hoping the peaceful surroundings would help to ease the ache in her heart.

CHAPTER TWO
LILY

Lily Weaver left the office feeling as if she could fly. Recalling the previous few moments, she smiled at the shocked expression on her boss's face when she'd told him an emergency had come up and she needed to take her vacation immediately—all three weeks of it.

David Bakeley started to protest, saying, "I'm sorry, but you can't do that. We need you here."

"I have to go. An emergency. I've asked for help for months, and you've refused to listen, forcing me to work weekends to try to keep up." She handed him a folder. "I've been keeping a list of people looking for work. I've selected several candidates you might want to interview."

"Where are you going? When will you return? How can I get in touch with you?" Each question was louder, higher-pitched, angrier, making her decision to go to Palm Desert even sweeter. Fighting her own anger, she realized the competence of which she was so proud had held her back. He and the others in the law office of Bakeley & Dibble had assumed that because she'd made it seem easy, it was. Now they'd finally appreciate how hard she'd worked for them.

"I've prepared a duty list along with detailed instructions for whoever takes over for me," Lily said. "That should make things easier for you." She checked her watch. "I have to leave now. I have a plane to catch. You have my cell number, but I won't be checking it on a regular basis."

David got to his feet and gave her a look of resignation. "I'm sorry about your friend dying. We're all going to miss you, Lily. Me, most of all."

"Thank you," she replied and turned and left, knowing she should've done something like this months, no, years ago.

Saying goodbye to her younger sister was a different story. Though ten years separated them, she and Monica were close siblings. At thirty-two, Monica was a single mom to three-year-old Isabel, a sweet little girl who was like the child Lily had always wished for. With no other family to help and the complete rejection by Izzy's father, Monica had asked Lily to move to New York and relied upon her help while she worked nights for a telecommunications company. Lily explained to her sister that she felt a deep need to go to Palm Desert to see Alec, but while she was away, she'd help pay for babysitters.

Outside her condo building, the sisters embraced.

"I'm going to miss you so much," Monica said, hugging her close. "Both Izzy and I will find it hard to have you gone."

"I'll miss you too. Izzy almost feels like mine." Lily held back tears. "But I know I'm doing the right thing."

Monica gave her a steady look. "I well remember how Alec Thurston hurt you, Lily. I hope you're not in for more heartbreak."

"It's not going to be that way. He isn't that kind of person," Lily said, confident that Alec, the man who still haunted her dreams, would never do anything so unkind.

"Better go," said Monica, gently pushing her toward the limo she'd hired to take her into the city to the John F. Kennedy International Airport terminal.

Lily moved forward with determination. Her life as she'd been living it was over. Of this, she was certain.

###

The flight from New York to Palm Springs seemed to take forever, with one stop in Salt Lake City before traveling on to California. As anxious as she was to get there, Lily reminded herself that worrying about it wouldn't help the situation. She'd trained herself to set worries aside, which may be one reason she'd stayed so long in her job. This change was exactly what she needed because she intended to break free from old living patterns. As sad as it was that Alec was dying, she felt as if he'd given her a multi-dimensional gift by asking her to come to see him.

No matter what he asked of her, she would willingly do it.

She'd been twenty-nine when she went to work for Alec Thurston as his personal assistant and was charmed by him from their first meeting. He had charisma and, more than that, a kindness that clearly showed. She'd jumped at the opportunity to work for him.

They'd worked together for several months before he asked her to join him for dinner. They had a pleasant evening of lively conversation while they enjoyed the delicious meal the chef at the hotel had prepared for them. It was her first taste of life without chaos, one filled with calm and love.

A few weeks later, Alec explained that while he wanted to spend more time with her, he was a widower who had no intention of ever marrying again, that they couldn't continue to see one another unless she agreed to those conditions. Hoping he'd change his mind, she happily complied.

Thinking of it, she sighed. Alec kept reminding her of the agreement, but she'd refused to understand how honest he was being. Finally, he'd told her it would be best if she found another job; he was worried she'd only become more hurt if the relationship continued. He'd found her a job in Phoenix with a business friend of his, and though she'd moved on, she'd always treasured that special time with him.

A voice boomed in the speaker above her with the usual announcement about stowing tray tables, turning off electronic items, and fastening seatbelts after securing any carry-on items before landing.

Heart pounding with anticipation, Lily stared out the window at the land below. Houses, desert sand, palm trees, and desert growth greeted her. She mentally embraced it all. It had been ten years since she'd last seen the area, and a lot of growth had taken place. She strained for a look at the Desert Sage Inn in the distance, but the plane was too far away on its approach into the airport.

When the time came for her to disembark, Lily stood in line holding onto her purse and carry-on bag, wondering if Alec would meet her at the airport as he wanted or if he'd had to send someone in his place.

Outside in the fresh air, the sun greeted her with a warm kiss. She lifted her face to it and then moved with the other passengers toward the terminal. Inside, she flowed with the stream of travelers to the baggage claim area where a brown-skinned man wearing tan slacks and a sage-green shirt held up a sign with her name on it.

Lily hurried toward the gentleman, rolling her carry-on bag behind her. "Hi, Pedro! Do you remember me? Lily Weaver. You're here for Alec Thurston?"

"Yes. Good to see you again. I'm to take you to him at the Desert Sage Inn."

"Is he ... is he worse?"

Pedro shook his head. "Each day he lives is both good and bad."

Lily clasped her hands together. "I'm so sorry to hear this. I've checked two bags. I didn't know how long I'd be staying. Each bag has a red ribbon on it to make it easier to see it."

"No problem. One of the other women is already here. The

last one will arrive before six."

"Other women?" Lily asked, feeling her heart drop to her feet. She'd thought she was the only one he'd asked to come.

"Yes, ma'am. There will be three of you." He walked with her to the baggage claim area and then went to the rotating belt holding luggage from her flight.

Lily tried to hide her shock over two other women coming to Alec's aid. She told herself to hold on until she found out exactly what or who awaited her, but disappointment ate at her.

She remained quiet and self-contained as they left the airport. Pedro drove her down Highway 111 from the airport through Cathedral City and Rancho Mirage to Palm Desert southeast of Palm Springs. She perked up as they entered the drive to the resort. The palms and colorful plantings on either side were as beautiful as she remembered. Her breath caught as a surprising thought came to her. This felt more like home than Ellenton, where her only family lived.

Pedro drove past the collection of hotel buildings to Alec's house in the far corner of the property. Seeing it with new eyes, Lily realized how beautiful, how elegant it was. It, too, hadn't changed much.

Pedro pulled the car up to the front of the house and hurried out of his seat to open the rear passenger door for her. Stepping outside, Lily wondered what awaited her. Trembling with excitement and worry, she moved forward.

The front door opened, and Alec stood beside it, holding onto the large, brass doorknob. The smile that stretched across his face seemed almost ghoulish on an abnormally thin countenance. Her breath caught.

"Lily, my dear, thank you for coming. It's so nice to see you," he said. His deep voice, so well-remembered, brought tears to her eyes.

She hurried forward into his embrace. Aware of how thin he'd become, she was careful not to cling. Looking up, she saw with relief that his gray hair was still intact. How she'd loved to thread her fingers through it.

"Pedro will bring in your bags. You must be tired. Come into the kitchen. Juanita will help you to anything you might wish. She'll assist you in getting settled in one of the guest suites. In about an hour, after the last one has arrived, we'll meet in the living room." He led her to a kitchen she'd always loved. Dark wooden beams crossed the high white ceiling above the white kitchen cabinets and dark-green granite countertops. The red Mexican tile on the floor was still appealing. Alec, she knew, was a conservative man who wouldn't be swayed by decorating fads but would stick to what worked for him.

"Juanita, you remember Lily Weaver," he said. "Please take care of her. I'm going to rest until our last guest arrives."

Juanita nodded and held out her hand. "Welcome, Ms. Lily. Would you like something to eat or drink, or would you rather get settled in your suite first?"

"I'd like some hot tea, thank you." She smiled at the short, plumpish woman with gratitude. "It's been a long day."

Juanita moved to the stove. "I'm glad you and Rose agreed to come so quickly. Alec needs you."

Lily's heart stopped and then spurted forward. "Rose? Rose Macklin?"

"Why, yes. Do you know her?" Juanita asked. She set a cup of hot water and a wooden box holding several assorted tea bags in front of her.

"I've heard of her. That's all," Lily answered. She knew Alec had dated Rose for six years, and they'd had broken up a year or so before she and Alec started dating. She'd always wondered if Alec had ever gotten over Rose, though it was he who'd ended things. Even now, she felt jealous of the relationship Rose had had with Alec.

"Alec said you were to choose which room you wanted. The Green Sage suite is already taken, but Blue Waters and the Sunshine ones are available."

"Thank you. I'll take the Sunshine suite." Lily couldn't remember each one, but she liked the idea of sunshine after living in the cold of the Northeast.

After she finished her tea, Lily followed Juanita to the room. True to its name, the walls were painted a bold golden yellow that didn't overpower the heavy, dark wooden furniture with an antique, carved-wood appeal. The duvet cover was as colorful as the walls with a print of desert flowers and birds. It was, Lily decided, a room dedicated to optimism. She embraced the idea. No matter what was going on with Alec inviting two other women, she'd stick it out, do her best to make him happy.

CHAPTER THREE
WILLOW

For Willow Sanchez, coming home was always a bit difficult. She grew up both loving and resenting the Desert Sage Inn. Her parents had worked at the hotel for as long as she could remember and for Alec Thurston in his house for almost ten years. As Alec's deceased wife's relatives, they were treated like family, though they took their jobs seriously. Alec had always treated her like a favorite niece and had encouraged her in everything she did. If he hadn't taken her under his wing, taught her what he knew about the business, and helped her get into the Cornell School of Hotel Administration, she might be floundering, still wondering what to do with her life. Because she'd chosen to be trained in management, it was always a little awkward to see her parents in their positions. Neither one ever mentioned it to her, but she believed they found it a little uncomfortable too.

After receiving his letter, she'd talked to Alec about coming back. He'd been adamant that she was to return as someone who was from a management position and would stay in his house with the other two women he'd asked to come to the hotel.

At the airport, she smiled at the sight of her father, Pedro, holding up a card with her name on it. He beamed at her, and her heart filled with love for him. Both he and her mother, Juanita, were kind, gentle, caring people who were proud of their ability to do excellent work.

She waved and hurried to him, suddenly wanting to feel his arms around her.

"Welcome home, *cariño*," he said, tugging her into an embrace. "Your mother is anxious to see you! It's been too long since you've come home."

She smiled. After hearing from so many students how fragmented their families were, she was well aware of how lucky she was. Her parents loved her. "I'm sorry. I should've come for the holidays, but I thought it was important to meet Jake's family. Too bad it didn't work out with him." She would never tell her parents how appalled Jake's snooty parents had been to learn the true status of her family. They thought of them as mere immigrants.

Her father took her arm, which shook off her memory of her horrible visit. "Come. I've got the car outside. Did you check any bags?"

"Yes. One big one. I didn't know how long I'd be staying." Her spirits drooped. "How's Alec doing? He told me things didn't look good, and Mom said he was really sick."

Her father shook his head. "They're not good. But other things are going on. I'm not sure what he's doing, but I think it's going to be important to you."

Willow felt a shiver across her shoulders. She and her father shared an ability to see and sense things others did not.

They waited silently for her luggage, and, after retrieving it, they headed out to the car.

Willow opened the passenger door to sit up front with her father, but he shook his head. "No, Willow. I've been given strict instructions to treat you like the other ladies. You're to sit in the back."

"Dad, this is stupid." Willow placed a hand on her hip. "What's going on? What other ladies?"

"Like I said, I don't know. Alec hasn't given me any details.

Let's take it one step at a time. Please do as Alec requested."

Willow reluctantly climbed into the backseat, uncertain what lay ahead. The thought of her personal hero dying filled her with sadness.

When they arrived at Alec's house, her father turned to her from the driver's seat. "Stay where you are. I'll get the door for you."

Willow frowned. "I'm perfectly capable of getting out of the car on my own."

Her father held up a finger of caution. "Please. This is what Alec requested. He told me he didn't want the other women to have any confusion about your status."

Willow remembered other times Alec had talked to her about presenting herself in a confident way and nodded. She was a bright woman who'd been taught she could do anything she put her mind to as long as it didn't hurt anyone else. That was a gift her mother and father had given her.

As he'd asked, she waited for her father to open the rear passenger door for her and stepped out of the car to face the luxurious house Alec called home, the place where her parents worked.

Alec opened the front door of the house and stood there, ready to greet her.

Suddenly, she felt like a child again facing him like this for the first time. Though instead of the flurry of heartbeats pulsing through her at the strong sense that he would play a large part in her life, her heart raced with concern to see how awful he looked. It had been over a year since she'd been home, and in that time, Alec had become a different person, bent and sick and weak. Tears sprang to her eyes.

"Welcome, Willow," said Alec, smiling at her. "Thank you

for coming."

She ran to him and stood before him until he reached for her. Then she settled in his weak embrace. As lucky as she was to have Pedro for a father, she was further blessed to have this other father figure.

"Come inside. You'll be staying in the Blue Waters suite. Pedro will bring in your luggage. After greeting your mother, I want you to meet with the two other women I've asked to come here. I'll wait for you with them in the living room."

Willow gave him a quizzical look, but he didn't respond. She hurried into the kitchen, anxious to see her mother.

Upon seeing her, Juanita's eyes filled, and she held out her arms.

Warmed by the sight of her, Willow hurried into her embrace. "I'm home for a while, *Mami.*

"I'm so happy to see you, but sorry it's like this with our Alec sick." Her mother hugged her tightly. "You'd better hurry into the living room. He's waiting for you." Her mother gave her one more squeeze before letting her go.

When Willow walked into the living room, two women were sitting there, observing her intently.

A tall, slender, beautiful redhead she remembered swept her gaze over her, neither approving nor condemning. She seemed to question her with a quizzical expression, and then a smile spread across her lovely features.

Sitting opposite the redhead on another couch, she recalled the younger woman with a pleasing face who studied her with a look of concern and clasped her hands.

Alec indicated the redhead with a wave of his hand. "So that everyone is acquainted or reacquainted, as the case may be, this is Rose Macklin." He nodded to the pretty woman sitting opposite her. "And this is Lily Weaver, and, ladies ..." he put his arm around her, "this is Willow Sanchez, my protégé, whom I'm sure you both remember."

The women murmured a polite "hello" to one another as Alec eased himself into an overstuffed chair that sat at the end of and between the couches.

He nodded to Willow. "Please have a seat."

Willow lowered herself onto the couch beside Rose, wondering what Alec had in mind. There was a self-satisfied look on his face that worried her.

Alec cleared his throat and smiled at them. "Ah, my lovely desert flowers—Rose, Lily, and Willow—three beautiful, talented women whom I'm asking to help me."

Like Rose and Lily, Willow stared at him with uncertainty. "Alec, darling," said Rose, "What are you talking about?"

"I have some time left, probably a couple of months or so. Maybe even longer. When I die, the inn will be sold to new owners based on its fair market value, which is yet to be determined. I believe they think with my illness, the inn will not do as well as it has recently, and they can pick it up for a price that would be entirely unfair after all the work I've done to make it a success."

"You're selling the hotel?" said Willow.

"Yes. The basic terms of the eventual sale, other than the final price, have been negotiated. Meanwhile, the buyers, The Blaise Hotel Group from Atlanta, have three months to complete their due diligence to familiarize themselves with all aspects of the inn's operation and to prepare their marketing and operating plans for the future. Current management will continue to operate the inn during this process, but with the Blaise people looking over their shoulders, so to speak. I'm asking you, my dears, to represent my interests for the next several months to ensure the unique characteristics that make the Desert Sage Inn the special place it is are not swept aside."

"How are we going to help?" Lily said.

"You each have different skills you bring to the table." Alec grinned at them, bringing a sparkle to his eyes. "We're going to show these greedy bastards who's smarter." He chuckled softly and then grew serious.

"I know I'm asking a lot of you, but each of you is very special to me. Your presence in my life has meant a lot. Looking back, I remember not only your business talents, but your very natures, and I want you here with me. I believe you can make a tremendous difference going forward. You will, of course, be well-paid for your help, but more than that, I hope your time here will re-energize each of you going forward into an even brighter future."

He went to each woman, kissed her on the cheek, and stepped back." My beautiful flowers—Rose, Lily, and Willow."

"What exactly are you asking us to do?" said Rose.

"I'm pairing you up with people the new company will bring into the operation of the inn. *You*, not *they*, will be in charge of the ongoing work of the inn. The outcome is important to me because most of the profit from the sale of the inn, following the usual expenses and deductions, will be used to set up a charitable foundation in my wife's name."

Willow noticed the other two women dart glances at one another. She knew from family gossip that both of them had thought at one time they'd be married to him. It was for that very reason Alec had broken the relationships, though there was still obvious affection between Rose and Alec. Lily was much harder to read because of her shyness, but there was a definite look of adoration when she looked at him.

"What are our jobs specifically?" Willow asked. She was trying to tell herself she was qualified for whatever he might have in mind, but the truth was, she didn't have enough information to know if she was up for the task. She had a degree in hotel management, but she'd been teaching business writing and accounting specifically geared to the industry. Did that count?

Alec beamed at her. "You, my dear, are going to be working with their assistant manager who, according to the paperwork I was given, is considered a hotshot in the industry, destined to do big things."

He turned to Lily. "You were an excellent assistant to me, keeping track of details in many areas. You'll work in my office as my new assistant overseeing the conversion team they have appointed."

"What about me?" said Rose.

Alec rubbed his hands together. "You'll be working with their social media guy. Or perhaps, I should say *against* their social media guy who will want to advertise the new company coming in and how they plan to change the image and marketing focus of this resort. Your job will be to see that the conversation about the hotel sticks to the Desert Sage Inn, not the one they're trying to create from it. There are other issues as well."

Rose let out a laugh. "I get it. A battle of words as well as wits. You've got it." Rose projected flamboyance compared to Lily and her; Willow couldn't help smiling.

Rose glanced at her and studied Lily. "We'll beat them at their own game. Right, flowers?"

Willow raised her fisted hand. "You bet!"

"Count me in," said Lily, giving them a thumbs up

Alec smiled. "Okay, my desert flowers, let's show them. I'm going to leave you now. Rose, you're in charge of pulling this group together. Enjoy yourselves. Cocktails and dinner will be served anytime you want them. To be clear, Pedro and Juanita are here to help you as family members of mine."

He stood, gave each of them a gentle hug, and left the room.

CHAPTER FOUR
ROSE

Rose sighed as she watched Alec leave the room. Full of mixed emotions, she faced the other two women. Lily was quiet, but a look of determination had crossed her face when she'd said to count her in. Willow Sanchez's dark eyes had shown with excitement. Interesting that Alec had made her a protégé. A stunning girl with long, straight, dark hair and skin the color of wheat.

"Are either of you as ready for a glass of wine as I am?" Rose asked.

"Yes. A glass of pinot noir sounds lovely," Willow said.

"I'd appreciate that more than you know," said Lily. "Later, I'm going to call my boss and tell him I'm not only taking all my vacation owed me, but I'm quitting." The smile she gave them brightened her features, making her beautiful.

"What kind of work have you been doing?" Rose asked, remembering how Alec had complimented her.

"Working for a law firm. Lots of sticky details to keep track of, with long hours and a lot of overtime because they were too cheap to hire extra help. But why should they? I did it all." She shrugged. "I guess it was as much my fault as theirs that they wouldn't cooperate."

"Doesn't sound that way to me," said Willow, giving Lily a look of concern.

"Nowadays, so many companies rely on their employees to work from dawn to dusk and beyond. And for what?" said

Rose. "I run my own company, so I can choose when and how and why I want to do things. Don't get me wrong; I'm busy. Very busy. But *I* run my life, nobody else." She turned to Willow. "What have you been up to?"

" As you know, Alec was a big supporter of mine as I grew up. And when I became fascinated with the hotel business, he trained me as much as he could and helped me get into the Cornell School of Hotel Administration. After I graduated, he told me to get different experiences. For the last year, I've been teaching business writing and accounting specifically designed for the hotel industry. I'd always planned, as he wanted, to eventually come to work here with him at the hotel." Her vision blurred, and she took a moment. "But that's obviously not going to happen."

"Except for doing this now," Rose said firmly. "Right?"

Willow's eyes widened. "Oh, yes. I'm on board. I don't want anyone taking advantage of his being sick when it comes time for someone else to take over the hotel."

"I believe his dedication to the hotel has always had something to do with the memory of his wife and child," said Lily, her voice soft with regret.

"And that's why we're going to help him," said Rose. She was well aware of Lily's love for Alec. It was written all over her face. "Now, let's see about that wine. I'll go check with Juanita unless you want to do it, Willow."

Willow shook her head. "No, you go ahead."

"No problem." *Good girl.* She'd wanted to make sure Willow wouldn't think that she, as the youngest of the group, had to wait on them.

As they sat sipping wine, Rose was able to get Lily and Willow to talk about themselves. It was an old trick of hers that she'd used as social director for the years she lived and worked here at the hotel. The truth was she liked people, was interested in their stories, and loved making others comfortable. She may not have gone through a professional hospitality program at a school, but she didn't need to because she was born to be in the business.

She thought back to when she first came to the hotel in 1998, an eager young woman ready to help acquaint people with the amenities at the hotel and the growing community of Palm Desert. Though many men had wanted to date her, Rose was always careful about who she spent time with. From the beginning, she was attracted to Alec. She saw him as a wounded man, someone who gave all he could to others and his hotel project. She knew the reason why, of course. Everyone had heard about the horrible fire that had taken the lives of his wife and unborn child. For that reason, she'd kept an emotional distance from him even as she stood in for that woman, acting as co-host at events, making it less awkward for him socially as he grew his business. Her thoughts skipped ahead to the time he told her their relationship couldn't continue. She'd known it was coming, had felt him inch away from their intimacy. He'd told her from the beginning that he would end it if they were in too deep. What neither of them understood was the damage it would do to her. He was the person she'd relied on to make herself believe she was loveable.

"Rose?"

She drew a deep breath and turned to Willow. "Yes?"

"Lily and I were trying to figure out what stage the hotel was in while you were here."

Rose smiled. "It was when Alec was doing some major renovations at the property. How about you, Lily?"

"I came to work right after you left and was here for only

two years. By the time I left, a lot of the major projects were completed. Alec found me a job in Phoenix, and after a couple of years there, I moved home to New York to be with my sister."

Rose's heart constricted at the pain that momentarily washed over Lily's features. She understood it.

"Shortly after, my parents took the jobs at Alec's house," said Willow.

"We have a lot of years of history tying us together," said Rose. "It's good that we're here to help him."

Willow nodded and then a smile spread across her face. "Let's have some fun doing it, too."

"Why not?" said Lily.

The three women grinned at one another.

That night, Rose lay in bed hugging the pillow beside her, feeling as if her emotions were playing a game of tag inside her. She swung from feeling happy to see Alec again to wanting to cry over his physical state, to being jealous that he thought as highly of two other women as he did of her. She told herself she was being immature, but she couldn't stop her circling thoughts as her heart expanded and contracted with every new emotion. She lay back and looked up at the ceiling, her eyes awash with tears.

Her thoughts drifted to her ex-husband. Poor Ron! She'd tried her best with him. Everyone thought he was the perfect man for her—fun-loving, wealthy. He should've been the right one, but, unfortunately, he wasn't Alec. She and Ron were both hopeful at the beginning that their marriage was going to work. And when it became obvious it wasn't going well, Ron became a different, destructive person. Though it had been several years since they divorced, she was still sorry about the way it had turned out. Since that time, she'd dated from time to time but wasn't interested in a permanent relationship with anyone.

CHAPTER FIVE
LILY

Lily sat in the dining room with the other two women eating a delicious meal of chicken mole and other Mexican dishes Juanita proudly presented to them. She'd forgotten how tasty Mexican food could be, but then upstate New York wasn't the place to find it.

Between mouthfuls of dinner, Lily did her best to concentrate on what Rose was saying. Rose was such a stunning, self-assured woman that Lily constantly fought insecurities in her presence. And Willow? A bright, attractive younger woman who had enjoyed a lot of Alec's attention.

"Is that all right with you, Lily?" Rose asked

"I'm sorry. What were you asking?" Lily felt the heat on her cheeks and knew they'd be turning pink. She'd tried and tried to train herself not to be so open but had never succeeded. One date told her he thought it was cute, but she knew better.

"Are you okay with meeting tomorrow morning, say, nine o'clock? We can gather here in the house in the kitchen."

"Sure. That would be fine. I'm as anxious as you to get started on Mission Save or whatever you want to call this."

Willow's eyes brightened. "I like that—Mission Save. Even better, I like desert flowers to the rescue."

"Do you remember that old television program about the man and his angels? We can be Alec's Angels," said Rose.

"Or like he says, we can be his desert flowers," said Willow, chuckling.

"Great idea," Lily said, liking the sound of it.

"Okay, we'll call ourselves the Desert Flowers. Let's all shake on it," said Rose, holding out her hand. Lily and then Willow shook it. "Now, it's official. Are either of you going to have any trouble staying here for an unknown period of time?"

"No," said Lily quickly. She'd already received a text wanting to know where certain things were in the office. She would help her replacement, and then she'd be free. She'd send her boss an email tomorrow morning to let him know she wouldn't be returning.

"I've made arrangements for my teaching assistant to take over for the next couple of months. She's highly qualified to do so," said Willow. "She's thrilled with the opportunity."

Lily studied the younger woman for a moment, admiring her beauty, the sense of calmness about her. Before she could stop herself, she said, "Did you and Alec ... I mean, were you and Alec ..." She stopped, suddenly aware of how awkward the moment had become.

Willow chuckled. "Were Alec and I together? No, he's like a father to me. Besides, neither one of us would've dishonored my parents in that way."

Lily clapped her hands to her cheeks. "Oh, God! I'm so sorry. That came out all wrong. I should never have had that second glass of wine."

"No problem," said Rose. "I'm sure we're all curious about our connections to Alec. He and I lived together for six years before going our separate ways."

"And I was with him for less than two," said Lily.

"He hasn't dated anyone else for any length of time," said Willow. "He told me he didn't want to continue to hurt anyone because of his devotion to his wife and child."

"Guess that says it all," said Lily.

Rose reached across the table and gave Lily's hand a

squeeze. "I understand how you feel."

Lily nodded, but she wasn't sure Rose understood at all. God help her; those feelings for Alec still lingered. She'd never loved anyone else.

The next morning, Lily stared out the window of her bedroom at the desert landscape. Some people thought desert scenes were so uninteresting, so plain. She liked that Alec hadn't succumbed to the idea of green grass. She loved the beige, sandy starkness of the land accented by a colorful plant, spiky cactus, or green tree here or there to add texture.

The sky was a bright blue that matched her sunny mood. She'd called her sister to tell her she was moving to California. Then she'd sent off a long email to her boss explaining that she would not be returning to the office and asked that her personal things, few as they were, be delivered to her sister.

Her boss's reply was quick and brief, acknowledging her work through the years, blah, blah, blah. More than ever, she knew she was right to make this move. She'd just turned forty-two and was young enough to begin a whole new life, wherever it might take her. First, she was going to help the man who'd proved to her that she didn't need to live in chaos all the time.

Lily fingered the drapes hanging by the window, loving the feel of the silky material. Her condo back home was suitable, but nothing more. The return to this lifestyle forced a promise to herself to enjoy life more, to live better.

She checked her watch. Time for breakfast and the meeting to which she'd agreed. Heaven knew what awaited her.

When she walked into the kitchen, she found Willow and Rose chatting comfortably with one another. Anxious not to miss out on anything, she joined them.

"Good morning! What a beautiful day!" she said, sliding

onto a chair at the kitchen table.

"Hey, there!" Rose said. "We were just talking about the need to set up a form to track any information we think Alec should know. I've already spoken to him about this, and he agrees. After breakfast, he's going to provide us information on the people we'll be working with. I can't wait to see it!"

Willow emitted a long sigh. "I've googled assistant managers at the company, and if the guy Alec mentioned is who I think it is, it's not going to be easy. I remember him from my time at Cornell. Unless he's changed, I'm in for a difficult time. He's not a nice guy."

"We'll soon know all about them." Rose stood. "Now, let's enjoy breakfast. Juanita has laid out a lot of choices, so we can help ourselves."

Lily went over to the breakfast bar suddenly feeling hungry. It felt great to have the time to relax at her morning meal. Usually, she was grabbing something to eat in the car on her way to work.

Sitting with the other two women, she felt a bond with them. The future ahead held no promise of easy things to come, yet they were all willing to face them together.

Willow smiled at her. "I like what you did with your hair."

Lily patted the twisted ponytail at the back of her head. "Thought it would be easier this way." She usually wore it down and shoulder-length.

Rose nodded with approval. "It looks perfect on you."

"Thanks," said Lily, grateful for their kindness. "I already like this relaxed lifestyle. I was more than ready for a change. How about the two of you?"

"I've always thought I'd be back here one day, so it doesn't seem surprising," Willow said.

"I'll still be working on my blog," said Rose, "and perhaps for a few clients of mine. But the bulk of my work will be for the hotel, of course."

"So, you'll be working mostly online?" Lily asked, interested in the idea of Rose facing off with another expert in social media.

"Yes and no," said Rose mysteriously. "It depends on who my opponent is."

Lily and Willow exchanged glances. Lily wouldn't want to oppose Rose for any reason. From the look Willow gave her, Lily thought she must feel the same.

CHAPTER SIX
WILLOW

After breakfast, Willow went back to her room to freshen up. It felt strange to be a guest in Alec's house, but she understood why he'd made those arrangements and was grateful to him for it. A few students at school had mocked her about her humble background. Hurt and angered by it, she'd done as Alec had suggested and ignored them. Besides, she was proud of all her parents had accomplished. They'd arrived in the U.S. with nothing but a determination to work hard and succeed. They'd done both.

Willow checked her phone. Jake Matthews had sent another text pleading for her to return his calls. She'd tried to tell him that after that awful holiday visit with his family, she never wanted to see or hear from him again. She had a lot more pride than that. Now that she'd stepped away from the relationship, Willow understood better that it had been doomed from the start. At this point in her life, she wasn't about to start dating a man who wasn't willing to accept who she was.

She brushed her teeth and stood a moment assessing herself in the mirror. Her skin looked as if the sun had kissed it with a glowing tan. Her shiny, straight dark hair hung just beneath her shoulders. Jake had once told her she was the most beautiful girl in the world, but then he saw only the outside of her, so it meant nothing.

She turned her back on her image and left the room.

When Willow walked into the kitchen, she was surprised to see Alec seated at the table with the other women.

"Good morning," he called out cheerfully, giving the impression it was going to be a good day for him.

"Hello," she replied and sat in the empty chair at the table. "What's going on?"

"I'm providing the three of you with the names of your so-called opponents." Alec's lips formed a crooked grin. "It's important to know who each of you will be dealing with. My Desert Flowers will stop the greed and prove to be winners."

"We hope so," said Rose. "The three of us have agreed to work together."

Alec handed her a photograph. "Rose, here's who you're going to battle. Henry "Hank" Bowers."

Rose looked at it and passed it to Willow.

Willow studied the picture of a tall, striking man with gray hair, classic features, and alert, steel-gray eyes that seemed to miss nothing.

"Hank is a hearty ex-football player—easy to talk to, glib, and with a strong, friendly handshake. He likes to be in charge," said Alec.

"Gawd! I bet he talks about everything in sports language," said Rose.

Alec looked surprised, and then he laughed. "Yeah, he does. Great guy, actually. "He's widowed, is the father of two daughters, and loves his three-year-old granddaughter." He raised a finger in warning. "He's sharp and has a lot of connections. You Desert Flowers are going to have to be careful with him."

"How about my opponent?" Lily asked.

Alec handed her a photograph.

After studying it, Lily passed it to Willow.

Willow studied the picture of a tall, muscular, athletic man in a T-shirt and jogging shorts. On his left leg, below the knee, he wore a prosthesis with a blade. His hair was dark brown, with a sheen of gray at the temples. His handsome face wore a cautious smile.

"Brian Walden is a Gulf War veteran and an honest guy," explained Alec. "He was in his early twenties when he lost part of his leg. He attended law school and decided not to go into practice. Instead, he consults for businesses making financial moves and acquisitions. He's clever and thorough. That's why I want you, Lily, to be present at meetings between my lawyers and him. You are extremely careful about details and may pick up information others might miss. They'll think you're just acting as my assistant, but we both know you'll be more valuable than they realize."

Willow smiled at the pride in Lily's face, the pretty pink flush on her cheeks making her attractive.

Alec turned to her. "Willow, the man you'll be battling is considered a real hotshot, a guy destined to be a big-time winner. His family's company might consider making him a manager of this hotel even though he's only two years older than you."

Willow filled with dread. "Is it Brent Armstrong?"

At Alec's nod, Willow sighed. "I knew him at Cornell, not that he'd remember me. He was part of a whole other group. Everyone thought he was a great guy. Me? I thought he was a pompous, racist ass."

She accepted the photograph Alec handed her.

A handsome blond-haired man stared at her with blue eyes. He wore a cocky smile she remembered from her days at Cornell when he'd walked past her without acknowledging her. She recalled too how he loved to put down anyone competing against him for an honor or even something frivolous like leading a discussion group.

"His father and his uncle, Duncan and Mitchell Armstrong, own The Blaise Hotel Group that is planning to buy me out. Like it or not, they're paving the way for him to succeed," Alec said with a note of disgust. "But, Willow, you're every bit as competent as he is. Remember that."

"Let me see," said Rose, taking the photograph from her. She studied it. "Looks like a little prick." Looking up at her, Rose said, "You do your thing, girl! Lily and I will be right there for you."

Lily accepted the photo Rose handed her, peered at it, and said, "We won't let him get to you."

"All right, then," said Alec, getting to his feet. "Looks like I'm leaving things in good hands."

Willow exchanged glances with the other two women and grinned. They'd already become a team.

At the edge of the living room, Alec stopped and turned around. "By the way, I've set aside time for the three of you to enjoy several days of teambuilding. My personal trainer will be handling that for me. Enjoy the rest of the day. Tomorrow you work with him."

"Really, Alec? You think we need to do that?" Rose protested, her expression troubled.

"I think you'll find it a great way to get to know one another," he said, grinning, and left the room. Willow glanced at the other two women. They looked as worried as she.

Rose stood. "Guess I'd better take advantage of today and head over to El Paseo to do a little shopping. I've been working at home, often in my pajamas. Time for me to look professional." She laughed. "And maybe a little sexy. Anyone else?"

"I wish I could, but I can't," said Lily. "I'm paying for a babysitter for my sister and am stretched for money."

Rose frowned. "I'll talk to Alec about that. He hasn't mentioned it, but we need to know how he's going to handle compensation."

"Thanks," said Lily. "I thought I was coming to visit a friend. This is much more than I'd prepared for." She turned to Willow. "How about you? Did you bring the clothes you'll need?"

Willow shook her head. "Not for this job," she said, wishing she'd known what she needed because she wanted to look professional when facing Brent.

"Hold on? I'll be right back," said Rose. "I'm sure it was just an oversight on Alec's part."

After Rose left, Willow turned to Lily. "That's nice of you to help out your sister. How many kids does she have?"

A smile crossed Lily's face. "Just one. A little girl of three named Isabel. We call her Izzy." She lifted her phone and showed her a picture of a sweet child with reddish-brown hair.

"She's darling," cooed Willow. "Do you have any kids of your own?"

A sadness filled Lily's eyes. "No, I wish I did. I'd want a little girl just like Izzy."

"Maybe you will someday," Willow said, seeing how much Lily seemed to care.

"It would have to be in a hurry. I'm almost forty-two, and time is running out."

"Time is running out for what?" Rose said, striding into the room.

"For me to have a family of my own," Lily said, letting out a long sigh. "But it hardly matters. I haven't found the right man for me."

"Ah, I understand," Rose said with sympathy. She sat at the table between Lily and her. "I thought I'd want kids too, but after marrying, I was glad it didn't happen. The marriage was wrong from the beginning. But, Lily, you have a family. That's something I don't have."

"You don't?" Lily said.

Rose shook her head. "Nope, I'm an only child, and my parents are gone."

"I'm sorry," said Lily softly.

"Me, too," Willow said, unwilling to think of a time when her parents might not be around.

"Your parents are great. Alec is lucky to have them helping him." Rose studied her. "And now you're working for him, along with Lily and me."

"It's a little odd for me," Willow admitted, "but it makes me happy to be able to help Alec after all he's done for me. And I'd love nothing better than to knock Brent off his pedestal. He was so dismissive of me at school."

Rose gave her a fist bump. "I'd love to see you take him down a notch or two."

"I'm going to try." Willow was determined to do her best to face Brent. Still, she liked the idea of having two other Desert Flowers around to give her support.

CHAPTER SEVEN
ROSE

O kay," Rose said facing the other two women in the living room, "I've talked to Alec about compensation, and this is how he wants to handle it." She handed each of the other women a credit card. "You have free rein to use these any way you want. He agrees we need to look our best, our most professional, but relax and enjoy ourselves. He knows us well enough to be certain we're not going to bankrupt him. We have all of the El Paseo district downtown for shopping, and there's a great outlet mall about a 30-minute drive away."

"What about the teambuilding stuff?" Lily asked. "That worries me a bit."

"Alec said we'd know in time that it was best to let things unfold naturally. He'll let us know when we're ready officially to go to work."

Lily turned to Willow. "Any guesses? You know him better at this time than we do."

Willow lifted her shoulders and let them drop. "I have no idea. One thing is for sure. He's thought this whole team thing out carefully. He doesn't make rash decisions."

Rose nodded along with Lily. That was the man she remembered.

The three decided to go to the outlet mall, which would provide them a wider choice of styles and, hopefully, some bargains.

Rose drove. Lily sat up front with her and Willow in the back.

She glanced at Willow through the rearview mirror. "What clothes are you looking for?"

"I'm going to have to buy some skirts and dresses. I pretty much wear pants for school," Willow replied. "How about you, Lily?"

"I think I'll be brave and add some color to my wardrobe. Even in a small town like Ellenton, New York, lawyers can be stuffy. I've worn grays and blacks to blend into the setting of the office." She chuckled. "Guess it might be time to step up my fashion a bit."

Rose grinned at the delight she heard in Lily's voice. "You'd look good in bright colors."

"We'll see," she said, giving her a beaming smile.

"How about you, Rose? What are you looking for?" asked Willow.

"Something a little flamboyant," she answered without hesitation. "If Mr. Hank Bowers is the male chauvinist I think he is, that should make it interesting."

When they arrived at the mall, and Rose had parked the car, she turned to the others. "How do you want to do this? Should we stick together or go our separate ways?"

"I'd appreciate input from the two of you," said Lily.

"Me, too," Willow quickly added.

Satisfied, Rose said, "Okay, we'll go together. It's been a few years since I fussed over my wardrobe, and I want to make each dollar spent count."

The three of them took off, a team already, Rose hoped.

As they entered the outdoor mall, Rose stopped and turned to Lily and Willow. "Our first stop has to be for workout clothes. That's the one requirement Alec made. If we haven't packed the proper clothes for a workout, we need to get them—T-shirts, shorts, sneakers, socks."

"Oh, you mean for the teambuilding stuff?" said Lily, looking aghast. "I'm not that athletic. I visit the gym once a week, and I try to take my niece for walks whenever I can, but that's all I've been able to do with my work schedule."

"No worries," said Rose. "I'm in that same category." She turned to Willow. "You look fit. Do you go to the gym often?"

"I swim twice a week," Willow said, "so I'm not exactly comfortable about what Alec may be proposing."

"Well, in that case, we'll all be understanding of one another," said Rose. "C'mon, let's get that part of our shopping done and move on to more exciting things."

They each were able to find the workout clothing they needed in one store, sneakers and socks in another.

Rose waited patiently while Willow and Lily tried on clothes. She was holding out for the stores at the far end of the mall, where there were several designer shops. During the day, she'd be working with Hank on social media. For a couple of evenings in the coming weeks, she'd be working as social director for special events involving the new hotel company—something she and Alec had discussed privately.

Lily was a conservative dresser as she'd mentioned, but both Rose and Willow agreed she needed to add some color and fun to her wardrobe. When she emerged from a dressing room wearing a brown-leather, knee-length skirt that had a becoming flare and a bright turquoise blouse with a V-neck that brightened her appearance and added a depth of interest, they both clapped their approval. Lily was a pretty woman, thought Rose, wondering about the relationship she'd had with Alec.

"That's perfect for you, Lily," said Willow, grinning at her.

"Yes. Let's look at a few more outfits along those lines. It's professional with a little bit of an 'I am a woman' tone," said Rose, making Willow laugh.

Color rose in Lily's cheeks. "Well, then, why not? I've never had fashion consultants before."

Lily purchased another skirt, several blouses, and a couple of dresses, all as discounted sales.

Willow wanted to see other selections. The three of them walked down the row of stores until she came to one that she wanted to go into. Racks of clothes were lined up according to styles, and while she dug into one rack, Rose and Lily looked through others.

Arms laden with outfits, Willow came over to them. "I'm going to try these on. Will you take a look at me in them?"

Pleased by the request, Rose and Lily nodded.

Willow was a perfect model. Her trim body made all the clothes look fantastic except for the few that both she and Lily agreed were too fancy or frilly for her.

"You're a natural beauty," said Rose. "You don't want anything to detract from that."

Smiling, Willow turned around and around, her black hair falling softly beyond her shoulders. "This is so much fun!"

Rose and Lily glanced at one another and laughed.

They waited while Willow dressed in her own clothes and paid for those things they'd all approved. Then the three of them moved on to the store Rose wanted to visit.

Rose knew that, with a self-imposed, limited budget, she needed a few essential pieces that she could mix and match. Like the other two women, she wanted to look both professional and ready for anything social. She recalled her days of working at the Desert Sage Inn as social director, and, with that in mind, she leafed through items hanging on the racks with a careful eye.

Later, as she studied herself in the mirror, she realized though her height helped her pull off some styles, she was no longer in her thirties and needed to dress accordingly. In her opinion, there was nothing worse than an older woman in clothes designed for someone much younger. Lily and Willow insisted, though, that she buy a black dress that straddled that border.

When they were through shopping, Rose suggested they get coffee before heading back to the car and the inn.

As they sat with all their purchases at an outdoor table, the sun shone down on them with a warmth that filled Rose with contentment. She looked at her fellow shoppers, pleased by the friendship that was beginning to develop between them.

"I've never been able to go shopping like this before," said Lily, setting down her cup of coffee and smiling. "I can't believe Alec allowed us to do this. I usually pick up one piece or another for my wardrobe at one of my favorite discount stores and then try to make everything come together."

"Alec is generous," said Rose, "but he has a purpose behind our shopping today. He wants us to represent him as successful women who are smart and resourceful."

"He insists all people who work at the hotel present themselves and the hotel well," said Willow. "He's pounded that requirement into my head. Crisp, clean uniforms make an important impression on guests. That, clean guest rooms, public areas, and a spotless back of the house."

"It's very nice that he took an interest in you and helped you into the field," said Lily.

Willow's eyes filled. "He's been so kind to my family and me."

Rose's thoughts flew back to her time working at the hotel. She knew then that Alec was a decent man and always would be. This was more proof of it.

She studied Lily and Willow, wondering how things would play out. They were pleasant women, but would each be able to win her battle in facing the so-called "experts" the Blaise Group would bring in to take over?

Lily's cellphone rang, and while she accepted the call, her face glowed with happiness as she talked quietly on the phone. There was a sweetness about Lily that Rose guessed had attracted Alec.

CHAPTER EIGHT
LILY

Lily couldn't help the stab of homesickness that struck her as she cooed and spoke to Izzy. She loved that girl like her own. After her last relationship ended, she'd pretty much decided that having a family of her own was out of the picture. Sitting outside in the sun in California, she felt a painful distance from her family, a feeling she'd never quite experienced before. Yet, she wouldn't trade being here with these other women for anything. Not if it helped Alec. She'd needed a change.

After clicking off the call, Lily secretly studied Rose, admiring the confident way she carried herself. She respected Rose's ability to take control without ruffling feelings and her determination to work for Alec. At first, it had hurt to see the undeniable connection that still existed between Alec and Rose, but she understood that, like her, Rose would always be bound to him in some way.

Lily had trained herself to listen and observe and often saw or heard small details that others did not. Alec was right to trust her to do that for him. Having grown up with a dysfunctional mother in poor circumstances and with the need to help rear a younger sister, she'd become watchful and had learned a lot that way.

Back at the house, Lily proudly carried her purchases into

her room. She sighed with pleasure at all the lovely things she now owned. She appreciated Alec's generosity but hoped to pay him back. If not in dollars, with work well done.

As she carefully hung up each item of clothing or placed it in a drawer, she thought of what the other women had told her about relaxing and enjoying life. She was such a worker bee! She couldn't remember a recent time when she wasn't working or stressing over something. Being here in the desert was her chance not only to help Alec but to decompress. She vowed to make this stay count. Feeling as if a new life awaited her, she left her room and went to find Alec.

Lily knocked on the door to Alec's private quarters and waited for an answer.

"Come in," Alec called to her.

Lily opened the door and stepped inside his living room. He was lying in a recliner.

"Hi, Lily," he said, smiling at her as he moved his chair into an upright position. "I was just taking a nap before dinner."

"It's important for you to rest," she said quietly. "How are you today?"

"Better than yesterday," he replied grimly. "It's a matter of good days and bad."

"Yes, I understand," Lily said, wishing she had the power to make him better. "I want to thank you for all the things I bought today. We went to the outlet mall, and I got some great bargains. But, Alec, I intend to pay you back."

He waved a hand in dismissal. "Don't worry about it. All part of the job you'll be doing for me. It's nice to see you. Please sit down. It's been a while."

"Just a little while," she teased, responding to his attempted joke.

"Even though we haven't seen one another, I've followed you on social media. I've learned a little about your job and your life." He smiled. "Your niece is adorable. I know from what you share on Facebook how devoted you are to her. No children of your own, though."

"No. I've never found a man I wanted to marry." She glanced at him and away. "I've had a good life, but now I want to make a few changes."

He studied her. "You deserve happiness. I haven't forgotten our time together. It's one reason I brought you here. That, and for the help you can give me."

"I wish things could've been different between us," she said, unable to stop herself. Even to her own ears, she sounded pathetic.

"I know," Alec said kindly. "Me too. But as I said from the beginning, we were just going to date, that nothing beyond it would happen. Don't let ending our relationship prevent you from enjoying others. Believe me, as you near the end of your life, friends and family are more important than anything else. You're still too young to give up on love."

"You've become a romantic?" she said, her voice lifting in surprise.

He gave her a sad smile. "That's my problem. I've always been one."

They both looked away and out the window, an uneasy quiet settling in the room for a few minutes. Then Juanita walked into the room ending the silence between them. "Time for meds, Alec. Hi, Lily."

Lily got to her feet. "Hi, Juanita. I'll leave you two now."

"Come back anytime, Lily," said Alec, smiling at her. "I enjoyed having you here."

"Thanks." She left and went back to her room, unsettled by her lonely life. Perhaps it was time to let go of her time with

Alec and embrace new chances for finding love.

Alec joined them for dinner in the formal dining room, though Lily noted he didn't allow Juanita to serve him any food. Still, it was pleasant to have him present. He added an interesting touch to the conversation. He spoke of the history of the hotel and how he'd converted what once was a small inn into a resort that was competitive with any of the smaller, upscale properties in the area. Lily and the other women listened carefully to the details that would serve them well in the days ahead.

"What about this teambuilding routine?" Lily asked. She dreaded the idea of a lot of physical exercise. She'd worked for one company that required new employees to spend a day with other new hires in a unique indoctrination program that included things like falling into one another's arms in an exercise as a matter of trust. She could never master that part.

"I think it's important for you three to be able to count on one another, to know each is dependable, and to learn to be friends," said Alec. "I chose you to work together for particular reasons."

"How long will this teambuilding last?" Willow asked.

"Until your instructor decides you're ready," Alec answered cryptically.

Lily glanced at the other women and sighed. Being here included a lot more than she'd thought.

The next morning, Lily was still snuggled in her bed when a loud, man's voice in the hallway woke her. Startled, she sat up and gazed around sleepily.

"Rise and shine! Time to get up," he shouted again.

Frowning, Lily checked her bedside clock. 6 A.M.

She climbed out of bed, ran to the door, cracked it open, and stared out into the hallway. A well-toned man in running shorts and a tank top was clapping his hands and calling out to them. "Get up, Flowers, and meet me in the kitchen in your running clothes. See you there in no more than five minutes."

Lily groaned. *Was this Alec's idea of a joke?* The only running she did was to her car, and that was a rare occurrence.

She closed the door and got dressed, remembering to put on her new sports bra. Without it, she'd be uncomfortable. When she emerged from her room, Willow and Rose were already heading into the kitchen. Both had tied their hair into ponytails. She ran back into her room and grabbed a baseball cap.

In the kitchen, Rose and Willow were talking to the man who'd so abruptly awakened them. He looked at her and nodded. "And you must be Lily. I'm Dan McMillan. I'll be working with you for the next week or so, helping you improve your physical condition as you work through some teambuilding exercises."

"Why do we need to be in physical shape for our jobs?" Lily asked, wanting to whine. Listening and observing didn't require much more physical skill than sitting still.

"It's about being healthy and settling into desert life," Dan said. "You'll find your outlook and approach to your responsibilities will be more focused and effective as you become more physically active and help each other through some difficult exercises."

"And your overall mental acuity will be stimulated as well," said a stunning, athletic, blond-haired, tanned woman entering the kitchen.

"This is my assistant, Tiffany Weber," Dan announced. "She's here to help you."

Lily's heart fell. This was serious business. She glanced at Rose and Willow, but they didn't seem the least bit worried.

She took a moment to study Dan. She supposed if she had to do some sort of workout, she might as well enjoy the view. Dan was a striking man with craggy features, bright blue eyes, and longish, dark-brown hair held back from his handsome face by a colorful sweatband.

Tiffany handed her a belt with a pouch holding a full water bottle. "The desert can be brutal. You'll always want water with you. Dan and I will carry extra, but each of you needs to wear a belt like this."

Lily buckled the belt around her hips. She'd meant to lose a few pounds but had been too busy at work to make that happen. Maybe, she thought, this exercise would be a healthy thing.

She followed Dan and Tiffany outside and stood beside Rose and Willow.

"I'll go first on the trail," said Dan, "to keep an eye out for snakes and other critters. Tiffany will follow us at the rear, making sure you're all doing okay. This first day, we'll go easy on you. It's more important to be part of the group than to be running on your own. Got it?"

Lily dutifully nodded, thinking she and Tiffany might become friends at the back of the line. Glancing at Rose and Willow, she realized she wasn't nearly as fit as they.

"Okay, ready? Here we go!" Dan jogged down the driveway of Alec's house and onto the road that led up to it.

Lily was grateful for the slow pace he established and kept up with the group. But just when she was beginning to feel comfortable, Dan turned to his right, left the road, and headed up a narrow, sandy trail on the hill beyond Alec's house.

As the climb became steeper, Dan slowed their pace to a walk. At the front of the line, he acted as if the arduous terrain was nothing. Lily could feel the muscles in her legs tighten until she had to call out to him to please stop.

Tiffany showed her how to stretch, and the pain that had knotted in her leg began to ease. "Just a short way to go before we get to the cabin," Tiffany said. She waved the others to go ahead. "We'll catch up to you in a few minutes."

Lily continued to stretch and massage her leg. "Thanks for helping me, Tiffany. I'm not used to this."

"I know," Tiffany said. "It'll take a while. But you're being a good sport, and that's important."

"Do you know what this is all about?" Lily asked.

"Sure." Tiffany smiled. "It's about the three of you working together as a team as much as it is improving your physical condition and stamina."

"Okay," said Lily. "I'm ready." No way was she going to be the laggard in the group. Rose and Willow seemed so confident, so close to Alec. She wasn't about to disappoint Alec or them.

Tiffany and Lily soon reached what Tiffany had called a cabin but was actually a small adobe building. Above the wooden door was a carved sign that said, "The Cabin."

They walked inside and found Dan, Willow, and Rose doing stretching exercises near a table placed to the right of the entrance. An adobe brick fireplace was built into the back corner, with a couch facing it. Along the wall opposite the table, a cot held a couple of quilts. There was no kitchen or evidence of running water.

"Whose cabin is this?" Lily asked, wondering why anyone would want to stay here.

"It's Alec's hiding place," said Dan, grinning at her. "A far cry from the comforts of his home, but a place to come when someone like him wants to get off the treadmill."

"I like it," said Willow. "I used to come here quite often."

Dan looked at her and nodded. "Me too." He turned to Tiffany. "Are we okay to keep climbing, or should we head down and do the tour of the property?"

"I think on this first day, a tour would be better," Tiffany replied.

"Don't let me stop us from doing anything you want," Lily said, sure they were worried about her.

"Okay," said Dan, giving her a devilish look. "We'll do the complete tour of the property."

"He's just kidding," said Tiffany. "We'll do that tomorrow. Today is about starting to get into shape. As we do these morning runs and walks over the next few days, you'll find it gets easier as your energy and stamina build."

"It's going to take me more than a few days," said Lily.

Rose laughed. "Me, too. I've found a few muscles I haven't used recently." She turned to Willow. "How about you?"

"Though I'm familiar with the area, it's been a while since I've run like this or used the cabin."

"You say you used to come to the cabin?" Lily said.

"Oh, yes," Willow said. "It's one of my favorite places. I've done a lot of studying and thinking here. Alec helped me get into Cornell but expected me to get a scholarship, too."

"And now, for a short time, you'll help manage his hotel," said Rose. "It's a wonderful story."

"So, you're smart, too?" said Dan, giving Willow a teasing smile.

Willow's cheeks grew pinker.

"She's very smart," said Lily, earning smiles from both Rose and Willow. *This whole team-building idea was a good one,* she thought.

CHAPTER NINE
WILLOW

At Dan's remark, Willow couldn't help the flush that crept to her cheeks—a heat that had nothing to do with the climb she'd just made up to the cabin. Dan McMillan was a super-hot guy. Too bad he was with Tiffany. But then, Willow reminded herself, she had only one man she needed to be thinking about, and that was Brent Armstrong. She'd dreaded hearing that he was the person she'd be watching during the due diligence process with the Blaise Group, checking every nook and cranny, every piece of paper concerning the operation of the hotel. All this, while the Desert Sage Inn remained open and running smoothly.

Dan stood. "Okay, ladies, let's be on our way."

When Willow stepped out of the cabin, the sun was a yellow orb rising in the blue sky, shedding light on the sand and rocks below. She knew that some people thought desert landscapes were boring, but she loved the different subtle tones of neutral colors and the play of light and shadow on the area around her. And when a desert flower appeared strong and colorful, adding to the landscape, her heart filled with joy because it seemed such a beautiful and generous gift.

A small bird flew nearby and landed on a purple prickly pear cactus. She watched as it pecked at a hole then flew away. Observing the bird's flight, Willow thought how, as a young girl, she couldn't wait to venture away from her home and see the world. Now, she realized how much she'd missed it. Yes, the desert was hot in the summer, but there were ways to cool down. Feeling unsettled about the future, she waited for the others to emerge from the cabin.

She looked out over the Coachella Valley. Mountains to the northeast bordered the valley along the southern border of Joshua Tree National Monument. To the northwest, San Gorgonio Mountain, the tallest peak in Southern California, reached for the sky with its snow-capped peak. Seeing the majesty of the mountains there and the San Jacinto Mountains to the west always made her realize how insignificant she was. Yet, as she'd been taught from a young age, she knew she mattered to those who loved her.

When they stepped outside, Rose and Lily looked tired. Willow was tired, too, though younger and in better shape. But it pleased her they'd all made the effort to do as requested. "Okay, down we go," said Dan. "Walking down can sometimes seem harder than climbing up, so watch your step."

An iguana scooted by.

Willow noted the horrified expression on Lily's face and held in a laugh. She'd take iguanas any day over meeting up with a tarantula or a rattlesnake or the likes of Brent Armstrong.

They hiked down to the service road surrounding the property and set out on another walk, a tour of sorts, before heading back to Alec's house.

When they arrived there, Dan announced, "Time to get into your bathing suits. We'll end the morning with some exercises in the pool to help keep those new muscles you have discovered loose and prevent unwanted cramping."

Willow exchanged glances with the other women, and sighing softly, went to her room to change. It had been a grueling morning, but she knew how important it was for all of them. Still, she hoped they'd have a chance to rest that afternoon.

Outside by the pool, Rose was talking to Tiffany. Willow thought Rose had an unmistakable natural beauty. Her figure was striking, enhanced as it was by her one-piece swimsuit with enticing cutouts. She'd tied her hair in a ponytail and looked like a woman half her age.

Lily stepped out of the house onto the patio wearing a two-piece swimsuit that she and Rose had insisted she buy instead of the simple one-piece black one Lily had originally chosen.

Willow smiled and gave her a thumbs-up.

Lily straightened and walked toward her wearing a smile. "What's next?"

Willow gave her a quick hug. "We'll see. Love seeing you in that suit."

"I'll get used to it," Lily said with a determination that Willow knew was forced. Whether she admitted it or not, Lily was a lot more beautiful than she thought. Sometimes it was hard to imagine Lily and Alec had been together; other times, Willow was drawn to Lily's kind nature and vulnerability. She was a sweetheart.

They turned as Dan stripped off his running shorts and stood in a Speedo brief that allowed them to see even more of his toned body.

"Wow," whispered Willow, unable to hold back her admiration.

"Ditto," said Lily, *sotto voce.*

Dan was oblivious to their stares as he turned to the water in the pool and dove in. After swimming a length of the pool to the shallow end, he stood in the water. "C'mon in."

Willow jumped into the water, enjoying the shock of the relatively cool water. When she surfaced, she treaded water and watched as Rose and Lily slowly climbed down the steps at the shallow end before allowing all of their bodies to get wet.

Dan waved her over. "Tiffany has left me in charge. We're going to do some simple exercises in the water to stretch our bodies and to keep sore muscles from tightening up."

Willow stood beside Lily and Rose and, for the next twenty minutes, followed Dan's instructions. By the time they got out of the water, Willow felt as limp as the other women looked.

Dan climbed out of the pool and gave them a salute. "See you same time tomorrow. Be dressed for another run."

They were silent as they watched him pick up his clothes and head out of the pool area.

After they had settled around a table under an umbrella, Rose turned to them. "What do you gals think?"

"If you're talking about Dan, I think he's one hot dude," said Lily in an imitation of a New Jersey accent.

Willow burst into laughter. Never in a million years would she suspect Lily had that humorous side to her.

"Are you from Jersey?" Rose asked Lily, her eyes twinkling with mirth.

"No, but one of my worst bosses ever was from there, and he had an accent like that," Lily said. "A work friend and I got so we were pretty believable imitating him."

"I'll say," said Rose, chuckling. "Willow, what do you think about all this?"

"The training?" At Rose's nod, Willow said, "I'm not sure it's required, but I understand that Alec has his particular ways about doing things, and if he thinks we need this, I'll do what he asks."

"Yeah, I'm a little puzzled by it but will go along with him," admitted Rose. "Besides, this team-building stuff is allowing us to learn more about one another."

Willow spoke up. "This whole thing is an opportunity for me to make some changes in my life. I've been stuck in a job I didn't like. Now, working here with you, I'll have the chance to rethink things."

"Me, too," said Lily. "Already, I can see what a rut I've been in. If nothing else, being here will force me to decide what to do with the rest of my life." Tears came to her eyes. "I've felt so trapped by my job and working day and night to help my sister."

Rose studied her. "Maybe it's time for you to do things for yourself."

"Yes, I know. After helping Alec, that's what I intend to do." Lily gave them a wobbly smile. "My life isn't at all what I'd imagined."

"But isn't that what life is all about, moving through one challenge after another?" Rose said.

"Are you saying we don't need to plan so we can meet those challenges?" Willow shook her head. Without establishing plans, she never would have gone to college, even with Alec's help. And if she hadn't already had plans to teach at Boston University, her breakup with Jake might've been devastating. As painful as it was, she'd moved on.

"All I'm saying," said Rose, "is that we must be prepared for challenges whenever and wherever they occur."

Willow nodded her agreement. Even the best-laid plans went awry.

Her mother came out to the pool area. "Are you ready for lunch? I have some fresh green salads and iced tea for you."

"That sounds perfect!" said Rose. "Thank you, Juanita. I'm ready."

"Me, too," said Lily as Willow nodded.

"Okay, then. I'll bring them out. It's such a pleasant day."

Willow observed the professional way her mother handled

herself—always polite, always encouraging to guests. Though it felt awkward to be treated as a guest, Willow stuck to Alec's plan to have her take on that role. Especially because she'd have to deal with Brent as an equal. Having been demeaned by Jake's parents, she was not about to be in that kind of situation again. She was who she was, child of Pedro and Juanita Sanchez, and she was proud of them and herself. She was pretty sure Brent wouldn't remember her, but she remembered him and the way he'd treated others outside of his group.

CHAPTER TEN
ROSE

Working with Lily and Willow, Rose sometimes felt old. They were becoming like younger sisters. She loved her independence, didn't need to be the center of an ongoing party, but still found something lacking in her life. Her blog was a godsend to her, allowing her to be at home or researching material for it while maintaining friendships with hundreds of social media participants. To an outgoing person like her who still needed her privacy, it was the best of all worlds.

Being here with Alec, flooded with memories of their time together, was a piercing experience, opening old desires for them to be together always. To someone else, his asking her to be present at this time might seem cruel. But he wasn't that way. He knew her well enough to know that in the end, she'd understand it was a gift of trust, caring, and a rekindling of sweet memories. It was a way to say a final goodbye.

It had taken her a while to move on with her life after she'd left him and the inn. And when she finally chose to allow herself to fall in love with someone else, he'd been Alec's total opposite. Their marriage had been doomed from the start. From there, she'd gone on to casual relationships, had even tried having a "friend with benefits," but that hadn't lasted long because she knew what real lovemaking was all about.

She lay on her bed and picked up the reading material Alec had given her. Willow and Lily had also received packets of information to study. No crying about what she couldn't change, she told herself, then focused on the project.

As she became immersed in facts about the hotel and leafed through various photos, she worked on producing several blogs about the place. She had an audience of thousands. Maybe she could beat the hotel company wanting to take over by raising the occupancy of the Desert Sage Inn by hundreds of room nights over the coming weeks. Smiling to herself, Rose got up and went to find Alec.

At his private entrance, she knocked gently. Hearing no response, she cracked open the door and peered in. Alec was lounging in a reclining chair, staring at her.

Startled, she managed a smile, though seeing him so weak always made her want to cry.

"Hi, Alec! Do you have a minute?" As soon as she said the words, she wished she could take them back.

His smile was weak, but his eyes were amused. "I apparently have more than a minute, but how many more we've yet to find out."

She laughed even as her eyes filled. "I have an idea I want to talk over with you."

"Pull up a chair."

She did as she asked and held up her notes. "You know I have the blog, 'You Deserve This,' right? I'd like to offer my followers a deal. For every three nights they stay here during the week, they get a free night. I think it would draw people. It's been a miserable winter to the north and east. I could call it a 'You Deserve a Desert Escape' plan, show plenty of pictures, and list some of the well-known people who come here. What do you think?"

"Weekdays only?"

"For the plan. But of course, I'd promote people spending the weekend here too, but make it seem such a bargain they'd be foolish not to make it a whole week. Those spending eight nights here would have two free nights making a 10-day vacation seem possible. 'Heads in beds,' as they say, is important to all the other operations at a resort."

"Spoken like a true hotelier," Alec said, beaming at her with some of his old energy. "Tweak the numbers a little, and let's do it." He grabbed hold of her hand and squeezed it. "You've always been the one woman I would've broken my promise for, but I couldn't do it. I hope someday you find someone who deserves you."

"At my age? Hardly likely," she retorted. "And I do like my independence."

Alec shook his head. "You're not that old. And you're beautiful and talented and fun."

Rose lowered her gaze and stared into her lap. She'd tried to find someone special but was never satisfied.

He patted her hand. "I have a feeling something positive will come out of all this. I certainly hope so."

Rose stared at him, not even bothering to hide her doubt. She'd long ago given up the idea of a knight in shining armor in her life. She'd been thrilled with her freedom after her divorce.

She watched as his eyes closed and then stood, put the chair back, and quietly left the room. If her notes on Hank Bowers were right, he was just the kind of man she detested. Maybe that's why Alec had her opposing him. He knew, if necessary, she'd fight him to the end.

As she walked back to her room, she saw Lily outside lying on a chaise lounge in the shade next to the pool, a stack of papers at her side. On an impulse, she decided to go talk to her. Alec had thought enough of Lily to date her for a couple of years; Rose wanted to know more about her.

As Rose approached, Lily raised her head and smiled. "Hi."

"How are you doing?" Rose asked, sitting in a chair beside her. "Looks like you have even more paperwork than I do."

"Believe me, this is more interesting than the usual legal documents I handle," Lily said. Another smile broke out on her face. "Or *used* to handle. I'm so glad I finally resigned from my job. Interesting how stuck we can get in a situation and then allow inertia to take over."

"Yes. I quit my job at one of the hotels a few years ago and set up my consulting practice doing social media campaigns for businesses, mostly small ones. I've never felt freer to do my own thing." Rose chuckled. "I like being my own boss."

Lily stared into the distance. "I don't know what I'll do after we're finished here. It's all so sad, and yet I'm pleased to be part of Alec's plan."

"You loved him, didn't you?" Rose said softly, touched by Lily's words.

"Yeah, I did. I've always thought he was a wonderful man. Still do," Lily admitted, her eyes filling.

Rose reached out and patted her hand. "We all do or we wouldn't be here."

Lily drew a deep breath and studied her. "He stayed with you the longest."

Rose remained silent, lost in the memory of the special relationship she'd had with Alec. Even now, it was frustrating to know that after all they'd shared, it hadn't prevented him from keeping a vow he'd established for his lost wife and child. "We almost made it," she said softly. "I've never found another man that matched those years with him. Sure, I've had plenty of dates and other relationships. I even married once, but it didn't work out. Just as well, I suppose, to be either free or with someone who can make me feel the way I did with Alec."

"I understand. I'm in the same situation." Lily studied her. "I used to be jealous of you."

"Really?" Rose said.

Lily nodded. "I knew how much Alec cared for you. I think he still does."

Overcome with raw emotion, Rose got to her feet. "Thanks for telling me. Guess I'd better get back to work." She walked away quickly so Lily wouldn't see the tears that escaped her eyes and trailed down her cheeks. Why, she wondered, was her life so screwed up? Was real love always going to be out of her reach?

Back in the safety of her room, Rose sat deep in thought. She was here to help Alec. Nothing more. She was content in her work and would figure out the rest as it came along. He'd asked all of them to come here for a reason. She had a feeling helping him at the hotel wasn't the only one. Time would tell.

At dinner that night, the conversation was brisk as Alec quizzed them on what they'd done with the information they'd been given.

Lily reported that she'd read through a lot of the paperwork but needed to make careful notes on several contracts. If the inn was to be sold, she wanted to be sure the reputation and integrity of the property were protected where possible.

"Not that I'm a lawyer, but I've learned enough to bring it to Alec's attention," Lily ended.

"Well done, Lily," Alec said, giving her a smile of approval. "Rose and I have talked about an advertising and marketing campaign she's putting together to bring in more guests. Rose, why don't you tell us what you've done with this?"

Rose cleared her throat and began. "I'm going to feature a special for my followers on my blog, 'You Deserve This.' If they stay three nights at the inn, they get a fourth night free, which means if people do this, chances are they'll add an extra couple of days onto their reservation to get a full week's vacation here at the inn. By building up our occupancy rate, we add value to the hotel through the additional room sales and increased revenues from all other guest services."

"Great idea," said Willow. "I joined your blog and will spread the news on Facebook and Instagram for all my friends."

"That would be great! If we can build a buzz, let's do it. We might even feature something on YouTube. I'll have to think of a cute event."

"We allow dogs in certain rooms, don't we?" Willow said.

"Yes." Rose grinned. "I've got it. We'll show a dog registering at the hotel. Or maybe a baby or both." She laughed with the others.

"And, Willow, what do you have for us? Have you thought of any plans for dealing with Brent Armstrong?" Alec said.

Willow frowned and let out a sigh. "I've read that he thinks he's a great golfer." Her frown was replaced with a devilish grin. "I thought I'd brush up on my game."

Alec laughed. "Willow was a state champion back in high school. I don't know how much golf you've played in the northeast, but by all means, spend some time on the golf course."

Rose glanced at Lily and gave Willow a thumbs up. It might be time for a certain cocky young male to get beaten at his game.

"I'll even caddy for you," said Lily.

Willow laughed. "Not to worry. I've got my own golf cart."

The more Rose got to know these women, the better she liked them.

CHAPTER ELEVEN
LILY

The next morning when Dan called to them to get up, Lily covered her ears. *"It couldn't be that time already,"* she groused. But as he continued speaking to them from the hallway, she turned over and stared up at the ceiling. She groaned softly as she got out of bed. Her muscles ached in new places. *"Why have I allowed myself to become such a softie?"* she asked herself and then remembered her usual hectic schedule at home. Full of determination to make some changes, she gamely took care of her morning routine and quickly dressed for another session of teambuilding.

Dan acknowledged her with a nod of his head. "Okay, we're all here. I thought you might enjoy running on the track at the high school. The girls' track team is working out, and they're dying to race you later this afternoon."

"You're kidding, right?" said Willow.

Dan shook his head. "Not at all. We're going to set up a three-person relay race with three of their top runners."

Lily glanced at the others. *Was Dan crazy?*

"Is this one of those lessons in humility?" Rose asked, giving Dan a steady look.

He laughed. "I guess that's something we'll soon find out. But you three are capable of much more than you think."

Rose turned to her and Willow. "Then, I guess we'll show those young girls exactly who we are. Right?"

Lily nodded and grinned, glad Rose was on her side.

#

That afternoon at the Palm Desert High School, home of the Aztecs, Lily followed Dan and the others onto the outdoor track. A group of a dozen girls, some wearing white hats with the round orange and gold logo on them, watched and giggled as they approached.

"Easy, peasy," muttered Rose, not bothering to hide her dismay.

Lily understood. The girls were young and in top shape. There was no way she and the other two women were a match for them.

Dan introduced them to the girls and then singled out each of the Flowers and told the girls a bit about them.

"I like how you call yourselves the Desert Flowers, and each of you has a name of one," said one of the girls.

The others murmured their agreement.

"We may have names that sound pretty, but all women have to be tough," said Rose. She couldn't stand the idea that some women depended on their looks to get by.

"Oh, yes, we know that well," said a tall, sinewy girl. "We have to be twice as fast as some of the guys on the team to get any recognition."

"You also have to be smart," said Rose. "Brains are more important than beauty." She turned to Dan. "What are the rules for this race?"

Dan shrugged. "It's simple. You women each have to run the length of the track and back, competing against someone from the high school team. The first team to cross the finish line in the races wins."

Rose stared into space, nodded, and waved Lily and Willow to her side. With a devilish grin, she drew them into a huddle.

"Okay, girls. This is what we're going to do," and she whispered her plan to Willow and Lily.

"Is that fair?" Lily asked, both shocked and pleased by the idea.

Rose grinned. "I believe it meets all the requirements as stated."

Lily couldn't hold back a laugh. Willow joined her.

"Ready?" asked Dan.

"Yep," said Rose. She walked over and got in place at the head of the track.

The tall girl who'd spoken up earlier lined up next to her.

"Okay, ready, set, go!" cried Dan.

Rose darted forward, quickly joined by Lily and Willow.

The girl looked wide-eyed at them, but the four of them kept running, up and back.

Though Lily was the slowest of them, she wasn't far behind. And toward the end, she ran in a burst of speed, joining Rose and Willow as they crossed the finish line behind the high school girl.

"We won!" cried Rose, lifting her arms in triumph.

"What? No," said Dan.

The girls from the high school shouted, "Cheaters! Cheaters!"

Rose held up a hand to quiet them. "The rules stated that we were each required to run against someone on the opposing team, and the first *team* to cross the finish line would win. We did that."

"But it was supposed to be a relay race," one girl protested.

"That was not made clear," Rose said. "Look! The whole point of our doing this was to demonstrate how smart women have to be in any competition. We don't have to cheat or twist the rules; we simply have to know what we're dealing with."

"Now," said Willow. "Let's do a real relay race and see how

badly you can beat our team."

Dan, who'd remained quiet during the entire interchange between the teams, laughed. "Well done, Flowers. You've demonstrated thinking outside of the box and exceptional teamwork. Now let's see how strong your competitive spirit is." His voice held a bit of teasing menace.

When it was time, Lily gamely took her turn running against a member of the track team though the outcome was inevitable. Still, she put her heart into it and decided she liked the adrenaline that filled her as one foot then the other pounded the surface, producing a certain soothing rhythm.

After the three races ended, Dan pulled a cooler out of his SUV and brought it over to the shade under a tree where everyone was taking a rest. He handed out water and power drinks and then sat down on the ground to join them.

The girls were talking about an event coming up at school and were asking Rose, Lily, and Willow if they'd be interested in coming to the school to speak to students about female empowerment.

"I know some of you may think it was weird how we went about the race at first," said Rose.

"But did it prove anything to you?" Lily asked, wondering what effect it had had on them.

"I'm going to listen better," said one of the girls.

"Me, too," chimed in another.

"I'm a legal assistant," said Lily. "As Rose had us point out, it's important to be sure what you're dealing with. Read things over or listen carefully, so you're not caught in a situation you don't like. I imagine some of you will earn scholarships with your skills. Make sure everything in writing is exactly as you want and have someone who understands contracts help you."

"I like this," said the tall, outspoken girl, smiling at them. "Women helping women. So how do you know one another?"

Lily exchanged glances with Willow and Rose. "Through the Desert Sage Inn." She didn't mention Alec's name because it wasn't her tale alone to tell.

She listened as a couple of girls mentioned having relatives work there and how much they liked it. Lily stored information away to use at a later date. The fact that employees were loyal was important, a bargaining tool, should it be necessary. The Palm Desert area with its abundance of hotels and clubs provided a lot of competition for finding and keeping employees well versed in the hospitality business.

Back at Alec's house, Dan ordered them into the pool to swim laps, competing against one another for fast times. As tired as she was from the races at the high school, Lily gamely jumped into the water and did as he asked, swimming as fast as she could, one length after another. A mere three days ago, she would've drowned. Now, she noticed how much stronger, how much more confident she was becoming. And there was something about Rose's competitiveness that made Lily want to do her best.

Later, sitting at the edge of the pool, kicking her feet in the water, letting the sun dry her skin, she studied Rose and Willow. They were such interesting women. Each day something more about them was exposed, like peeling the skin off an orange and discovering something sweet.

For the next several mornings, Dan repeated his 6 A.M. calls to action to get the women up and out for more jogging, hiking, and other exercises intended to build stamina and improve physical conditioning. Each session ended with time in the swimming pool to stretch newly used muscles and to cool down carefully to prevent any cramps or muscle pulls. At the end of a week of these sessions, each of the women felt more energetic and admitted they had gotten to enjoy their early morning routine and planned to start their days going forward with some form of physical exercise. At the end of a week of this, Dan announced that he felt they were ready to move ahead with their responsibilities working with Alec and the Blaise Group team for the ownership transition.

CHAPTER TWELVE
ROSE

After the last morning of Dan's workouts, Rose finished drying off by the pool and headed into her room to get dressed. She needed some time alone. Later, she planned on visiting Alec. Like the other women, she always found a moment or two to spend time alone with him. After all, he was the reason they were all there.

After changing into her clothes, Rose lay down on her bed, content to rest and contemplate her life to this point. Everyone described her as outgoing, friendly, and fun to be with. Little did they know it was all an act to cover up the insecure, unloved young girl that made an unwelcome appearance now and then inside her.

She was an only child of parents who'd made it clear they'd never wanted her. Instead, they wanted comfortable routines. Rose's natural curiosity and excitement over new things fought with their insistence on peace and quiet. To this day, Rose sometimes found herself purposely doing outrageous things to satisfy the feeling that she'd somehow escaped their cruel, cold ways. Both dead now, her parents would never understand why she was helping Alec. He had, after all, broken her heart. To make up for that, though, he'd given her a sense of self that she'd always sought. In his eyes, she was a perfectly endearing human being, worthy of being loved, not the child her parents hadn't wanted. She knew he still cared about her. And though they'd never marry or get the chance to grow old together, she'd always be grateful to him for all they'd shared.

Rose sighed, got up, and went over to the window to look out at the desert scene. A tiny hummingbird, fluttering its wings, suspended in the air near the brilliant red blossoms of the espaliered bougainvillea against the wall at the edge of the lawn.

She'd had love in her life. Men found her spontaneity, her sexuality intriguing. But she was so much more than her physical beauty. Only Alec had been able to reach inside her, to touch her soul.

Thinking of him, she turned around and walked to his end of the house. A report on how his "Flowers" were doing on forming a team was due him.

After gently knocking on his door, she entered his living quarters. "Alec?" she called softly.

"In here," he answered.

She walked into his bedroom. Fully dressed, he was lying atop his bed reading a book. When he saw her, a smile broke out, briefly lighting his haggard face.

"Rose, come sit by me," he said, patting the bed beside him.

She grinned. "I can do better than that."

A look of delight softened his features, allowing her to see a bit of the younger man she'd loved so dearly.

Sliding onto the bed beside him, she lay next to him, wrapped her arms around him, and drew him close.

"Ahhh, how I've missed this," he whispered. "I've always loved you."

"I know," she answered, unable to keep the sadness out of her voice. She lightly caressed his back with the palm of her hand, rubbing gently in comforting circles. If only life were different. If only he weren't dying, maybe then she could convince him that as noble as the idea was, he didn't need to give up happiness because of guilt over his wife and child. Now, no matter what, it was too late.

She continued to hold him, well aware of how thin he was, how fragile. He'd always been an athletic man. That made it even sadder that he'd become like this.

He lay on his back, and she cuddled up next to him, aware of the pleasure her closeness brought him.

He turned his head toward her. "So how are you Desert Flowers doing? Are you becoming friends? Learning to trust one another?"

She nodded and looked up at him. "Yes, we are. But, Alec, I know you well enough to know you have something planned for us. Something unexpected. Am I right?"

His lips curved. "You'll see."

"You aren't going to say anything more about it?"

His smile grew wider even as his eyes filled. "Nope."

She sighed. He always kept to his word. "In the meantime, we'll do what you ask and keep the resort going strong. When are we going to be introduced to the staff?"

"Soon," Alec replied. He patted her back. "Thank you, Rose, for being you."

Her heart welled with love for him.

That afternoon, Rose was sitting outside, studying past advertising campaigns for the resort, when Willow approached the table and sat down.

"Am I interrupting you?"

Rose smiled at her. "Yes, but I need a break. What's up?"

Willow slumped down in a chair facing her. "I've been thinking about the trick we played on the girls from the track team. It was a smart lesson, something I'm going to need in the days ahead. I haven't told my parents or Alec, but at school, I was harassed for being Mexican, a female at that. People, including Brent Armstrong, called me 'Enchilada' under their breaths and made certain to let me know they didn't think I should be there. I called out the worst of the girls on it, but I could never work my nerve up to face the guys."

Rose straightened in her chair and studied her. "Wow! I can't believe they could get away with that."

Willow rolled her eyes. "People like that are sneaky about how they do it. Sometimes they talk to you as if you're beneath them, or they just look at you funny, or turn their backs, or..."

"Roll their eyes?" Rose said, arching an eyebrow.

Willow chuckled. "Yeah, that too."

Rose reached across the table and patted her hand. "None of it is acceptable when it's aimed to hurt you. I'm sorry you've had to deal with that mistreatment. How are you going to handle going face-to-face with Brent here at the hotel?"

"I'm not about to let the past rule my future. I don't come from the same kind of background a lot of those students did, but that doesn't make me less than them ..." Willow began.

"No, my dear. It makes you something better," said Rose, interrupting her. "You've had to work harder, do more to succeed. You've already proved how strong you are. You know you can take on Brent Armstrong. That's how you're going to handle that little prick—by being you, strong and confident."

Willow's eyes widened. "Have you experienced something like that?"

Rose nodded. "In more subtle ways, perhaps. But I suppose each of us has to discover what inner strength we possess to follow dreams. Even if it's in a twisted way. Mine was a determination not to be cold like my parents, to overcome their lack of love for me. Weird, huh?"

"I'm sorry. That must have hurt. My parents have been so wonderful to me."

Rose smiled. "They're lovely people, so full of life. You're a lucky woman."

Willow straightened. "Thank you, Rose. You've helped me more than you know." She stood and gave her a quick hug.

Her eyes stinging from withheld tears, Rose hugged her back. She realized how much she loved the idea of becoming close to Willow and Lily. Alec was a smart man who must've known this. If she only knew what was behind his plans for them.

As Willow walked away, Lily approached her. "Is everything all right? Willow looked like she might've been crying."

"Close to it," Rose admitted. "She's been bullied in the past, and we were discussing how to handle Brent, her counterpart. She's strong enough to stand up to that little bastard, but if he's as entitled as we've been led to believe, she's going to need us to support her."

"I definitely agree. She was right to come to you. I can't imagine your letting anyone get the best of you." Lily gave her a warm smile.

Rose shifted uncomfortably. "I'm not as strong as you think. It's important for all of us to band together when the occasion arises."

Lily sat down at the table. "I've been making a few notes about the strengths of the resort. When I'm finished, would you mind taking a look at them? As someone savvy in communications, you might be able to add to it."

"Sure. No problem," Rose said, inordinately pleased by Lily's confidence in her.

Lily grinned. "By the way, I've signed up for your blog. What a fun way to learn about some great things. How did you come up with the idea?"

"I met a lot of people during my job as a hostess at one of

the big hotels in Vegas. So many people who were used to spending a lot of money were eager to find out about different places to go for eating and shopping that I started a blog for Vegas and then included other places I've heard about or, preferably, visited. From there, I chose cool 'in' things to purchase for both home and for personal use. The blog has grown like crazy. I'm grateful because I now have advertisers willing to pay for a spot on it."

"And you'll put the Desert Sage Inn there?"

Rose grinned. "I've already worked up a post for tomorrow. Once we're introduced to the staff, I'll do a couple of personal interviews with them and share those as well."

"Great idea." Lily got to her feet. "Guess I'll go lie down for a while. See you at dinner."

Rose watched Lily walk away. Now that she'd had a chance to get to know her a little and had seen how determined she was to do her share to bring them together, Rose felt a growing friendship toward her. There was no reason to believe any rivalry existed between them regarding Alec. Rose knew that though they'd both moved on, she and Alec still shared something special. And if the others did too, she didn't mind.

Later, Alec joined them for dinner, taking a seat at the head of the table. Though a plate of food was put in front of him, Rose knew it was just a formality. His menu consisted of healthy drinks and a few favorites that Juanita cooked for him throughout the day.

"Love to see my 'Flowers' looking so bright and ready for work," he said, giving each of them a smile. "Tomorrow, we'll have you join me for a staff meeting at the hotel, and I'll introduce you to everyone. After the meeting, you can pair up with one of my staff so that you'll be ready to meet with the buyers' due diligence team next week."

"So soon?" Willow said, glancing at Rose.

Rose gave her an encouraging nod. "You'll be ready, Willow. You are now."

Willow shot her a smile. "You're right."

Alec's eyebrows shot up. "Am I missing something?"

Rose shook her head. "Just a matter of confidence. We're all going to be just fine."

"Excellent," said Alec, nodding emphatically. "I've put my trust in you."

Rose once more had a sense that there was more to it than that, but she remained quiet.

The following day, Rose was glad to see she wasn't the only one who'd dressed for the occasion in business attire. Until now, they'd worn mostly running clothes or swimsuits with cover-ups.

Now, Willow was wearing a black skirt that came to just above the knees, a crisp white blouse, and a light-weight blazer in bright green that looked great against her skin. Lily wore a turquoise linen sheath with capped sleeves that was both tasteful and sexy. Her eyes picked up the color of the dress and illuminated her face. Rose was wearing black slacks and a light sweater in a soft green that went well with her hair. All in all, they were an attractive threesome, toned from the workouts in which they'd been forced to participate. Rose hoped their appearances would hide the brains behind them. She liked the idea of catching people in the industry off guard.

They gathered at the front door waiting for Alec to show up. He'd insisted on taking them to the meeting himself. When he appeared, Rose stifled a sob that came from the heart. Alec had always been an impeccable dresser. Now it was evident that though his navy blazer and gray slacks were of the highest quality, his pants were more than baggy, and the gap between his neck and the collar of his blazer appeared much too large, leaving a space between cloth and skin.

"' Morning," he said pleasantly. "You all look terrific—professional and yet truly beautiful. Rose, Lily, and Willow—true desert flowers."

Pedro appeared. "The cart is ready for you. Ladies, if you'll please follow me. Alec has chosen to transport you aboard the large golf cart this morning. It will help to create a dramatic entrance for you." His eyes swung to Willow, and Rose could read the pride she saw in them. Willow was a stunning young woman. Better than that, she was smart as a whip, able to handle many details at once. After she faced Brent, Willow would, she was sure, be able to stand her ground with him.

Rose followed the others to the front circle and stood by to climb aboard the golf cart. Fortunately, there was no wind to mess with her hair or to kick up desert dust. She'd forgotten how dusty the desert could be. She brushed off a vinyl-covered seat with her hand before sitting down.

After everyone else was in place, Alec got behind the wheel and turned to them with a grin. "We're off!"

The cart moved quickly, quietly along the paved path skirting the golf course. Guests playing on the course lifted their hands or golf clubs in friendly salutes as they rolled by. Rose studied the landscape, smiling at the sight of a rabbit hopping across the grass and then freezing in place as they drew closer. Hummingbirds fluttered by blooming cacti, and a bird of some kind pecked at a hole in a tall, prickly cactus. A desert landscape was no less active than many others.

Alec made a special gesture by driving them up to the front entrance of the hotel. The resident manager and a few of his staff stood ready to greet them.

Rose helped Alec off the cart, and she, Lily, and Willow walked beside him to meet John Rodriquez and his staff. She'd read about John and knew he was a retired military man who'd received a graduate degree in Hospitality Management from the University of Denver. Observing his straight posture and dark brown eyes that seemed to miss nothing, she could easily imagine how well he did in the service. He had medals to prove it.

Curious about the man who'd been at Alec's side for several years as the resident manager, she held out her hand in greeting.

His smile was warm as he shook it. "Rose Macklin, welcome. I'm pleased you're part of the transition team."

She returned his smile, liking him already. There was a quiet dignity about him. She knew he wouldn't accept any nonsense from anyone.

After all the Flowers were introduced to him, John and Alec exchanged man hugs, and then John led them inside. Rose studied the lobby with approval. Even with normal activity going on, the lobby was clean and tidy. Attentive housekeeping staff went about unobtrusively doing their chores. She made a mental note to use this information in another blog.

John took them down to the ground level to a large room set up for a staff meeting. When she and the others walked into it, she saw from their uniforms that it was filled with people from all departments, who all stood as they entered the room.

Five seats in the front row remained empty. Before Alec sat down, he turned and waved to the group. A resounding wave of applause filled the room, bringing tears to Rose's eyes. As she'd always remembered, the staff loved him.

John motioned for the staff to be seated and for Rose,

Willow, and Lily to face the audience. He then introduced them one by one. "These women will be actively involved both before and during the transition phase, which officially begins next week. I want each and every one of you to cooperate by answering all their questions and providing them with any information they might need. Rose will be working on social media and advertising. Lily is going to be in my office assisting Mr. Thurston and me. And Willow will be working with the young man heading the executive team."

Rose smiled as a round of applause broke out, and then she took her seat.

John described the process that would take place, the need for strict confidentiality outside the hotel, and the hope that by doing a superb job, staff members would be assured of continuing their careers at the hotel. "That decision won't be ours to make, but we plan to put pressure on the Blaise Group to have a place for each of you." He glanced at Alec. "Mr. Thurston has made that very clear from the beginning."

Rose and her fellow Desert Flowers joined in the round of applause that followed John's remarks.

Aware of Alec's inability to stay for much longer, John closed the meeting by handing out a schedule of events for the week and an announcement that a surprising number of reservations were being requested due, no doubt, to Rose's latest "You Deserve This" blog. He motioned for her to stand.

Rose got to her feet. "For those of you who haven't signed up for my blog, you'll find it easy to do so. I'll make sure Mr. Rodriguez has the information posted on your hotel news site." She wasn't the least bit ashamed to promote herself. That's what social media was all about.

Following the meeting, John invited them upstairs to Joshua's, the informal dining room, for lunch.

Eager to see if the food was as delicious as advertised and

finally to have a meal that wasn't part of the team building menu, Rose glanced at Lily and Willow and gave them a conspiratorial wink.

Lily gave her a thumbs up. "I get it. I really do."

"Me, too," said Willow, laughing. "I already know I'm going to order fries."

Feeling like a school girl let out of school early, Rose laughed with them.

Joshua's was as desert-themed as the name implied. The walls and wood trim were painted in tasteful beige tones. Green accents were popped with bright-pink color throughout the room in the fabric on the drapes and the compatible tablecloths and napkins. The gray-green vinyl on the seats of chairs and the benches lining the booths reflected desert tones, matching the color of some of the various cacti native to the valley. Rose loved it.

A table in the corner of the room had been reserved for them—a convenient place, Rose knew, to observe the activity of guests and the competence of the wait staff.

After the waitress passed out menus and took orders for drinks, Rose eagerly looked at the food choices and immediately decided on the Southwest Shrimp Cocktail made with tomato, cucumber, red onion, cilantro, avocado, tomato juice, lime. Lily, she noticed, ordered a grilled chicken sandwich, and Willow ordered a burger with fries. Rose decided to forgo fries and order dessert instead after seeing a lemon chiffon tart delivered to a nearby table.

While they waited for their orders to be delivered, Lily asked John about his career at the Desert Sage Inn.

John talked easily about his need to do something positive with his life after leaving the service and spoke eagerly of his time at the University of Denver, learning about the business. A native of California, he decided to return. "And when I met

Alec, I knew I'd made the right choice. I was an older, inexperienced student, but he saw potential in me."

"He's a good judge of character," said Willow. "As you know, my parents and I are devoted to him."

John nodded. "A better man never existed."

Hearing such praise, Rose felt her heart clench. So many people loved him. Soon, he'd be gone.

CHAPTER THIRTEEN
WILLOW

Willow listened carefully to John. He, like her, had received Alec's confidence, giving him an opportunity in the hospitality business. She was tempted to ask him how to deal with people who judged her too quickly and then decided, as her father had told her, she had to prove to others how competent she was regardless of her background. Coming from an immigrant family like theirs, she'd tried to face challenges with the same dignity as her parents.

She tuned into the conversation. Rose was talking about the changes at the hotel. It was still called an inn, but, in reality, it was a full-blown resort with what they all liked to think of as an intimate, luxurious feel.

After lunch, they were taken to the executive offices, where each Flower was assigned a person to introduce them to standard operating procedures. John worked directly for Alec with a staff of department heads and two assistant managers. Willow would become the third one whose job would help the transition team as a fresh set of eyes and ears.

John reintroduced her to his assistant managers, Sarah Jensen and Tim Kneeland. She knew already that Sarah was the mother of a two-year-old boy and had come home when the Army deployed her husband to Afghanistan. Her family had been part of Palm Desert since the early days when people like Edgar Bergen, the famous ventriloquist, first moved into the area. Tim was in his early forties and was in charge of the front desk and reception areas. Both were effusive in their welcomes to her, which made her wonder how easy John was to work for.

Tim walked with Willow to the lobby, where they stood watching the activity. "As much as possible, we like to get our arriving guests into their room ahead of normal check-in time. It makes them happy, and as long as Housekeeping can keep up with the demand, we're glad to do so."

He nodded toward the front entry, where a doorman was holding the door for a young couple who'd just arrived. "Listen carefully," Tim said to her softly.

The doorman, an older man with gray hair, greeted the couple politely and followed them into the lobby. He then directed the gentleman to the front desk to check in and suggested to the woman that she might like to have a seat nearby or have a drink from the pitcher of ice water atop the table in the seating area.

"We like to make sure that each employee here, regardless of station, feels as if the property is their own to share. It takes a lot of training, but when it happens, the guests love it."

"Sounds like a lot of effort," said Willow. "Some people are naturally shy."

"Those who find it uncomfortable to do the job are placed elsewhere or let go. John is a stickler for protocol, and if Alec wants something done, he makes sure we do it," said Tim.

"So, he's difficult to work for?" Willow asked.

Tim shook his head. "As long as you follow his orders, he's great. An old Army guy like him demands discipline. I don't mind it."

"Thanks for telling me," said Willow.

"Sure. He would do anything for Alec, as we all would."

Willow smiled at the thought of so many people being

devoted to Alec and followed Tim through the public areas of the building.

Sarah joined them. "Thought Willow should tour my end of things."

Tim grinned. "I take the arrival process; Sarah handles the 'keep the guest happy' part. Better her than me."

"Diplomacy with a capital 'D' is required," said Sarah. "Not always easy. Our guests are pampered, which is exactly how we want them to feel. I work part-time, every other day, which is convenient because it's a demanding job and I've got my son, Henry, at home. Thankfully, my parents help out with him, and the rest of the time, he's with a sitter who comes into their home."

"You're living with your parents?" Willow asked.

"Just until my husband returns. Then we'll decide what we're going to do. This tour of duty is going to be his last. My parents want us to move here permanently. We'll see." Sarah rolled her eyes. "You know how it is to come home again. Are you back here to stay?"

Willow paused. She hadn't thought much about it, but the idea was inviting. She'd felt dissatisfied at her last job and wanted to be in operations where the action was. Maybe one of the other hotels could use her. Chances were strong that the new hotel company already had someone in mind for any management position she'd take. Besides, if they wanted Brent Armstrong to be part of the executive team, she didn't believe she could work for someone like him.

"I'm open to moving back," Willow responded, pleased by the thought.

"It would be wonderful if you did," said Sarah. "With my having Henry to take care of in addition to this job, I need a friend who understands the lure of the business. You know?"

Willow smiled and nodded. Sarah, she was sure, could have

as many friends as she wanted. She was that kind of person. On an impulse, she said, "Why don't the two of you join me and the other two 'Desert Flowers,' as we call ourselves, for cocktails tonight at Alec's. Any chance of doing it?"

Tim shook his head. "Sorry. I've promised my girlfriend I'd take her to dinner. But another time, that would work."

"It's my night off, so I'd love to do it," Sarah said, her face lighting up. "Let me make a call to see if Nita, my babysitter, can stay late, and I'll let you know. I'll be right back."

After Sarah left them to make the call, Tim said, "I'm glad you two are already getting along."

"Thanks. As she says, it's helpful to have friends in the business who understand the demands of the job. Where does your girlfriend work?"

"She owns a store on El Paseo—Elle. Do you know it?"

"Oh, yes. Great clothes for women, but a little pricey for me." Elle was one of what Willow called her favorite "I Wish" stores. Maybe someday she'd be able to afford to shop there, but not yet.

"I'll make sure to introduce you to Marietta and get you a discount," said Tim, grinning. "She loves helping local women out."

"Thanks," said Willow, not about to pass up an offer like that.

Sarah rejoined them. "Did I miss anything?"

Willow broke into a smile. "A discount at Elle."

"Oh, sweet. I've already got one, thanks to Tim. Marietta is a doll."

For the first time since she came home, Willow felt as if she might truly belong here. She loved Rose and Lily, but Sarah and Tim were not only hoteliers but also part of the community.

"I've cleared the time for me to come for cocktails," Sarah

told her. "What time should I be there?"

"I'm thinking five o'clock, if that's possible." Willow hadn't cleared it with Rose and Lily, but she was sure it wouldn't be a problem. That was the time of day they all normally regrouped.

Sarah beamed at her. "That'll give me time to get home and see Henry for a bit. I don't like missing times like that."

Willow studied Sarah. She was a pretty woman with stylishly cut blond hair swinging at her shoulders, and her blue eyes sparkled. Her open face, pleasant demeanor, and friendliness were magnets attracting people. She understood why Alec had hired her and why the guests loved her. In some respects, Sarah was a combination of Rose and Lily.

Tim left them to go back to his office, and Sarah and Willow took off to walk through Sarah's part of the hotel.

Chatting like an old friend, Sarah introduced Willow to the gentleman at the concierge desk and told her about the various deals they offered guests for tours of the area, including the ever-popular tour of the homes of Hollywood stars in Palm Springs.

"We try to encourage guests to do everything from taking the Aerial Tramway up the mountain to visiting the Air Museum in Palm Springs, to shopping and dining on El Paseo, and to go to places like the Living Desert Wildlife Park. All things you know about, I'm sure. This area is full of interesting opportunities for guests to discover," said Sarah, sounding like someone from the Chamber of Commerce.

"I can hear how much you love the area," said Willow.

"Oh, yes. My grandfather bought property here from Cliff Henderson and was in on the early growth of the city in the 1940s. It was an interesting time. Not many know that General Patton trained his troops here in 1942 and 1943 for desert warfare. A lot has changed since then."

"My family and I have been here for almost twenty-five years, and the growth has been unbelievable," said Willow, feeling a new sense of pride.

They walked out to the pool area, where there was a small poolside bar that served refreshing drinks and a few snacks. "We try to do everything we can to make our guests comfortable. The head of food and beverage is fantastic. You've yet to meet him, but you will."

Willow watched as a waiter carried a drink over to one of the guests sunbathing on a chaise lounge. "I'd forgotten how classy this hotel is, what a wonderful feeling this place has. How is the new company going to compete with this?"

Sarah's expression turned grim. "That's what we need to impress upon them. We don't want the reputation of this hotel destroyed. Not after all the work that's been done to make it this way."

Rose joined them. "Mind if I tag along? I want to see as much of this part of the operation as possible. Information for my blog."

Sarah and Rose exchanged greetings, and they headed over to the spa area. Located in a separate building, the spa was a full-service one with a little pool for relaxing between procedures. At the end of the building, in an area of their own, were the exercise facilities.

As they approached it, Dan McMillan walked outside. "Hey! What are you doing here? Ready for more exercise?" He looked at Willow and gave her a sexy grin.

Willow could feel her cheeks warm as her pulse sped up. In his workout clothes, his muscular body was so ... so ... appealing. She quickly worked to gain control of her reaction to him. Tiffany was nowhere in sight. Even so, she wasn't about to become involved with someone who was already in a relationship. She had enough problems facing her.

Rose stared from her to Dan and back again, and the corners of her lips curved. "I think we all could use a break."

Unaware of the undercurrents playing with Willow's emotions, Sarah said, "Working with Dan pays off big time."

Willow and Rose exchanged glances.

"I know," said Rose. "Right, Willow?"

Willow pasted a neutral look on her face and nodded. Someday she was going to pay Rose back for teasing her like this.

As if she knew what Willow was thinking, Rose grinned and gave her a little hug.

CHAPTER FOURTEEN
ROSE

Rose helped Juanita place appetizers on the table outside on the patio, pleased that Willow had made plans for Sarah to join them for their usual cocktail hour. A smile crossed her face when she recalled the interaction between Dan and Willow. They were both nice, attractive people obviously taken with one another. But as she'd learned, life can intervene and make things difficult.

She returned to the kitchen and mixed up a batch of Texas Margaritas, a favorite of their small group. Lily, Willow, and Sarah arrived as she was finishing up.

"Just in time. We have appetizers set up outside, and I've got the blender full of Margaritas ready to go."

"Great," said Lily. "I'm almost blind from going through documents and drawing up lists of things to discuss with Alec. Is he going to join us?"

Rose shook her head. "Not tonight. He says it's girl time."

Lily laughed. "Well, I'll get to it in the morning. The buyer's team isn't scheduled to arrive for another couple of days. Right?"

"Yes," said Rose, heading outside with the others.

The February evening was pleasant with only a light breeze to disturb the warmer-than-usual air. Still, Rose wore a sweater because, as pleasant as it might be during the day, the desert cooled quickly as night approached, and they'd have only a short time before the sunset. The standing gas heaters on the patio would help, but no doubt she and the other women would end up in the living room.

The four of them pulled chairs to the table and sat. After introductions were made, Sarah asked Rose and Lily where they'd come from and how they were connected to Alec. Rose was again reminded of their unique situation as Lily spoke. Few men could pull off the friendships Alec had made through the years, producing many loyal friends, even with old lovers.

"How about you, Sarah? How long have you known Alec?"

She smiled. "Since I was a little girl. My father, George Goodrich, and Alec are friends—golf buddies, actually."

Rose drew up in her chair. "I remember him. A very pleasant man."

"Thanks," said Sarah. "He is. Both my parents have been kind to me, and they adore Henry."

"When is your husband due home?" asked Lily.

"Eric has another eleven months to go," said Sarah, sighing softly. "You never get over it, having someone you love in danger."

"I appreciate his service to our country," said Rose. "You, too. It's hard on spouses and families."

"Yes. I try to talk to Henry about his father and show him pictures, but it isn't the same. That's one reason Eric is leaving the service after this tour."

"When do we get to meet Henry?" Lily said. "My three-year-old niece is at such a darling age. I miss her like crazy."

Sarah chuckled happily. "Don't worry; I'll introduce you to him. Then you'll be begging me to leave him at home. He's a terror and into everything."

Seeing the pride that crossed Sarah's face, Rose suffered a pang of remorse. At one time, she'd thought she wanted children of her own. But that hadn't happened, and now she was too old.

"I hope you won't mind," Rose said, focusing back on business, "but I'd like to roam in your management territory tomorrow to see what else I can use for an advertising campaign."

Sarah shrugged. "I'd love to see what you come up with. I'm off, but Tim will keep an eye out for any problems that might occur."

"Okay. I want to have a lot of ideas ready for when the buyer's transition team comes in for due diligence." Rose winked. "I apparently have a tough adversary."

"I can't imagine that will be a problem," said Lily sweetly.

Rose laughed good-naturedly.

"Just what is your job going to be?" Sarah asked her.

"I'll be working with the man who's going to head up the social media campaign for the transition to the new hotel brand. Alec doesn't want to disappoint his regular guests by having the new management team destroy what he's built by changing everything at once. That's something they'd agreed to in their negotiations."

"Frankly, I'm worried about it. A big, successful hotel company is going to want to do things their way. I'm afraid they won't understand the atmosphere we've built for both staff and guests," said Sarah. "I've only been with the Desert Sage Inn for less than a year, but I understand completely how important it is to keep the same sense of cooperation and service. It's what has made the inn so special. I remember coming here as a little girl and loving it. I still think it's a unique, extraordinary place."

Rose tapped her hand against the arm of her chair. "I get it. That's why I'll be working hard on this."

The next morning, Rose awoke with a new sense of

purpose. Today she'd dress like one of the guests and remain a shadow among them, testing specific areas of service, studying the grounds for backdrops for ads, and gathering inside information for her blog followers.

She pulled on her jogging shorts and a T-shirt, added socks and sneakers to her outfit, and headed outside. Dan had shown her and the other Flowers how pleasant an early-morning walk could be.

Outside, she breathed in the cool air and let out a sigh of pleasure. The sun was rising in the east, casting a pretty pink glow to the clouds hovering close by the mountains. Birds were caroling on the branches of trees or flitting between the plantings outside Alec's house.

She headed down the sidewalk at a brisk clip, taking in the sights and sounds around her.

A little deer mouse scurried across the path and headed into a desert honeysuckle whose orange blossoms were just beginning to emerge. She smiled at the sight of it. One creature she hoped to avoid was a rattlesnake. At the moment, it was probably too cold for them to be slithering about. Later, she thought, the sun's warmth would tempt them into activity.

She walked quickly and then broke into a run for the return trip back to the house.

When she walked into the kitchen, Juanita was already there, fixing breakfast for Alec. An early riser, he still liked to have a cup of coffee upon awakening.

"This is for Alec?" Rose said.

Juanita nodded. "First of the day." As she spoke, Rose noticed a sadness cross Juanita's face.

"Mind if I take it into him?" Rose said.

Juanita shook her head. "I'm sure he'd love to see you. He always perks up when one of you women visit."

"I'm glad we're here for him," Rose said.

"Me, too." She handed Rose a mug of coffee for Alec. "Here's his coffee, just how he likes it."

Rose accepted the mug and walked to the far end of the house, where she gently knocked on the door. Hearing no response, she opened it and went to Alec's bedroom.

Dressed in a terry robe with the hotel logo on it, he was sitting up in an overstuffed chair by the sliding glass door that led out to a private patio. He saw her and smiled. "Ah, a lovely way to start the day. Come sit with me. I'm enjoying the early morning glow in the sky."

She handed him his coffee and kissed the top of his head. "I've just returned from a short walk and have been admiring it myself." She took a seat opposite him. "This is a better day for you?"

He gave her a crooked smile with a touch of humor. "Well, I'm still here. I count every morning a blessing."

"Me, too, for you," she said. "Today, I'm going undercover at the hotel. I thought it would be a different way for me to get some ideas."

He chuckled softly. "Leave it up to you to come up with that."

"I want to be able to surprise Hank Bowers."

Alec's lips curved. He gave her a knowing look. "I think you'll do just fine."

Rose got to her feet. "I'd better get going. Juanita is in the kitchen waiting to prepare your breakfast, and I've got to take a shower before I head into the hotel."

"Good luck, my dear," Alec said, accepting her kiss on his cheek gracefully.

She left him, returned to the kitchen, grabbed a cup of coffee for herself, and headed into her room to get ready for the day.

###

Later, dressed in one of the outfits she'd bought on sale at an upscale shop on El Paseo, Rose studied herself in the mirror. Wearing white jeans, a floral shirt with turquoise colors, and turquoise sandals, she looked the part of a tourist/guest. The addition of silver jewelry helped too.

She tied her hair back into a loose knot and, satisfied, went out to see what the other women were up to.

Rose found Lily in the kitchen in jogging clothes. Surprised, she said, "Are you taking Dan's training seriously too?"

Lily laughed. "I decided to make a change in my life and be more active. Out here with all sunshine and warm air, it feels great."

"Wait until summer," said Rose.

"I know, I know, but right now, it's perfect," Lily said. "You look nice, like a guest, as you wanted. Have fun today at the hotel. I will stay right here and look over some documents Alec's lawyer thought I should see. All to be prepared ahead of time."

"Oh, dear! That sounds boring." Rose was happy to work on the creative side. Reading documents sounded awful. But then, Lily was used to that kind of work. A natural detail person.

"It isn't always fun, though usually, I discover something interesting," Lily said, waving to Willow, who walked into the room wearing a tank top and short pajama bottoms.

"Why is everyone up so early?" Willow mumbled, going to the coffee maker and pouring herself a cup.

"Rose is doing her detective work, and I'm reading documents to prepare for the introduction to the transfer team by the end of the week," said Lily.

"I'm meeting Tim, John's assistant, later," said Willow,

"but I'm basically on my own today."

"Relax and enjoy it while you can," said Rose, knowing the stress Willow was about to face. She understood that Willow was addressing many personal issues, and it was about to get more complicated. Still, she couldn't help teasing. "You can always go to the fitness center. Dan might be there."

Color crept into Willow's cheeks.

"Yes. A workout might be just what you need," said Lily, playing along.

Willow shook a finger at them. "You thought he was hot too."

Rose fanned herself with her hand. "Too hot for me!"

"Just right for someone a little younger than me," Lily said, adding fuel to the tease.

Willow waved away their jabs at her. "He's dating Tiffany. Fantasizing about him and me being together will get the two of you nowhere."

Rose exchanged glances with Lily, sure now that Willow was attracted.

Willow joined Rose and Lily at the kitchen table. After chatting a few minutes, Rose got to her feet. "See you later. I've got to be on my way. I want to get there bright and early."

As she hopped on the golf cart to get to the hotel, she thought about the incoming transition team. So far, for confidentiality, most of the paperwork shown to them identified the hotel company as Hotel XYZ. However, Alec had earlier told them it was The Blaise Hotel Group, a hotel investment and management company known for their success with what the company referred to in their advertising campaign as ordinary people as in, "Ordinary People, Extraordinary Places." It was precisely this that concerned Rose. She wasn't a snob, but she knew the Desert Sage Inn catered to people who enjoyed and expected the kind of service they gave. A person's wealth or lack of it didn't concern her or the hotel staff. Neither did race nor religion. Her concern was the new team might think they wouldn't have to keep up the excellent service or that their guests didn't deserve it.

She drove the cart to the staff entrance and climbed out, eager to see the property from a guest's perspective. She hurried through the executive offices, past the employees' cafeteria, and up the stairs to the main floor and lobby.

As she entered the lobby, she noticed an older gentleman holding the hand of one of the cutest little toddlers she'd ever seen. Wearing a pink sundress and a white hat that barely covered her red ringlets, the little girl babbled and pointed to several objects.

She drew closer.

"That? That?" the little girl said, pointing to a cactus.

"Cactus," the man answered, smiling.

"That?" The little girl pointed to Rose.

The man glanced up and paused before saying, "A pretty woman."

"Me pretty too," the girl said, pointing a finger at her chest.

Rose and the gentleman laughed together.

"Hello," said Rose. "Beautiful morning, isn't it?"

"Yes," he quickly agreed. "I love sharing this time with my granddaughter, Leah. "I'm ..." he hesitated, "I'm Papa B."

"Is there a Papa A?" Rose asked before she could stop herself.

He laughed. "Indeed, there is. But it doesn't mean I'm second-best. Leah and I have a special friendship. That's why I'm out of bed early so my daughter and son-in-law can sleep in."

"A devoted grandfather. I love it."

"You're welcome to join us for a little walk outside. We're

probably going to end up studying the stones around some of the plantings, but you never know what you'll discover."

Rose smiled. "I'll try to catch up with you later. Right now, I'm headed into the restaurant."

"Enjoy." After her grandfather spoke to her, Leah waved a hand at her, "' Bye, 'bye!"

Still smiling, Rose entered the restaurant to see how things were going there. Though it was crowded and people were lined up at the breakfast buffet, everything was in order. She wasn't surprised. Martin Schnabel did a great job heading the food and beverage department.

After checking the restaurant, Rose entered the lobby, which was quiet. She walked through it and out the sliding glass doors to the patio overlooking a putting green. She noticed Papa B and Leah standing just beyond the patio, studying the flowers. Observing them, Rose assessed the man who was so devoted as a grandfather. He was a tall, well-built man who was still muscular and erect. She wondered if he was a retired sports figure. Her gaze traveled to his face. His baseball cap and large sunglasses hid most of it, but she could see enough of his features to know he was a nice-looking man. In fact, there was something familiar about him. She guessed he was someone famous, not unusual at the inn.

He noticed her and waved her over.

Thinking she might ask him a few questions about his stay, she went to him.

"Thought you might like to share in a few discoveries. It seems we've found some special stones." He smiled at her. "At this age, everything is a bit of a miracle. That's why I like being around Leah. It makes me think about the important things in life, like finding a colorful stone or one that is perfect to hold in my hand."

"A lovely thought. We all need reminders like that."

"So, what are you doing here? Just a vacation, or what?"

"I'm sorry. I didn't introduce myself. I'm Rose Macklin. I'm here to rest and relax." She couldn't let him or anyone else know her real job was to spy on the hotel, to look for flaws.

"Nice to meet you, Rose." He handed her a stone. "Isn't this a beauty?"

She looked at the small yellow stone in her palm. It shimmered with an orange streak. "It's lovely."

"Just a simple piece of washed gravel, but unique in its own way. Sort of like looking at grains of sand under a microscope. It's amazing what you see."

Rose smiled at him, and a wave of longing washed over her. At one time, she'd thought she and Alec would be together, maybe even share children and grandchildren.

Leah looked up at her and smiled, holding a stone out to her.

"Oh, that's a pretty one," said Rose, kneeling beside her. The little girl's blue eyes rested on her. Then she reached out and patted Rose's hair. "Pretty."

"My hair is red like yours. Right?"

Leah nodded and tapped her head several times.

Laughing, Rose came to her feet and rocked back off balance as the heel of her sandal slid on the loose stones.

"Steady there," said Leah's grandfather. He grabbed her elbow to keep her from falling.

Her flesh burned where he'd made contact. Fighting to hide her reaction, she quickly pulled away. "Thank you. Enjoy the rest of your morning. I'm off to check out the fitness center."

His eyebrows rose, but he simply nodded. "Nice to meet you. Have a good day."

She lifted her hand in response and hurried inside. She felt like a teen with a huge crush. *What was that all about?*

When she got to the fitness center, Dan was doing a private session with someone while two other people were using the facilities. She watched a moment, thinking that Willow and he would make a cute couple.

She checked the golf and tennis pro shops and then headed back to the pool. Things should be picking up there.

As she approached the pool, the sound of tropical music met her ears. The poolside snack bar was open, and a couple of staff members were placing chairs around the pool, even as a few guests had already staked a claim on some of them.

She looked for Leah and her grandfather but saw no trace of them. But later, when she saw them sitting by the fountain out front, she joined them, drawn to the grandfather in a way she'd never felt before. His kindness, his view of his granddaughter's world had touched something inside her. And there was no denying how attractive he was, how his smile had warmed her.

"Now you're discovering the joy of water," she said, smiling at him.

He nodded and patted the empty space on the bench near him. "Have a seat. Leah loves watching the water fountain. If you look carefully, you can see tiny rainbows in the spray from it."

She peered at the fountain. "Oh, yes, I see them!" she cried, then laughed at herself. He was making her feel like a kid again.

Leah pointed at the water. "Pretty."

"Yes, the droplets look like diamonds in the sunlight."

He turned to her with a teasing grin. "You like diamonds?"

"I enjoy the sparkle. What woman doesn't? But things like that are not that important to me."

His smile grew wider. "I'll be through babysitting duty later. Perhaps you could join me for a drink."

"Thanks," she said, "but I can't this evening. But if you're going to be here for the next several days, perhaps we can try to do that then."

"Fair enough," he said, then turned to Leah, who was pointing something out to him.

Walking away, Rose was surprised by her willingness to try to meet him. It wasn't like her to be so open to dating a stranger, but he was someone special.

CHAPTER FIFTEEN
ROSE

Rose straightened her skirt and brushed an imaginary piece of lint off her blazer jacket. She wanted to look perfect for today's series of meetings. She checked herself in the mirror once more and went to join Willow and Lily. The three of them were going to meet Alec in his room for what he called a pep talk.

In the kitchen, she grabbed a second cup of coffee, wanting that little bit of energy to keep her spirits high. So much about what they were going to do was attitude.

When Willow and Lily walked into the kitchen, unexpected tears stung Rose's eyes. They both looked lovely—professional and beautiful at the same time. In the short weeks they'd been together, she'd grown fond of them. But then, that's what Alec had planned all along with his teambuilding program.

"You look gorgeous!" Lily said to her.

Rose gave her an impulsive hug. "You too." She reached for Willow. "And you. We're going to wow the other team."

Willow let out a long breath. "I hope so."

"Ready? Let's go say 'bye to Alec," Rose said, setting down her cup of coffee.

When they got to Alec's end of the house, the door to his apartment was open. They tiptoed inside.

Alec was dressed in a robe and sitting on a lounge chair. "Ah, my Desert Flowers! You look lovely."

Rose, Willow, and Lily each bent to kiss him on the cheek,

and then stood in a line in front of him.

"I wanted to see you before you headed to the hotel to meet the other team. I wanted to remind you why we're doing this. As you know, I've put my heart and soul into this project for years. Finally, it's at a point where I'm satisfied with the property, the staff, and the hotel's reputation. Then I contracted cancer. It's best that I sell the hotel. That's a given. But what I want is for The Blaise Hotel Group to understand what Desert Sage Inn is all about. You're here to help me see that they don't take what I've built and destroy it by turning it into a hotel like their others. I'm attempting to discuss their developing a new brand of upscale hotels starting with Desert Sage Inn."

"That would be fantastic," said Rose. "In wandering around the hotel *incognito* yesterday, I learned how much all kinds of people love it, whether they're traveling with family, on their honeymoon, or just here to relax for a few days."

"And it's paying off," said Willow. "I've checked the sales figures with John, and we're doing the right things."

"I want to ensure that this subject is discussed throughout the process both in person and in writing," said Lily.

Alec beamed at them. "I knew I was right to bring the three of you into the transition. You're my best hope of dealing with them. To each one of you, thank you. Now, go do your thing."

Rose left with a great sense of purpose. At one time, Alec had given her a chance to learn the business, and later, had shared a special love with her. It was time for her to pay him back. When they got to the hotel, John directed them to a conference room on the second floor of the hotel. Eager to meet the man Alec had said would try to control her, she felt her pulse quicken.

She followed John into the room to find two gentlemen talking in the corner with their backs to her. A young man she figured was Willow's counterpart was seated at the table alongside a young woman who was typing on a computer's keyboard. Rose knew this was only a small part of the transition team. Others, like experts on structure and construction would be sweeping through the hotel from time to time for the next 90 days, familiarizing themselves with the details of the building and the operation, looking for any flaws or upgrading needs.

She studied the men in the corner. One was tall and muscular; the other short and stocky with quick, emphatic movements as he talked. She figured him for a lawyer.

Hearing their arrival, both men turned to face them.

Rose studied the taller man. There was something familiar about him. She mentally placed a baseball cap on his head and sunglasses on his nose. An image of Papa B filled her mind.

"Hey, everyone, that's Henry Bowers, a social media consultant working with the Blaise Group, and the Blaise attorney, Simon Nickerson," John explained.

"You!" Rose said before she could stop herself. "You're Papa B. Why didn't you tell me who you really are?"

"My name in the family is Papa B," Hank said, approaching her.

"But you knew who I am. Considering our circumstances, I think you should've revealed who you are."

"And spoil the fun? I don't think so. Look, no real harm has been done. I was simply being Papa B with my granddaughter."

John Rodriquez said, "You know each other?"

"I thought we did," said Rose, reining in her dismay. She couldn't let anyone see how upset she was, how much she felt a fool. She silently vowed not to let Hank Bowers get the best of her again.

The smaller of the two men approached her.

John said, "I want you to meet Simon Nickerson. He's the lead attorney for the Blaise Group on the transition phase."

Rose forced a smile and held out her hand.

"Pleased to meet you, Simon." She ignored Hank's gaze on her and turned as more introductions were made. As she'd suspected, the young man seated at the table was Brent Armstrong. Blond and blue-eyed, he was as handsome as his photograph. His self-confident smile hinted at condescension. She told herself not to judge too quickly but decided she'd keep an eye on Willow to make sure she was all right working with him.

The young girl sitting at the table on her computer was introduced as Jessica Hart, a legal secretary who usually worked in Simon's office.

Just as they were ready to sit down, another man entered the room.

"Ah, here's Brian. Now we can begin," John said. "Okay, team, meet Brian Walden, the hospitality consultant whose client is the Blaise Group and who is running this show for them."

Rose shook hands with him and sized him up. He was tall and made no effort to hide the fact that the lower part of his left leg had been replaced with a light-weight, metal prosthesis with a shoe. His brown hair, graying at the temples, was cut in a boyish, tousled style that suited him. She looked up at his face, which displayed craggy features and light-brown eyes that contained an air of gentleness that she liked.

"Everyone, please be seated. I'm sorry to be late, but it was such a beautiful morning, I took advantage of it for a run," said Brian, taking a seat at the head of the table.

John sat at the other end of the table. Rose sat between Lily and Willow opposite the other team. As luck would have it, Hank faced her.

Lily brought out her laptop, plugged it in, and got ready to take notes.

"All set?" Brian asked. At Lily's nod, he continued, "Rather than think of us as opposing teams, I'd like for us to think of ways to help one another through this process. Teams of inspectors will be going through the property. John, I assume your staff has been alerted and will cooperate."

John nodded. "Of course. Our main concern is not to disrupt the guests. Sometimes, we will require inspectors to make special arrangements, particularly for access to guest rooms, depending upon our bookings at the hotel. We will set aside blocks of guest rooms for your inspections over the next several weeks and will permit no access to any occupied guest room. But we will be as flexible as we can."

"Understood," said Brian. "Let's see, Rose and Hank will be working on transitional publicity. Is that correct?"

Rose met Brian's intent look and nodded, wondering if it was a mistake, given her distrust of Hank.

"No problem," said Hank with a pleasant, buoyant note. "We'll make a great team."

"Willow, you and Brent will be working together on scheduling and tracking all inspections and checking off other requests as they arise and coordinating with John. Right?"

"I'm taking the lead on that," said Brent, straightening in his chair.

Willow tensed.

Rose reached under the table and gave Willow's hand an encouraging squeeze.

"Brent, there is no lead required," said Brian. "You and Willow are working together. Understand?"

"I'm prepared to do whatever is necessary to oversee matters," said Willow.

Brian's eyebrows rose. He nodded at her. "That's the kind

of cooperation we're looking for."

Rose noticed the petulant look that crossed Brent's face and shook her head. He was going to be a troublemaker.

"But I represent the executives," Brent said, unwilling to drop the matter. "I was specifically assigned to this project by them."

"Indeed," said Brian, looking directly at Brent. "So was I. And my job is to ensure all aspects of this transition are completed cooperatively and on time. I've managed several major hotel ownership transitions, and I can do it now, with or without you. Until the Blaise Group takes title to the hotel, final decisions regarding the scheduling of all inspections rest with the current owners."

Though he spoke almost pleasantly, Rose heard his firm tone. No doubt Brian had had to deal with Brent before.

Brent puffed out an angry breath but said nothing more.

"We have ninety days to make all this happen," Brian continued. "Let's get to work. John has been gracious enough to give us all places to work in an empty conference room downstairs. We can come and go from there. Everyone has my contact number, and I've got yours. I will be staying at the hotel from time to time as we all will. Alec's representatives are living at his house for the duration. Is that right, Rose?"

"Yes. That's how he's arranged it."

"Well then, ladies and gentlemen, we can begin. I've drawn up a procedural plan. Take a look at it and let me know if there are any questions. I'll be meeting with John to review and modify it as necessary for most of the day. The rest of you can do your thing. Willow and Brent, I'd suggest you tour the property together and then go over the plan."

Rose knew from the set of Willow's shoulders that she was trying to be professional and gave her an encouraging smile. Willow wasn't the only one with challenges to face.

CHAPTER SIXTEEN
WILLOW

Willow returned Rose's smile and got to her feet, filled with determination. Brent Armstrong may not know it yet, but she wasn't about to let him steamroll over her.

Brent stood. "Ready?"

"Yes. I'm well acquainted with the property, so I can show it to you without wasting a lot of time."

He studied her. "You look familiar to me. You were at Cornell at the same time I was. Right?"

"Yes, two years behind you."

He snapped his fingers. "Now I remember. You used to ... We called you ..." His cheeks turned red. "I'm sorry ..."

"You and your friends teased me about being on scholarship. You used to call me 'Enchilada' because of my background." Her defiant stare drilled into him. "Let's get something straight. The only reason I agreed to work with you was because of my loyalty to Alec Thurston."

Brent held up his hands. "Whoa! I'm sorry. That was then. This is now. I'm hoping to be given the job of resident manager here, so I don't want you screwing up my chances."

"I think you can take care of that on your own," Willow replied, sure she'd never come to like the man. She headed out of the conference without waiting to see if he'd follow.

He caught up to her. "Can we at least pretend to be friends?"

She heard the note of desperation in his voice but said, "No, we can't be friends, but we can be civil and work together on this transition."

As she led him through the property, Willow delivered the lines she'd rehearsed about how well things functioned in the various areas of the hotel due mainly to the staff's training and commitment to give a high level of service.

He listened—sometimes nodding, sometimes shaking his head.

They stopped for lunch at the pool bar. "Even here, we do an exceptional job of coaching staff to feel as if this is their hotel, and they're here to ensure their guests have a delightful stay."

"Pie-in-the-sky kind of stuff, as my Dad would say," said Brent. "It's all about numbers. Getting guests in and hoping they'll come back. Our hotel company is one of the biggest in the business. We didn't get that way by messing things up with too much touchy-feely stuff."

"Still, repeat business is important. We have a high rate of return guests."

"Alec Thurston is an old-fashioned hotelier," said Brent. "Most times, we can't afford to do some of the extra things he does for his staff."

"That's what keeps them loyal," said Willow. "Most of the staff have been here for years. They and their families depend upon us to provide them with a decent living and benefits." She sighed, wondering how she could get through the rest of the day.

They finished their sandwiches in silence, and then Willow said, "Let's keep going as there is a lot more to see."

When they got to the fitness center, Dan stopped talking to one of the guests outside and walked over to greet them. Willow couldn't help the smile that spread across her face. He looked ... well, yummy.

He grinned at Willow. "Are you here for a workout?"

Brent glanced from him to Willow and back again. "I'm here representing the new hotel company."

"He and I are on the transition *team*," Willow said, emphasizing the word 'team.' "This is Brent Armstrong. Brent, Dan McMillan, head of the fitness program here at the hotel."

Tiffany joined them.

"And this is Tiffany Weber, Dan's assistant. Tiffany, Brent Armstrong."

Brent's eyes traveled over Tiffany's body in a way Willow found disturbing. He was a handsome guy and no doubt had women falling all over him, but in her mind, he was a pig.

"Better watch it," Dan said to him after noticing Brent's reaction. "If Tiffany doesn't like you, she can toss you around in about five seconds."

Laughing, Tiffany extended her hand. "Hi, Brent. No worries. Pleased to meet you." She turned to Willow. "We've missed seeing you around. Maybe we can catch up one of these mornings."

"Thanks. I'd like that."

"While you're here, let me show you around," Tiffany said to Brent.

After he followed Tiffany inside, Dan turned her. "Is that guy the jerk I think he is?"

"Afraid so," said Willow. "I'm doing my best to be polite because of Alec, but Brent is truly a pain in the butt."

"Any time you need help to reduce your stress working with him, stop on by; a workout does wonders for people."

She gave him a grateful smile. "Will do."

When Brent emerged from the gym, he was grinning. "Ready? I want to get this tour over with. Tiffany's agreed to meet me for a drink."

Surprised, Willow checked Dan's face for a reaction, but he didn't show any sign of concern. *He and Tiffany were together, weren't they?*

"Have fun," Dan said to them, keeping a steady look on Brent. "Remember my warning."

Brent ignored him and continued to talk to Tiffany.

Willow asked softly, "Aren't you dating Tiffany?"

Dan's eyebrows shot up. "Me and Tiffany? No way, she's my step-sister."

Willow didn't know whether to laugh or not. She'd imagined them together so often it was difficult not to think of them as a couple.

Dan winked at her. "I'm her big brother, though, and if anybody messes with her, they'll have me to face."

"I see," said Willow smiling at the thought of Brent having to deal with Dan. There was no doubt about the winner of such a confrontation.

CHAPTER SEVENTEEN
LILY

Lily watched Rose and Willow leave the room with their counterparts and shut down her computer. When she looked up, Brian was standing by, waiting for her. The others had left the room.

"Are you coming?" Brian asked her. "Why don't you join John and me in his office so you can take notes for Alec. I want everything to be wide open and fair."

"Thanks." Lily quickly gathered her things and followed him out of the room. As they made their way to John's office, she noticed how easily Brian managed his prosthesis and couldn't stop herself from asking, "How did your injury happen?"

He turned to her but kept walking. "Afghanistan, a number of years ago."

"You do very well," she commented.

He grunted an indistinguishable reply.

Lily immediately felt contrite. "I'm sorry. I shouldn't ask. I can't imagine how difficult it must be to be reminded of it every day."

He stopped and looked at her. "Funny, most people don't think of it that way, but you're exactly right. If only they had an operation that could remove all the bad memories."

Lily studied the anguish in his expression, and her heart went out to him. "Thank you for your service. I know how inadequate that is, but I mean it. I have a little niece whom I adore, and knowing there are people like you willing to keep her safe means the world to me." She blinked away the sting of unexpected tears. *She was making a fool of herself.*

"Thank you, Lily," he said quietly and turned away, leaving her to try and catch up to him.

CHAPTER EIGHTEEN
ROSE

Rose turned to Hank. "Where should we work? In the room they have set up here?"

"Unless you want to work in my suite," he answered.

Rose hesitated, uncertain she'd heard correctly. "Are you suggesting ..."

Hank cut her off. "Rose, I understand you're upset that I didn't reveal who I was, but I have no intention of acting in an ungentlemanly way. Leah would be disappointed in a grandfather like that."

Rose felt her anger leave her like air from a leaky balloon. *Why was she acting this way?* As soon as she asked herself that, she knew the answer—she was attracted to Hank Bowers like she hadn't been to any man since Alec, and it scared the hell out of her.

She realized he was waiting for a response. "You're right. She wouldn't like Papa B being rude. Leah is one of the sweetest little girls I've ever met."

The smile that crossed Hank's face lit his steel-gray eyes and gave her a pleasurable feeling. Struggling to hide her reaction to him, she picked up her laptop. "Let's go. We'll have total privacy in your room."

"My suite has plenty of space for us to work comfortably."

"Is your family still here?" she asked as they headed to the elevator.

Hank nodded. "They leave tomorrow. I was hoping you'd agree to join us for cocktails and dinner. As long as we'll be working together for the next three months, I want them to meet you. We can explain to Leah why Papa B won't be around as much."

At the idea of meeting his family, Rose felt a shiver of anticipation begin to cross her shoulders and quickly stifled it. She was making this seem more than it was.

"Thanks," she said in a noncommittal voice.

"No family you need to inform about the job?" Hank asked gently.

Rose shook her head. It was true. No one cared about where she was or who she was with unless you counted her blog followers. The thought hurt.

"Well then, it'll be nice for all of us to be together," Hank said.

Hank's suite was spacious with plenty of room for them both to work at a long desk. Rose was anxious to show Hank a few of the ads she'd made up to carry them through the next ninety days.

But after they were seated, Hank said, "I'm a member of your blog. I must say, it's impressive." He grinned. "I've used it for ideas as to what gifts to give my daughters."

Flattered, Rose brought it up on her computer screen. "Then you've no doubt seen what I've been showing and discussing online about the Desert Sage Inn."

He nodded. "You're good at this job, Rose. I know going forward, we won't agree on all things, but I do want you to know that."

"Thank you. I appreciate it," she said sincerely. "These are the topics I plan to put up this week. I want my followers to understand that as my blog title says, they deserve a place like this no matter where or how they live."

"Realistically, though, not everyone can afford a place like the Desert Sage Inn. What do you do about those followers?"

"I try to find them deals or places similar to it. It's not about money so much as it is about sharing ideas for unusual things and interesting places at all prices."

Hank ran a hand through his graying hair. "I don't know. The Blaise Hotel Group feels they offer everybody excellent service at affordable prices. That's what they want me to emphasize."

"And that's where we're going to have a face-off," said Rose. "We need to keep the reputation of the inn intact before they take over. We hope that after seeing the results themselves, they will buy into our philosophy."

Hank shook his head. "Sorry. Wish we were on the same team because it might get ugly. My clients are committed to making the inn theirs in every way."

"What about the idea of a whole new, upscale collection?" Rose asked with growing concern. The determination in his voice made his position clear.

"That idea remains to be seen. Better show me what you have in mind for how we can combine both points of view."

"All right," said Rose. "But remember, the inn is still Alec's until the sale goes through."

"Yeah, I know. We're both paid to do our jobs," said Hank, giving her a steady look.

She nodded, but he had no idea how committed she was to Alec's wishes. She'd drawn up several different ads based on three specific ideas – quality, value, and experience.

"These are clever," said Hank, looking at each ad carefully. "But I have to be honest; I can easily twist these into something for the Blaise Group. After all, they're promoting the same ideas."

Rose couldn't hold back a sigh. "You know they're not the same."

Hank held up a hand of caution. "We both understand in the advertising business, this kind of manipulation takes place all the time. But I want to be fair. Let's work together on developing a style of presentation more like the Blaise Group is accustomed to having."

"I'm going to do my best to convince you otherwise. Keeping the Desert Sage Inn's reputation is important to Alec and all of us who work for him. We've all bought into the idea that it truly is different, offering guests a unique kind of stay. Sort of like the service Nordstrom has always given its shopping customers."

"Personally, I like the idea of the formation of a brand of higher-end properties for the company," said Hank. "Maybe we can do both; work on promo for that too."

Rose's eyes widened with surprise. "Really? That would be wonderful!"

Hank's cheeks reddened at her enthusiasm and the way she was beaming at him. "I think we'll make a great team for this work. Even hit a home run or two."

She laughed. "Right. Teammates."

Hank grinned at her.

While they were discussing the project, Hank received a phone call.

Rose stood and walked to the sliding glass door to give him some privacy. At the end of the call, when she turned, he said, "I've told my family about working with you and suggested they meet you. It's official. Will you do us all the honor of joining us for cocktails and dinner tonight?"

"Thanks. That would be nice," she responded, wanting to know more about him and his family.

Later, before they parted that afternoon, Hank asked her to meet him in the hotel lobby at six o'clock before they joined his family. Though it had been a frustrating day working with and sometimes against his ideas, Rose agreed. She'd need a little time to get past the mental tug of war between them. She was used to having clients rave about her work, be thrilled with her creative ideas. Compromise with an opposing viewpoint was difficult and emotionally exhausting.

At Alec's house, all was quiet. She figured Alec was napping, and Juanita was on a break and decided to cool off both mentally and physically by taking a swim in the pool.

After changing into her bathing suit, she walked out to the patio, tossed her towel on a chair, and dove into the water. Gasping with pleasure, she paddled to the side of the pool and caught her breath. It felt relaxing to be in the water, feeling its silky coolness against her skin.

"Hey, did you just get here?" said Lily, walking out onto the patio. "That looks so refreshing; I'll join you."

"Please do," Rose said. "It feels great."

A few minutes later, Lily and Willow came out to the pool together in their swimsuits.

"Ah, the Desert Flowers are together again. How did everyone do today?" Rose said, hanging onto the side of the pool and kicking playfully, loosening tight muscles.

"Let's just say I'm ready for a swim myself," said Willow. "Working with Brent Armstrong is a physical and mental test of its own." Without saying another word, she dove into the pool, her dark hair spreading in the water behind her like the black wings of a bird.

"I hope you had a better day," said Rose, looking at Lily.

"I did," said Lily. "A bit boring, but nice otherwise." She sat on the top step of the pool, splashed water on herself to get used to its coolness, and then slid her entire body into the pool with a soft groan.

After they'd each had time to move around in the water, they sat together on the wide steps leading into the pool at the shallow end.

"How was your day, Rose?" Lily asked her. "I know how upset you were this morning with Hank. Did the rest of the day go better?"

"Yes," said Rose. "We've agreed to disagree as we go forward, but we're trying to cooperate. We're going to work on the proposal Alec talked about concerning the formation of a high-end group of hotels under a separate banner. We'll see if we can pull that off."

"Wow! Sounds like you two are working together, like Brian wanted," said Willow. "I can't imagine that happening with Brent and me. By the way, he's meeting Tiffany for drinks."

"What?" said Lily. "I thought she and Dan were together."

"So, did I," Willow said. "But it turns out she's his stepsister. Weird, huh?"

"Maybe a good thing for you," said Rose, nudging her playfully.

Willow shook her head. "I don't think so. As I was leaving, a woman approached him making sure he was going to meet her later."

"He's a hottie," said Lily. "I can't imagine he has any trouble getting dates."

Rose noticed the disappointment Willow tried to hide and let it go. Willow would have to work it out on her own. Dan might be considered a hottie, but Willow matched him in every way.

After a while, Rose climbed out of the pool. "Guess I'd better get dressed. In the spirit of things, I've agreed to meet Hank and his family for drinks and dinner. Because he'll be away so much of the time for the next three months, he was anxious for them to meet me."

Lily and Willow stared at her.

"Is that what you're telling yourself?" Lily said. "I saw the way he looked at you, even when you were mad at him."

"Please," said Rose, hoping she sounded stern enough. "Brian wanted us all to get along. That's what this is all about. Nothing more."

"Uh, huh," said Willow giving Rose a wide, teasing smile that brought a happy laugh out of her.

CHAPTER NINETEEN
LILY

I think Rose is only fooling herself if she thinks Hank wants her to meet his family just because they're working together. There's something tangible going on between them."

"If only Rose will relax and let it happen," said Willow. "She likes to be in charge."

"Definitely," said Lily. "She's had to fight her own battles all her life. She told me her parents never wanted her, never understood or approved of her desire to try new experiences and do things differently."

"Yeah, I can't imagine having parents like that," said Willow. "Rose may be a bit quirky, but she's one of the nicest, most fun people I know. I love that she's a free spirit."

"There's more to her than that, though," said Lily with a frown. "I think she's been hurt enough in the past to use it to cover up her sensitivity. Have you seen how careful, how loving she is with Alec?"

"Does it bother you to see them together?" Willow asked her.

"No. I always knew they had something special. If Alec were ever going to allow himself to move forward, it would've been with her."

"He's steadfast in his beliefs, but I admire him for it."

"Me, too. Now, how does a margarita sound?"

"Like music to my ears," said Willow, giving her a grin.

Lily laughed. Neither was a big drinker, but after the day they'd had, it sure sounded perfect.

Before she left, Rose came to the kitchen dressed for dinner.

"How do I look?" she said, twirling in front of them, a worried note to her voice that Lily took seriously.

"Stand still. Let me get a better look." She studied the sleeveless turquoise-linen sheath Rose wore. Rose's body was lean and trim, curved in all the right places. The skin around her eyes, slightly lined, reflected the smiles she often gave others. Otherwise, her features were those of a younger person. And there was a casual elegance to her that Lily found attractive. No wonder Hank seemed interested.

"Rose, you look smashing," she said honestly. "I'm sure Hank's family is going to be very impressed."

"I hope so," Rose said. "I haven't done much socially lately."

"They're going to be wowed by you," said Willow. "Believe it."

Rose gave them each a smile. "Thanks. I love you guys.

Lily returned her smile. She loved her new friends, too.

CHAPTER TWENTY
ROSE

Rose drove to the hotel, chiding herself for being nervous. Hank had made it plain it was a work commitment. She'd certainly met enough men doing business that she shouldn't be the least bit concerned, especially because his family would be present.

She parked the car in the employees' area and then walked over to the front entrance of the hotel. Pausing a moment to study the lines of it, the classic way plantings, large pots of flowers, and other decorative items enhanced it tastefully, she murmured a little prayer that she could save the best of it for Alec and those who would follow.

As she entered the lobby, she saw Hank standing and talking to a younger gentleman. Hank looked dashing in tan slacks, a bright green golf shirt, and a navy blazer. Reminding herself that he was, in some respects, the "enemy," she moved forward.

His face brightened when he saw her. He hurried to her. "My! You look lovely. Come meet my son-in-law. My daughter and Leah are outside looking at flowers."

Rose studied the young man who was standing aside. Tall and thin, with thick brown hair that waved gently, his blue eyes regarded her with interest.

"Rose, this is Rob Garland, my favorite son-in-law. Rob, Rose Macklin."

Rob smiled and shook his head at Hank. "His *only* son-in-law." He held out his hand as Hank gave him her name. "How do you do, Rose. Pleased to meet you."

"Thanks. Hank was anxious for you to know who he'd be working with for the next three months. He didn't want Leah to think he'd abandoned her."

Rob laughed. "Papa B and Leah are very close. It's touching to see. Especially with him being alone."

"She sure fills my time when I'm at home," said Hank. "It's great to be with her, and it helps out Sam."

Rose caught the eye of a young woman who was approaching them holding Leah in her arms. Surprised by the look of annoyance on her face, Rose forced a pleasant smile as she waited for them to get closer.

"Ah, here's Samantha now," said Hank, beaming at his daughter.

A smile replaced Samantha's previous frown as she hurried to Hank's side and nestled up against him. Leah held out her arms to Hank. He easily swung her into his embrace and onto his hip. Watching his ease with his granddaughter, Rose was once again filled with longing for a family. Even though both of her parents were dead now, they'd left her wounded by their lack of love. Now she wanted to change, perhaps because of Alec's situation, perhaps out of pure loneliness. She would shrivel with embarrassment if anyone found out how she was feeling. Most of all, Hank.

"Sam, I want you to meet Rose Macklin, my co-worker on the project for this hotel. I thought you'd like to meet her."

"Indeed," said Sam, holding out her hand to her. "It's nice to meet you, Rose. I know you'll be spending time with Dad, but we at home need him too. Now that my mother is gone, it's important for our family to stick close together. All part of the healing process."

Rose froze. Sam couldn't have made it any clearer if she'd

carried a sign that said, "Go away!" Even Hank looked uncomfortable.

"Now, Sam, it's been almost two years, and I've made it perfectly plain that business is what this dinner is all about," he chided quietly, but Rose knew there was a whole lot more that wasn't being said. She'd read stories about daughters who didn't want their fathers to date after their mothers' deaths. Apparently, Sam was one of them.

She took a moment to study her. With burnished brown hair that met her shoulders, Sam was of average height with a trim, but broad athletic body that Rose thought must have come from Hank. Her face, though pretty, wasn't remarkable. Her green eyes were, however. Large and round, they studied her with intensity.

In the awkward silence that followed, Rob cleared his throat. "Well, let's go have that drink before dinner."

"Good idea," said Hank. "I've ordered a bottle of wine to be delivered to my room, along with some appetizers, so Leah can play there while we sit and talk to get to know one another better." Hank led them to the elevator. Feeling unusually uncomfortable, Rose stuck to his side, determined not to let Sam ruin the evening.

Upstairs, while the family got things organized, Rose stepped out onto the balcony. It was a pleasant evening, but she was glad she'd brought along a light-weight shawl for later. Looking out at the mountains in the distance and admiring the rosy glow of a sunset that coated their peaks like the blush on a baby's cheeks, she felt a new peace envelop her. The mountains always had that effect on her. She considered them a sign of strength and a reminder to her to be strong.

She heard footsteps behind her and turned.

Sam smiled at her. "Pleasant evening, isn't it?"

"Very nice," Rose replied. "Hank told me you were leaving tomorrow."

"Yes, back to Atlanta and the rat race there," Sam said, coming closer. "I need to ask you something. How well do you know my father? Had you known each other before now?"

"Your father and I are working together on this project for the next three months. I don't believe it will last longer than that. And no, before now, I've never met your father." Rose was shocked by the question. She knew Sam was asking much more than that, but she wasn't willing to say anything else. Heaven knew she didn't want Sam or her family to know of her attraction to Hank.

Hank stepped out onto the balcony. "Here are the beauties. Rob and I have been wondering what you're up to."

"Just chatting," said Sam. "I wanted to make sure there would be no surprises. You know how protective I am of you." She entwined her arm around his. "Let's enjoy our last evening together for a while. We're going to miss you so."

Hank glanced at Rose and followed Sam inside.

Well done, thought Rose. Sam had handled herself like a pro. No doubt she'd had plenty of practice. Hank was a catch. She went inside, well aware of the game Sam was playing and was determined not to react.

She took a seat on a chair next to the couch, ignoring Hank's invitation to sit by him on the couch.

Leah toddled over to her and lifted her arms. "Up. I wanna get up."

"Hi, Leah," Rose said, smiling at her. She was adorable in a pink sundress that looked as if it cost more than many of Rose's bargain buys. She lifted Leah into her lap.

Leah smiled at her and patted her hair. "Pretty. Pretty lady."

"Yes," said Hank, smiling at them. "Very pretty lady."

"Pretty Leah," said Rose.

"Oh, no! We don't like to say things like that to her," Sam softly scolded. "We don't want Leah to think her appearance is all that matters to people. Right, Rob? It's so shallow."

Rose bit her lip, forcing herself to remain quiet. She hadn't meant any harm.

Hank winked at her. "So different from when Sam's mother and I were raising children. But then that was some time ago."

Rob rolled his eyes. "A compliment now and then never hurts anyone."

"Well, I'm sure you, Rose, understand what I meant," Sam persisted, making a bigger point of it.

"Oh, yes," Rose answered, knowing exactly what Sam meant. It made things easy for her. Rose had no desire to get involved with Hank's family. Not that she was afraid to fight for something she wanted. But, in this case, there was no need to go there. She and Hank were working together on a project, period.

She asked Rob what he did for a living, and conversation perked up. He was a financial analyst and had a lot to say about the fluctuating stock market. She listened, fascinated to know that people like him put a lot of time into studying it. In the end, she suspected, they did as much guessing as anyone else. She herself had a knack for finding profitable deals that had little to do with research but simply reading the news and connecting the dots. Not that she had much money to play with. She'd made a good life for herself, but it didn't include a lot of extras.

"It's time for dinner, folks," said Hank, getting to his feet. "I've reserved a table at Sage, the premier restaurant here."

There was a knock at the door.

"That must be Julie, the babysitter," said Sam. "I'll get it."

She hurried to the door and opened it.

An older woman with gray hair and a plump figure entered the room wearing a big smile. "Hi, there, Leah. Remember me?" She held up a stuffed lizard. "Lizzie and I are here to read more books with you."

Leah clapped her hands. "Books!"

Rose thought back to her childhood. It had been filled with books. That was one thing her parents had done for her, given her a chance to read as much as she could from an early age.

With a sweep of her arms, Sam waved her, Rob, and Hank out of the room and stood by as Julie got settled on the couch with Leah. "We'll be back soon, Leah. Have fun!" said Sam, firmly closing the door behind her.

Rose waited for crying and screaming, but after a few words from Julie, all was quiet. "That was easy," she said to Sam.

"Tonight, this was easy. We go out quite a bit at home, so Leah understands we'll be back."

Rose wondered if Sam did anything wrong. She seemed like the perfect mother.

Hank took hold of her elbow. "I'm anxious to try Sage. Traveling with Leah, we usually stick to family restaurants. Nothing worse than a screaming child or having one run around the room while you're trying to have a pleasant, quiet meal."

"I agree," she said. "I've had only one meal at Sage, and it was delicious. I'm excited to eat there again. The chef worked in San Francisco at one time and came here for warmer weather. His food is excellent."

Hank gave her a warm smile. "I'm happy you could join us, Rose. It means a lot to me."

"I'm pleased to meet you, but it's going to be an early evening," said Sam.

"Yes, we've got work to do," Rose said.

"My father is quite an expert in his field," Sam said, giving him a big smile.

"So is Rose," said Hank, holding open the door to the elevator so they could join others there. "Did you know that Rose, here, runs the 'You Deserve It' blog?"

Sam's eyes widened. "Really? I follow that blog. So many interesting ideas."

"So, do I," said a young woman whose skin looked red, as if she'd been out in the sun too long. "That's why Rick and I decided to come here for our honeymoon."

"Not that we've seen too much of the place," her young husband said, making his wife's face turn even redder.

Rose hid a chuckle. "Glad you like the Desert Sage Inn. It's one of a kind."

Hank stirred restlessly at her side. Rose knew he was dying to tell the guests about The Blaise Hotel Group taking over, but before he could mention anything, the elevator door opened, and they all got out.

Sam took hold of Hank's arm. "C'mon, Dad. We're late."

Hank held onto Rose's hand as they walked to the restaurant's entrance, making it an awkward line of three.

The hostess in the restaurant greeted them at the door. "Welcome to Sage."

"I have reservations for four under Bowers," said Hank.

The hostess checked her list. "Oh, yes. You're all set. Juan will show you to your table."

Juan was a middle-aged man who obviously loved food. The sage green tie he wore with a crisp white shirt curved over his round stomach.

"You're in for several treats tonight," Juan said, holding a chair for Rose. "Enjoy!"

Hank hurried to hold a chair for Sam opposite her. Then he

returned to Rose's side.

Rose looked around the restaurant, admiring the southwest feel of the room. The stucco walls were painted the lightest shade of sage green. Dark wooden beams in the ceiling offset the white surface and matched the tables covered with crisp white cloths and the chairs whose seats were covered in a rich green fabric. In the center of each table was a small crystal vase filled with wild flowers in bougainvillea pink, deep gold, and bright yellow. Crystal and silverware sparkled at each place setting. At one end of the room, flames flickered in the gas fireplace.

She looked out the windows along the outside wall onto the expansive patio where more tables were set for dinner. Patio heaters were strategically placed among them.

"It's going to be hard to go back to reality," said Sam. "This is lovely, and the aromas have my mouth watering."

Hank beamed at her. "I'm glad you're enjoying it. Too bad Nikki couldn't join us." He turned to Rose. "Nicole, my oldest, is a physician working in Atlanta. She's dedicated to her cancer patients."

"She must be an angel to do that kind of work," Rose said with feeling. "I think it would be depressing."

He nodded. "Me too, but she loves it. And she wins the battle quite often. It's amazing what they've done with medications fighting cancer." His features drooped. "Nothing could help my wife, Leigh. It was too late."

"I'm sorry," Rose said, aware of how much he must have loved her.

"Losing Mom was awful," said Sam. "She was the best mother in the world. Right, Dad? The best at everything."

"I'd like to think so," he answered quietly. He picked up the leather-bound wine list that Juan had left at the table. "How about wine to accompany dinner?"

"Sounds great," said Rob. "How about you, Rose?"

"Lovely," she said. Talk of Hank's wife was sad for them and awkward for her.

Their waiter arrived with an offer of a selection of water. After ordering sparkling water for the table, Hank asked to see the wine steward. A few minutes later, a gentleman came to the table to discuss wines with Hank.

The dining room was full, but service seemed to be running smoothly. Best of all, the sound of happy conversations filled the space. That, and the aromas wafting from the kitchen and other tables pleased her. Alec could be proud of what he'd built.

"Any idea what any of you are going to order? Meat or fish?" asked Hank.

"Seafood for me," said Sam. "Probably steak for Rob."

"I don't know," Rose said. "I want to peruse the menu."

"Okay, I'll order a bottle of white to begin. We'll go from there." Hank nodded at the wine steward. "I'll take your suggestion and order the sauvignon blanc."

"Good thing we're not driving," said Sam. "Mom would think we were in trouble."

Hank glanced at his daughter and turned to Rose with a smile. "Are you going to need any help getting back to Alec's?"

Rose chuckled. "I think I can manage."

Their wine came. Hank went through the routine of tasting and approving, and after wine had been poured in each glass, he lifted his.

"Here's to health and happiness."

"For all of us," Rose said, clicking her glass against his.

He smiled at her, and even as his gaze remained on her, he took a sip.

It was quiet at the table when Rose put her glass down. She realized from the clamped-mouth expression on Sam's face that she hadn't liked the way Hank had looked at her.

Ignoring her, Rose opened the menu the waiter had placed in front of her.

As predicted, Rob chose a New York strip steak, and Sam chose salmon.

Rose turned to Hank. "What are you having?"

"I'm going to join Rob and have the steak. How about you?"

"I'll join Sam and have seafood. But instead of salmon, I'll have the glazed sea bass with ginger butter sauce."

"Better watch that butter sauce," warned Sam, patting her flat stomach.

Rose pressed her lips together. Drawing a calming breath, she said politely, "No need to worry. On occasions like this, I allow myself a few treats."

Hank nodded and smiled at her. "I like a woman who enjoys food."

"But Mom ..."

"Sam, that's enough," Hank said firmly, bringing tears to his daughter's eyes. "That was then. This is now."

"Oh, but ..." Sam sighed. "I'm sorry, it's a difficult time for me."

"We're trying for another baby," said Rob quietly.

"And so far, no luck." Sam's lips trembled. "It's been almost a year."

"I'm sorry," Rose said. "I understand how stressful that could be."

"Oh? So, you know ..."

"I couldn't have children," Rose said, surprised by the pain she felt. At the time, married to the wrong man, it hadn't bothered her. But now, as she was aging, it was becoming more painful.

"It'll work out, honey," Hank said to Sam. "I'm sure of it."

"Thanks, Dad. We'll see. But please don't let me ruin this

dinner. I know you and Rose need this time together to do the project. One of those home runs you always talk about."

Hank laughed. "Yes. Rose and I will load the bases with all kinds of ideas and hit the ball out of the park."

Rose's lips curved. She'd always heard he tended to talk in terms of sports. She thought she'd be annoyed by it, but he made it seem so natural she loved it. She settled down to enjoy a delicious meal.

CHAPTER TWENTY-ONE
WILLOW

After sharing an early light supper with Lily, Willow decided to take a walk. The last of the day's golfers were putting out at the 18th hole when she approached. She stopped to see them. Golfers were a group unto their own, taking advantage of every playable moment of daylight on the course. She moved on and stopped again when she heard her name being called.

"Willow! Wait up!"

She turned to find Dan running toward her.

"Hi," she said, pleased to see him.

"Where are you headed?"

"Nowhere. Just letting off some steam and trying to get into a better frame of mind for tomorrow."

He frowned at her. "What is it with you and Brent Armstrong? When he came to pick up Tiffany after work, he was very polite to her and me. Is it something between just the two of you?"

"Mostly," she admitted. Brent was cocky and full of himself like some guys his age who acted that way when trying to prove themselves in business. It didn't make Brent more likable, but she understood that others might think of him in a better light. Soon enough, they'd discover the mean boy beneath the polished man. It wasn't up to her to make sure they did.

"Mind if I walk with you?" Dan asked.

"No. I'd enjoy the company." Her voice held a note of pleasure she couldn't disguise.

His lips curved into a smile that showed a dimple. "I'd like to get to know you better."

"Not much to tell. I'm an only child whose parents work for Alec. Because of him, I went to the hotel school at Cornell. I've been trying to decide where to go from there. I was teaching at Boston University before Alec requested that I come home."

He laughed and shook his head. "Your attempt to make it seem boring has only piqued my curiosity. There's a whole lot more to that story, I'm sure."

She grinned. "Tell me about yourself."

"Like you, nothing much to tell. You already know Tiffany is my stepsister. I have a much younger stepbrother, too. Mom's second husband is a nice guy. My dad? Not so much. But it's all good. No big complaints."

"Sounds like things are pretty normal. How'd you get into the fitness program?"

"I played all kinds of sports in high school and then hurt my knee. When I was undergoing physical therapy, I realized I wanted to know more about the field. I studied it in college and practiced for a few years. When I met Alec, and he offered me the chance to run a fitness program here, I thought I'd try it out. I've been here for almost a year, and I love it."

"You gave Rose, Lily, and me a tough workout program. We bonded pretty quickly during the sessions."

"They seem like exceptional people," said Dan. "But then, they must be if Alec wanted their help." His gaze rested on her. "You too."

She felt warmth rush to her face. "Thanks." She hadn't realized how much she'd needed to hear his compliment. It was nice to be acknowledged.

In comfortable quiet, they reached the hotel.

Dan turned to her. "I have to go. I have an early appointment tomorrow morning. But, Willow, will you go out with me sometime?"

She looked into his eyes and nodded. "Yes. Give me a call."

"Thanks, I will," said Dan.

She waited and watched him go to his car, then turned and sprinted along the lit walkway, heading back to Alec's feeling as if she could fly the whole way home.

CHAPTER TWENTY-TWO
ROSE

Sitting in the dining room with Hank and his family, Rose couldn't help wondering what it would be like to be part of such a scene permanently. The thought of it, which might have scared her earlier, was surprisingly pleasing. Sam was a problem, but she'd softened quite a bit after announcing the reason she was under such stress. Rob was a great guy with whom she felt comfortable. And Hank? He was the star of the show, easily keeping conversation upbeat and enjoyable.

She was amused by the sports terms he used—terms she was getting used to. But when he said, "Okay, team, what is everyone having for dessert?" she laughed.

Sam rolled her eyes before joining her laughter.

"Let's hit a home run and order whatever we want," teased Rob, making them laugh even harder.

Hank joined their laughter. "All right, enough."

They ordered a variety of desserts, and later, while Hank was looking over the bill, Sam said, "Guess we'd better get back to Leah."

"She's such a darling," said Rose, smiling.

Sam nodded. "She's named after my mother. That makes her even more special to us."

"I see," Rose said, disappointed by the lukewarm tone of Sam's voice. She'd thought they'd gone beyond that stage.

"Leah likes you, Rose." Hank smiled at her.

Though Rose returned his smile, she knew any relationship with him would be difficult. Sam was frowning.

They all stood.

"You guys go on ahead. I'm going to walk Rose to her car," Hank said to Sam and Rob.

"It was nice meeting you," said Rob, smiling at her.

"' Night, Rose," Sam said politely.

"Safe trip home," Rose said. "Enjoy springtime in Atlanta. The flowers and flowering Bradford Pear trees there are so beautiful at this time of year."

"Thanks," said Sam, with a warmer note to her voice.

After Sam and Rob left them, Hank walked out to her car with her. "I'm sorry about Sam's over-protectiveness. You know how close fathers and daughters can be."

"Actually, I don't," said Rose. "My father and I didn't have that bond."

He studied her. "I'm sorry to hear that. How about your mother?"

Rose shook her head. "I was never supposed to happen. It was not a happy household."

"Wow, that's sad," said Hank. He leaned over and kissed her cheek. "Is that why you are alone?"

"Partly," she said, staring into the distance, not wanting to get into any discussion of her relationships.

Hank turned her toward him and tilted her chin up so he could look into her eyes. "I like you, Rose. A lot."

She knew he was going to kiss her and let it happen. There was something so appealing about him and the way he made her feel.

His lips on hers were soft, sure. Rose reached up and slid her arms around his neck, wanting to hold onto him and this moment for as long as she could because she doubted this relationship was going far. Hank was a family man, and his daughter had made it plain how she felt about his being with Rose.

When they pulled apart, Hank smiled at her and brushed a tendril of hair away from her face. "I want to start seeing you."

In an attempt at humor to cover up her uncertainty, she said, "You're going to be seeing a lot of me. Every day at work."

"Hey, that's not what I meant, and you know it," he said softly. He kissed her once more, and, God help her, she responded even as she told herself she was being foolish.

He stepped away and let out a long sigh. His thumb rubbed her cheek in a sweet caress. "I've wanted to kiss you from the first time Papa B met you."

She cocked an eyebrow at him. "That was a dirty trick, and you know it."

He chuckled. "The truth was, I was afraid if I mentioned my name, you'd back off without letting me explain. You have a reputation as being very independent and strong."

"Yeah? Well, I've had to be." She tried to hide the pain behind her words. She'd been pretty much alone in life, even when she was married. It turned out the man she thought she'd wedded was quite different from when they'd first met, and he courted her. Not nice at all when he realized she didn't love him the way he loved her. They were both better off apart.

"Rose, I like your strength and independence, the way you handle yourself. My daughters choose to remember my wife at her best. I admire that. But they don't know about the bad times when Leigh and I hid our unhappiness from them. With you, I know I'm going to get the real you. The good and the bad."

"And the ugly," Rose said, feeling such a relief that she wanted to cry. Not since Alec had she found a man willing to see her for who she was, and it wasn't all pretty. "Let's take it easy and see where it goes," she said. "In any case, we have to work together. That will be a way to know if we're going to take this thing ... whatever it is ... any further."

"This thing you're talking about is me wanting to get to know you better. Alec is the one who thought we'd make a great team."

"Really?" Rose couldn't hide her surprise.

"Yeah. He knew how talented you were, how much you'd loved working here at the hotel. And he knew how honest I am in my work. He told me you'd respect that."

She gave him a thoughtful look and nodded. "Yes. He knows that about me."

Hank's face softened as he continued to study her. "Well, then, let's move forward both with work and with this 'thing.' Shall we?"

"One step at a time," Rose said. She turned and unlocked her car door, sorting through her feelings. "I'll see you tomorrow."

He stood by as she got into her car and then lifted a hand and waved goodbye.

She returned his smile and drove away, eager to talk to Alec.

Back at the house, she went to check on Alec. His waking hours were erratic, with his sleeping during the day altering his nighttime patterns.

She tapped on the door and opened it a crack to find the place well-lit and Alec sitting up in his chair.

"Hi," she said softly. "Okay if I come in?"

"Yes," he said. "Just the person I wanted to talk to. How did it go with Hank?"

She walked over to the couch near him and sat down. "He's a lovely man. I've just come from dinner with him and his family. We've agreed to disagree about a lot of the upcoming advertising. Still, I have him thinking about the idea of using the Desert Sage Inn as a prototype for a new, upscale group of hotels for The Blaise Hotel Group. He's open to the idea. We're going to draw up plans and an advertising campaign to present to them about it. And we'll be working on ads that set the inn apart from the others in the Blaise Group. However, he also must follow through on the ideas he's already presented to them about adding the inn to their list of hotel properties, branding it like the others."

Alec nodded. "I like the idea of making the inn unique, as you well know. If the two of you creative people can't do it, I don't know who can."

Rose was quiet, almost too hesitant to ask the question that was rubbing her mind raw. "Alec," she finally said, "why did you plan for me to work with Hank? He said it was your idea. Are you trying to play matchmaker?"

Alec's eyes widened, and then he chuckled, which had him coughing. When he could catch his breath, he said, "You're attracted to him?" His eyes lit with excitement.

Rose nodded. "He reminds me a lot of you when we first met. Remember?"

His face became somber. "Yes," he said softly. "Sometimes, I think I was such a fool. Other times, I know I was right to pull away from you and Lily. Life is full of choices. I'm still not sure what I'd choose to do if I had the chance to do everything all over again. Pretty damn sad if you ask me."

Rose got up, walked over to his chair, and, sitting on the arm of it, hugged him. "I should've fought harder, for you, for us. But you know why I couldn't." Her parents had made her believe she was unlovable. For her to reach out against his wishes at that point in her life was something she wasn't equipped to do.

"Yes, I do ..."

Rose cut him off. "Did you know I went into counseling after I left you? Even after all those visits and all these years, I still feel uncomfortable about commitment. I know why I have all those feelings, of course, but being aware of them doesn't always change things. Not completely."

Alec wrapped thin fingers around her hand and squeezed it. "Don't waste any more time on the past. The problem wasn't about you. I'm sorry I made you doubt yourself. Embrace the future. That's what I would wish for you. Especially now when I see so clearly the limits I placed in my own life and that of others. Don't be afraid to see where this goes."

She let out a sigh from deep within her. Alec was right. Leaps of faith were part of living. Without them, how did people move forward?

The following day, Rose awakened and stared up at the ceiling fan twirling slowly above her. She'd tossed and turned through the night, but awake now, she decided to let her attraction to Hank play out. Nobody knew her better than Alec, and he'd reminded her she'd be foolish to let old insecurities and hurts play a part in choosing what she wanted for the future.

She climbed out of bed with a new spring of hope in her step.

After grabbing a cup of coffee, she walked out to the patio and sat in the morning sun, letting its warmth take the chill out of the air. She liked this time of day when she felt as if she had the world to herself. A small iguana raced out of the bushes nearby and stretched out on the warm surface of the patio, a sunbather like her.

She turned as Lily came out, dressed in running clothes.

"Hi," Rose said. "Are you going out for a run?"

"More like slow jogging," said Lily, "but I'm learning to like the early morning exercise. My morning exercises at home consisted of getting up and getting ready for the office before heading off to work to try to catch up from the previous day. Pretty lame, huh?"

Rose nodded. "Sounds like a rat race to me."

"As I've said before, I'm not sure what I'm going to do after this stint here, but it's not going to be that." Lily gave Rose a little wave and headed out.

Rose watched her, surprised by the changes in Lily. But then they'd all changed since coming to Alec's aid.

Later, on her computer in her room, Rose typed content for her blog. Her followers expected to hear from her regularly. Today she talked about a new sun cream she'd brought to California with her to try out. That and a new recipe she'd adapted from one of Juanita's recipes for a pork taco would be enough for today.

She answered her email, sat back, and sighed. Running a blog wasn't as easy as she'd initially thought. It required a lot of research, building a list of advertisers, a willingness to respond to everyone's questions and comments, and a creative way to put a new spin on things day after day.

She checked the time and hurried to get ready. She and Hank were to meet at ten o'clock in the lobby, after he'd had a chance to say goodbye to his family.

In the shower, with warm water sluicing over her body, she thought of him. It had been interesting to see Hank with his family, so different from what she'd initially heard about him. He was a sweet, tender guy. She remembered his lips on hers, the taste of him, and the way he'd cradled her in his arms, making her feel safe and cherished. As she thought of it, her body turned liquid. But she didn't allow herself to linger too long on those thoughts. She'd been fooled before.

She stepped out of the shower and towel-dried, trying not to focus on her image in the mirror. At fifty-two, she was in decent shape. Still, perky breasts and a flat stomach were things of the past. She pinched her stomach and reminded herself not to be pressured by social media into thinking she and other women her age were not desirable.

At ten o'clock, she strolled into the lobby. Hank was saying goodbye to his family. Seeing her, Leah ran over to her. "Hi!"

Rose squatted beside her. "Hi, Leah! Are you going on a plane ride today?"

"Yes. In the clouds."

"What fun to be way up high like that."

As Rose straightened, Sam approached them. "Come, Leah. The limo is here." She held out her hand, and Leah took it.

"Have a safe trip," Rose said.

"Thank you," Sam responded as she hurried toward the front entrance.

"It was nice to meet you, Rose," said Rob, stopping by her. "I hope to see you again."

She smiled. "Thank you. I enjoyed meeting you too."

Hank came over to her and put his arm around her as his family left the hotel. "It's always hard to say goodbye. In the time I'll be away, Leah will have learned so many things without me."

"You'll have to Facetime every day," she said, aware of how sincere he was.

He smiled at her. "Yes. It's a relief we can do that. Now, what's on the agenda for today?"

"I thought we'd better talk about some of the transitional material we'll give guests after the hotel is sold. Rather than have new management make it seem as if nothing will stay the same, we want to assure guests that the original style of service will remain." She smiled at him. "I thought maybe I could show you around the hotel so you can see it through my eyes."

"What? You don't trust mine?" He gave her a teasing grin.

"No, no," she said. "I merely want to point out a few things many people wouldn't notice. And you can tell me your ideas about your approach."

"Fair enough," he said agreeably. "First, can we grab a cup of coffee? I didn't sleep all that well last night."

She wondered if he'd thought of her as much as she'd thought of him.

They joined others in the lobby and helped themselves to coffee at the special station set up for that purpose. In the afternoon, large containers of iced lemon or cucumber water would replace the coffee machine.

"Let's sit a moment outside," said Rose. "From there, we can watch activity in the pool. It's adult swim time. A great chance for real swimmers to get in some laps."

"An excellent sales point," said Hank, taking a sip of coffee. "This is the kind of thing you want to show me, right?"

Caught at her game, she laughed. "Plenty more to come."

They settled in chairs side by side on the patio and looked out at their surroundings. Rose wanted him to capture the colors and care that went into the landscaping. It didn't happen haphazardly. Maintenance of the hotel grounds was an essential part of its elegance, appreciated by many of their guests. A local magazine had showcased the property recently for this exact reason. It was this kind of setting their guests craved.

"Ahhh," said Hank. "Quiet, peaceful, and all that. But a lot of younger guests want a little more action."

"Yes," said Rose. "They can find it here too, just not in this spot, where so many share the space."

They got up and walked to the pools. Adult swim time was officially over. The poolside bar opened, and music played softly in the background as staff moved about realigning the lounges and chairs. A couple of families moved into the pool area, tossed towels on unoccupied chairs to claim them, and moved standing umbrellas to give them better shade. She watched a mother rub suntan lotion on a little boy, desperately trying to keep him still long enough to get the job done. He was hopping about in his excitement to get into the shallow end of the pool specifically designed for kids.

"Leah is just like him," commented Hank. "She loves the water too."

"She's so darling," said Rose. "I hope Sam and Rob can have more children. I bet Leah would love being a big sister."

"Or not," said Hank, cocking an eyebrow at her, making her laugh. "Being a princess can be tough duty when you're suddenly told you have to share the kingdom."

"Is that what happened with your daughters?" Rose asked, curious about his family as they left the pool area.

"No, Nikki thought Sam was her own special doll," said Hank, smiling at the memory. His face suddenly changed, erasing all signs of happiness. "I talked to Nikki last night. She called to ask about you. Sam told her you and I were dating."

"That wasn't exactly true," Rose said. "We hadn't even talked about it until after dinner." Though she was irritated by Sam's interference, she tried not to let it show.

"Yeah, I told Nikki we weren't dating."

"Is that how you left it?" Rose asked. *Hadn't they agreed they'd give dating a try?*

Hank sighed. "I thought it would be the best thing to say at this time."

Rose's heart stopped and then raced. This couldn't be happening to her. Not after she'd finally decided to take a leap of faith. Feeling sick, Rose stared out at the scenery, seeing nothing.

"Rose, I want to date you. You know that," he said quietly.

She glared at him, "If you want to go out with me, you can't hide it and pretend with your daughters that it's not happening. What kind of person would that make me?"

"Or me," he said calmly. "Don't worry. I'll set things straight with both of them. It's time they accepted that I want to date."

"You haven't dated before now?" Rose asked, surprised.

"Not really," said Hank. "I've been working hard to keep the family together." His breath came out in a long sigh. He kicked at the grass with the toe of his shoe and then faced her. "Nikki thinks she should've recognized Leigh's cancer symptoms earlier. And Sam and her mother got into a fight about having a baby so soon after marriage, and then Leigh fell ill and was diagnosed. So, in part, the girls blame themselves for their mother's illness and quick death."

"Families can be so complicated," said Rose, stunned by what she'd heard. Maybe dating Hank wasn't the best idea. She didn't want to get in the middle of such drama when she was already unsure about him.

CHAPTER TWENTY-THREE
LILY

Lily trotted along the path by the golf course breathing in the clean air, listening to the birds sing, and feeling at home in her surroundings. There was a lot she liked about desert living. She heard a strange noise behind her and turned.

"Hey, there!" Brian said, moving quickly toward her, the metal blade of his prosthesis striking the pavement in a steady rhythm.

He came to a stop beside her. "I'm surprised to see you."

"Since being here, I've come to enjoy getting out for a walk or a short run in the mornings. When we first came to the inn, Alec insisted that Rose, Willow, and I work out in the mornings with Dan, the inn's physical trainer. Instead of hating it, I've learned to like it."

"These morning runs are important to me. Gets the blood going. Mind if I walk with you for a few minutes before taking off again?"

"Not at all. I'd enjoy the company." She tried not to react to seeing him in his jogging clothes. He was a real hottie. And the prosthesis was interesting.

He grinned. "Amazing what this can do." He wiggled the metal blade of his prosthesis.

"It certainly hasn't slowed you down any." She smiled at him, not the least bit uncomfortable talking about it. He made it seem so natural.

Studying him as they walked, she wondered what it would be like to make love with him and felt her face flame with heat as images of them together swirled through her mind in vivid detail.

"It sure gets hot quickly," he said, glancing at her.

She patted her cheeks. "Yes," she agreed, grateful to be able to use that excuse to cover up her reaction to him. Flustered, she tripped.

Strong hands caught her before she did a face plant on the pavement. "Whoa! Be careful!"

After she regained her balance, they walked on.

"How do you think this transition process is going to work out with the new owners coming into the hotel?" he asked. "I know you, Rose, and Willow are working for Alec. What's that all about? I hear he calls you his Desert Flowers."

"Yes. It's sweet. We're here to make sure all of Alec's hard work doesn't go to waste. We don't want the Blaise Group to change it into one of their regular properties immediately."

Brian's eyes widened. "That's a loaded statement."

"It may sound that way, but it's how we all feel."

He studied her. "Are we going to be enemies then?"

"Not necessarily," she answered, flirting a bit, which wasn't like her at all.

"Well, we'll have to see about that. It seems as if there's a challenge ahead of us." He tipped his head. "I'd better be on my way. Sounds like I'm going to have my hands full dealing with you."

They smiled at one another.

As he sprinted away, Lily thought she just might like having his hands on her.

CHAPTER TWENTY-FOUR
ROSE

Rose and Hank continued their tour of the property, but the sparkle of past conversations was missing. She kept looking at him, wishing she felt differently about the idea of dating him. Just as she was ready to take a leap of faith, common sense was yanking her back, telling her it would only be a struggle with an uncertain outcome. Hank's dedication to his family was admirable, but like the situation with Alec, trying to be with him could end up with her getting hurt.

A new aura of sadness had enveloped him. He sighed. "I'm sorry, but I need time to myself. Can we continue this tour another day? There are some personal things I need to take care of."

"Sure. I understand. Maybe tomorrow will be better. I'm going to work on some materials we can give to arriving guests to explain what is going on. I'll do them to my specifications, aware that you might want to make a lot of changes."

"Sounds fair," he said. "Thanks. See you later."

She watched him walk away and waited until he was back inside the hotel before going to her car and driving back to Alec's house. She had a lot to think about too.

When she arrived, she found Alec sitting outside under the shade of an umbrella.

"Hello!" said Rose. "How nice to see you outside. How are you feeling?"

"Better than some days. Seeing a beautiful woman always makes me feel even better," he said with some of his old charm. She loved him for it.

She pulled up a chair near his. "I'm going to work at home today. Hank needed some personal space."

"How are things going between the two of you?"

Rose studied him. "Are you sure you're not trying to be some sort of matchmaker?"

He laughed and waved away her suggestion. "You already asked that. You're just two people I like working together."

"The truth is he's been dealing with some family issues with his daughters. It seems as if they'd been blaming themselves for their mother's death. They have some issues they need to work out to help their healing. He's spent a lot of time making sure they're all right."

"Admirable," Alec commented.

"Yes, but now his daughter Sam has made it crystal clear she doesn't like the idea of his being with another woman. Even though Hank and I have talked about dating, I don't think it's a smart idea."

"Time takes care of a lot of things," Alec said, patting her hand with his bony fingers.

"Life certainly throws you a lot of curves," she said sadly, then held in a chuckle. Hank would probably tell her something like, you have to handle a lot of curveballs before you hit a home run.

"You'll be fine, Rose. You're a strong, independent woman."

"Yes, you're right. I'll be fine." But her heart wasn't in it. For once, she wished someone would see how vulnerable she was. But she'd put up such a strong front through the years she wondered about the difference between being vulnerable or just plain weak.

She kissed Alec's cheek and said, "I'd better get back to work, or my boss is going to be unhappy with me."

He laughed. "Never."

Still smiling, she left him and went to her room. She'd been sketching some ideas, and now, with greater determination, she wanted to introduce them to Hank.

It wasn't until her stomach rumbled that Rose realized she'd worked through lunch. She got up, stretched, and walked into the kitchen.

Juanita looked up from where she was chopping vegetables. "Are you finally ready for something to eat? I didn't want to disturb you."

"I didn't realize it was so late. I think I'll just grab some yogurt and fruit. I'll be eating here tonight." She walked over to the counter where Juanita was standing. "What are we having?"

"I thought I'd make a vegetable soup, and then Pedro said he'd grill up some chicken for us."

"The chicken with the lime marinade?" Rose asked hopefully.

Juanita chuckled and nodded. "One of your favorites, I know."

Rose leaned her back against the counter and studied Juanita. "You and Pedro have been married a long time. How do you do it? You do great work, have a lovely daughter, and are always cheerful."

Juanita set her knife down on the counter and turned to her. "So much of living is up here." She tapped her head. "There are choices to be made every day. Some days it seems as if nothing will ever go right, that the future looks dim, that the past won't let go. That's when you decide if you're going to move forward or stay in place. Or, God forbid, tumble backward."

"I'm talking about you and Pedro. I've seen how you look at one another, the way he touches you when he walks by. How do you keep that up?" said Rose. "You've worked together to raise your daughter; you even work together for Alec. And yet, I sometimes get the feeling that you're alone, together, in the room." Her voice became wistful. "It's beautiful to see."

"Ah, I understand where you're going with this. You're talking about love." Juanita's eyes filled with tenderness. She reached out to touch Rose's cheeks. "That, my dear, is a different story. In that case, love is all about the other person, even when you're trying to protect your desires and needs."

"I grew up in a house that had little love," Rose said, wondering if that's why the thought of being with Hank scared her so. "My parents weren't close, and they certainly showed nothing but duty toward me. I was clean and fed and clothed, but they'd never actually wanted a child. Me."

"I'm so sorry," said Juanita. "But because you weren't shown love, it doesn't mean you can't give it. I see the way you and Alec treat each other."

"Yes." Rose's eyes filled. "He's the one person I let get close to me. I've tried with others, but it hasn't worked out."

"Until now?" Juanita said, her dark eyes piercing her.

Rose gasped. "How? ..."

Juanita smiled. "I notice things about people, and I saw your excitement when you went to dinner last night. That's all."

"I don't know if I'm capable of opening up to someone else."

Juanita took her hands in her own. "Rose, you are a lovely person who has much to give other people. I read your blog too. There, it's evident what kind of person you are. Maybe it's time to trust yourself ... and life itself."

"Is that why your marriage works so well?"

Juanita chuckled. "Heavens, no. It works because we each give in to the other's wishes about 80 percent of the time."

Laughing, Rose hugged her. "You are such an amazing woman. I love you."

"Love you too, Rose. Love all of you women who came back to help Alec."

Rose grabbed her yogurt and a few raspberries and headed out to the patio, deep in thought. She might have come from a loveless background, but it didn't mean she couldn't love someone. That, she realized, was her gift to give.

CHAPTER TWENTY-FIVE
WILLOW

One afternoon a few days later, Willow sat in John's office listening to him talk about the transition team he intended to put in place until the actual change of ownership.

"To assist me, Willow is going to oversee procedures, along with Sarah and Tim. We don't know who will be leading the team for the Blaise Group, but I suspect you, Brent, will be part of it."

"I probably will. I have the experience," Brent said with confidence.

Willow observed the tightening of John's jaw and said nothing. It surprised her that Brent didn't recognize others' reactions to his making statements like that. Sarah and Tim had each spoken to her about their dislike of him. She understood. Brent was irritating even when she didn't believe he was trying. Maybe it came from his privileged background. Instead of it making her angry, it made her realize that with his lack of people skills, he'd have trouble becoming an effective leader.

"In that case," said John quietly but firmly, "I'm having you assist at the front desk. You'll begin by taking the evening shift, working with Sarah."

Willow felt her eyes widen but again said nothing. Sarah might not like Brent, but she would be a strict teacher and wouldn't hold back on correcting him when necessary. Willow knew this because they'd worked a shift together, and Sarah was particular. Better yet, Sarah was accustomed to people like Brent, who felt entitled to be in charge and have every creature comfort.

"Willow, I want you to start working with me, going through my routines, looking through more of the financials and that kind of thing," said John. He managed a smile. "You can be my assistant for a while."

She returned his smile, confident she'd learn a lot from him. Returning to the inn to help Alec was good for her, as was being back in operations.

After the meeting, Brent said, "Hey, Willow, want to go get a drink?"

She shook her head. "No, thanks. I'm headed home. It's going to be a busy day tomorrow. Besides, you'll be working at the front desk soon."

He waved away her concern. "No problem. I'm going to sweet talk Sarah into letting me off. I know how front desk operations work."

She frowned at him. "Every staff member takes his or her duty seriously, Brent. That's what we're trying to get you and the company to understand."

"My company is extremely successful. We don't need the people at a hotel we're acquiring to tell us how to handle all of ours."

Willow shrugged and walked away. Sarah would take care of him. She wasn't a military wife for nothing.

As she left the main building, Willow decided to head to the fitness center. At Dan's suggestion, she kept a locker there where she could change into her workout clothes. Brent's cockiness stressed her.

When she got to the center, it was quiet except for a male guest who was doing a private session with Tiffany. Willow waved to her and went into the locker room to change.

Later, she entered the main room and noticed Dan with a young man Willow recognized as someone who'd been talking to Brent earlier. A little older than Brent, he had the same blond coloring and clear blue eyes. But there was a noticeable difference in his manner. Friendly, with a kind expression, he smiled at her.

"Willow!" called Dan. "Come on over and meet Trace."

Curious, she joined them.

Still smiling, Trace held out his hand. "Hi, I'm Trace Armstrong."

She shook his hand. "Nice to meet you. Any relation to Brent?"

"Brent is my cousin. I've been sent here to clean up after him. I understand he's already causing problems."

At his frankness, she blinked in surprise.

"Go ahead and tell him, Willow, why you're here at the fitness center," said Dan. He turned to Trace. "I set her up with a locker so she can leave her job and work off her stress from working with your cousin." He indicated Tiffany with a nod of his head. "My sister doesn't have much good to say about him either."

Trace made a face. "Sorry about that. My aunt and uncle have spoiled Brent since he was small, telling him he's perfect no matter what he does."

"He believes he's going to take over management of this property," said Willow quietly.

"No way. Not if I can help it. My dad and Brent's father don't see eye to eye about many things, but I'll make sure to do my best to see that they agree on this. This is my first visit, and I like what I see."

"I'd be happy to show you around," said Willow.

Trace nodded. "Thanks. I'd like that." His blue-eyes settled on her.

"Okay, then. We can meet tomorrow morning."

"Great. And then how about joining me for dinner someday? Friday, Dan and Tiffany are taking me to one of their favorite places."

Willow turned to Dan. "Tico's?"

He grinned. "The best Mexican food around."

"All right. I can't resist. I love their *Pollo en Mole*. What time?"

"Meet us there at six. We'll grab a table on the patio."

"Sounds like a plan." She left Dan and Trace talking to one another, liking the idea of Trace facing off with Brent.

CHAPTER TWENTY-SIX
ROSE

Rose awoke the next morning determined to carry on with or without Hank. Late last night, he'd sent a text announcing he wouldn't be able to meet today. Heaven knew what he was up to. She told herself she didn't care, but she wondered what was going on with him.

She dressed in jogging clothes and padded through the house and out the door. The sun was rising in the sky, sending shards of pink through the early morning clouds hovering at the tops of the mountains. It seemed the forecasters might be right, and the day would be a gray one with showers.

Listening to the sounds of the birds around her, Rose paused before breaking into an easy jog. The pattern of her feet hitting the pavement was comforting. She moved along in rhythm to the sounds of the awakening world.

She stopped in surprise when she saw Lily and Brian walking together ahead of her. Quietly, so as not to disturb them, she turned around and walked away. *Lily and Brian?* The thought made her lips curve. Lily was such a sweet person. She deserved some happiness.

Later, when Rose returned to the house, she took a cup of coffee into her room. It would be, she decided, another workday at home. She didn't mind. She had another idea worth developing.

###

She'd just taken a shower after spending the entire day in exercise clothes when she got a text message from Hank asking her to meet him for dinner. She reread the message and stood at the window of her bedroom, staring out at the desert scene. The heat of the day had settled on the landscape, washing it with a peaceful stillness. Did she really want to get involved with him?

Is this about business? she texted back.

Yes and no, he answered. *There's someone I want you to meet.*

She sighed. When had she ever been this afraid simply to work with a man? It was silly to make much more of it than was realistic.

Okay. What time?

He answered promptly. *Seven. At Sage. Thanks. See you then.*

She clicked off and went to her closet.

When she walked into the restaurant, she saw Hank sitting with a young woman at a table tucked into a corner of the room. Curious, she moved forward. As she drew close, Hank got to his feet, and the woman with dark hair pulled back into a severe bun looked at Rose as if inspecting her.

Self-conscious, Rose smoothed the lines of the black dress that hugged her hips. She'd brightened the V-neck opening of the dress with some silver and turquoise necklaces. On her wrist, she wore a simple silver bracelet.

Hank smiled and reached for her elbow. "Rose, I'd like you to meet someone special in my life. This is my daughter, Nikki."

Rose held out her hand. "Hi, Nikki. I'm Rose Macklin."

Nikki shook her hand crisply. "Pleased to meet you." Her

smile was lukewarm.

Hank helped her into a chair.

She looked up at him. "What's the occasion?"

He glanced at Nikki. "I wanted both of my daughters to meet you. We'll be working together for several months ..."

Rose sighed. *What is he up to? Was he going to take that stance again?*

Nikki shook her head. "Dad, please. That isn't the reason I flew here from Atlanta to be with you." She turned to Rose. "For the first time since my mother died, Dad is interested in dating someone. He brought me here to see for myself why he likes you so much."

Rose blinked rapidly to fight the stinging sensation in her eyes. She turned to him. "You'd do this for me?" she asked softly.

He reached over and covered her hand with his. "I would," he said simply.

She thought he might kiss her, but he didn't.

"Let's relax and enjoy dinner," said Hank, glancing from her to Nikki. "It's great to have the two of you together, and, Nik, you're going to love the food here."

"Yes, Sam told me this place is great," Nikki said agreeably. She studied Rose. "She also told me you run the blog called 'You Deserve This.' How did you happen to do that?"

Pleased to be asked this easy question, Rose began, "I've been in the hospitality business for most of my career. Working on marketing campaigns, most of all. As satisfying as that is, I wanted to create something for my own purposes. I've met many people, and in talking with them, I realized they all want the inside scoop on places to visit, the latest things to buy, and other things to know about. I gather the information for them."

"Do you ever provide medical information?" Nikki asked.

Rose shook her head. "I don't feel I'm qualified to do anything like that except to repost official reports online. But, if some medical person asked me to help get information out, I'd be glad to cooperate."

"It's hard sometimes to get people to pay attention to the signs of cancer," said Nikki. Her mouth turned down. "I wish I'd been more alert to my own mother's condition."

Rose nodded sympathetically. "I can imagine how you feel. I had a dear friend who died of pancreatic cancer, and I still wish I'd pushed her to go to the doctor sooner than she did."

"Thank you for not throwing a lot of platitudes my way. I appreciate it," said Nikki, regarding her with interest.

Rose remained quiet as a waiter appeared at the table. He handed out menus and took an order for sparkling water.

"What's everybody hungry for?" asked Hank.

"I'm going for the swordfish," said Nikki.

"I'm going to order a filet of beef," said Rose. "It's been ages since I've had something like that."

"The N.Y. strip looks perfect for me," said Hank, waving away the frown on Nikki's face. "Look, Nik, it's a favorite of mine."

She laughed. "Okay, it's the doctor in me that can't help warning you about red meat. I'll relax."

"Thanks," said Hank. He waved the wine steward over, and after consulting with him, Hank ordered a bottle of cabernet from California and a glass of sauvignon blanc for Nikki.

While they waited for their wine, Hank said to Rose, "When I was away, I had a conversation with a friend of mine who runs a small, upscale group of hotels, and I have some ideas about how we can approach The Blaise Hotel Group."

"Great. I've got the beginning of a campaign to show you tomorrow," she responded, pleased that he'd taken the time to follow up on their discussion.

Hank winked at Nikki. "Rose is very competent at her job."

Rose smiled at him and turned to Nikki. "Tell me more about your work. Your father is so proud of you."

Nikki straightened in her chair. "I'm a doctor at the Piedmont Hospital in their oncology program, specializing in the diagnosis and treatment of breast cancer."

"Such strides have been made in the treatment of it. That must be very satisfying," Rose said sincerely. "It used to be some years ago that when a woman was diagnosed, it usually meant death."

"Yes, but now we're discovering through focused research there are more and better ways to treat it, and we're able to give women some choices about both surgery and non-surgical treatments. Still, I'm hoping for the day when we can take those at risk and prevent it entirely through genetics. We're working on it, but it will take time."

"Such a rewarding job," commented Rose.

Their wine came. The steward and Hank made a little ceremony of having Nikki taste and approve the white wine, and then Hank said, "Why don't you taste the red, Rose?"

Flattered to be asked, she took the task seriously, swirling the wine in its glass to inspect its color and clarity, inhaling the wine's bouquet, taking a small sip of it, and letting it settle in her mouth for a tiny bit before swallowing. "Lovely," she declared.

The wine steward poured red wine into glasses for her and Hank. "*Bon appetit!*" he declared as he left the table.

Hank raised his glass of wine. "Here's to two lovely ladies!"

Rose glanced at Nikki and smiled. "Here's to all of us!"

The table filled with meaningless conversation about the weather in Atlanta, the condo Hank owned in Buckhead, and Nikki's upcoming vacation with a girlfriend.

"No special man in your life?" Rose asked Nikki.

Nikki let out a long sigh. "Waiting for the right guy. You know?"

Rose nodded, directing herself not to glance at Hank.

"If you ladies will excuse me, I see someone I need to speak to." Hank got to his feet. "I'll be right back."

As soon as Hank walked away, Nikki leaned toward Rose. "I've wanted a moment alone with you. I don't know what exactly is going on, but I've never seen Dad this way. He insisted I come to California for a couple of days of rest, but more specifically so I could meet you."

"Your father and I have discussed dating," said Rose. "Your sister made it clear she wasn't comfortable with that."

"Yes, she called me," said Nikki. "I think she didn't realize how serious Dad was. Sam's the baby of the family and was extremely close to my mother. She still believes if she and Mom hadn't been arguing for weeks, Mom might have been able to fight the cancer better. It's twisted thinking, I know, but I've struggled with her death too. Sam and I ended up not speaking for some time, which Dad felt he had to fix. In short, we've all been a bit of a mess these last two years."

"I'm sorry," Rose said. "I have no family, but I understand how that can happen. I have no idea if our seeing each other will turn into anything more for either Hank or me. All I can tell you is that I like him a lot."

Nikki studied her. "May I give you a piece of advice?"

Rose shrugged and nodded. "Shoot."

"Don't change. Whatever it is he sees in you is good for him. He doesn't think I know my parents weren't always happy. They worked hard to make Sam and me think they were. Samantha recently told me she overheard him talking to a friend on the phone, saying this is the happiest he's been in years. It pleases me to hear that. Don't worry. Sam will come around."

Hank reappeared. "Have I missed anything?" he asked as he took his seat.

Nikki and Rose glanced at each other. "No," they said in unison.

He laughed. "Okay, then, let's enjoy the wine. Our dinner will be here soon."

As they made their way through their meal, Rose tried to hide the elation she felt. It meant the world to her that Nikki not only didn't mind her father seeing her but was encouraging it. That made the situation seem much better. Not that either she or Hank needed permission to date from either Nikki or Sam.

When they finished the last of their meal, Nikki rose. "Thanks for dinner, Dad. I'm going to go ahead and go up to my room. I've made an appointment at the fitness center for seven tomorrow morning with a man named Dan."

Rose grinned. "You'll love him. When my two co-workers and I first came to the inn, Dan was in charge of a teambuilding program for us. It was great!"

"I need to get out in this fresh air and work off the meal. I have another couple of months before I go on vacation for real." Nikki kissed her father on the cheek and held out her hand to Rose. "It was nice meeting you. I'm sure I'll be seeing you in the future."

"Thanks. I enjoyed meeting you too."

"If you want to join me for lunch, honey, I'm available."

Nikki grinned. "Spoken like a true gentleman. I'd love it. Please stay and enjoy your coffee."

Hank drew a deep breath and let out a sigh of contentment as he and Rose watched Nikki make her way through the restaurant and out the door.

"She's lovely, Hank," said Rose, grateful for Nikki's support.

"Thanks. I've spoken to Sam about the rude way she treated you." He leaned over, cupped her face in his broad hands, and gazed into her eyes. "I'm willing to fight for you, Rose." He kissed her on the mouth.

Not caring who saw them, she responded, feeling as if Hank had just ridden into the room on a white horse, her own knight in shining armor.

CHAPTER TWENTY-SEVEN
ROSE

Rose and Hank walked hand in hand outside the restaurant.

"I want to show you something," Hank said. "Come with me. My car is parked over there."

She followed him to a black Cadillac Escalade and waited while he opened the door for her. Sliding into the passenger seat, she said, "Where are you taking me?"

He grinned and went around the car to the driver's seat. "It's a surprise. One I think we're both going to like." Still smiling, he drove out of the hotel's gates and into a nearby neighborhood, where he pulled up in front of a one-story house with a red-tile roof and a beige-stucco exterior.

"What's this?" she asked, admiring the beautiful landscaping outside the solid wall that lined the property.

"I'm renting the house for the next few months. I got to thinking it would give me more privacy." He gave her a wink. "I should say give *us* more privacy. If we're going to spend time getting to know one another better, we need to have a place of our own away from the hotel."

She beamed at him, loving the idea. At work, she'd be as professional as she usually was. But here, she could allow herself to be open and comfortable with him. Anticipation curled inside her.

"C'mon. Let's go inside. It's fully furnished. I think you'll like it."

He went around the car, opened the door for her, and then led her to the wrought-iron front gate and unlocked it. He waved her through it with a flourish of his arm.

She stopped and stared at the enclosed, flood-lit front yard, which was covered with landscaping stones and highlighted with several cactus plants and a tree whose branches drooped with ripening, bright yellow lemons. "This is beautiful," she said, loving the idea that green grass had been replaced in this fashion to accommodate less need for water.

He walked up to the heavy, carved-wooden front door and unlocked it. She followed him inside and looked around after he switched on some recessed ceiling lights.

"Oh! You have a pool and a private backyard," she exclaimed, walking across the living room to a large, sliding-glass door and looking out.

Hank unlocked the door. "Come see. The pool has a spa, and the surrounding deck is an open place to catch some sun rays."

Rose breathed in the fresh air and looked up at the dark sky, admiring the glittering stars that seemed to wink at her with the promise of good things to come. Hank's thoughtfulness was touching. He'd turned on the lights in the pool, and in the dark, the turquoise waters reminded her of the silver and turquoise jewelry she loved.

"It's lovely," Rose said.

"I figure we can relax here after work," he said.

"Sounds like a plan to me," Rose said, happily envisioning themselves having a drink by the pool.

Inside, Hank showed her the living and dining rooms, the fully equipped kitchen, and the three bedrooms and en-suite baths.

"There's enough room for the family," he said. "Might as well make use of the space. I figured maybe I could convince

Sam to return in a few months."

Rose didn't say anything. Hank and Sam would have to work out their differences themselves. Heaven knew where she might fit into it, if at all.

"Care for coffee or an after-dinner drink?" Hank said. "I have some Sambuca. That should help settle your meal."

"That sounds perfect," Rose said. She'd always liked the anise-flavored liqueur.

Hank poured tiny amounts into two small glasses and handed her one.

They settled on the couch in the living room and faced one another.

"Tell me," said Hank. "Why aren't you married? I see how great you are with Leah, and you're a beautiful, smart woman."

Rose took a sip of her drink and found the words. "I was married for a short time to a man who was wrong for me. We each realized it was a mistake early on."

"Weren't you with Alec for several years?"

"Yes. We had a very special time together, but he hadn't fully recovered from the tragedy of losing his wife and unborn child in a fire. The split was painful for us both. If I'm honest, he still holds a special place in my heart."

"I know romantics say there's just one person in your life who's right for you, but I don't believe it," said Hank. He covered her hand with his. "I'm hoping the months ahead will prove my point."

Staring into his steel-gray eyes, Rose saw a vulnerability she appreciated. Apparently, it was hard to take chances like this for him too. They talked of dating one another, but Rose knew taking this step meant much more than that. At their age, it meant not waiting too long.

When he set down his drink and reached for her, she placed

her glass on the coffee table in front of them and took him in her arms. As they leaned into one another, Rose inhaled the spicy scent of his aftershave, felt the strength of his embrace, and allowed herself the thrill of being with him.

His lips met hers. Their warmth and the taste of him created a moan of excitement within her she couldn't hide.

When they broke apart, Hank smiled at her. "This seems so right. I'm glad we met. I hope this is only the beginning."

"Yes," she murmured. "I'd forgotten it could be this way."

He kissed her again, and when one of his hands cupped a breast, she sighed with pleasure. As he'd said, it seemed so right.

Later, after necking on the couch like horny teenagers, they sat and stared at one another.

"As much as I'd like to stay, I can't," Rose said reluctantly. "I hope you understand."

He nodded and brushed a lock of hair off his forehead. "We've got time, and I can be a patient man."

"Thank you," Rose said, well aware of how fast she was falling for him.

"I missed you here last night for dinner," said Lily the next morning in the kitchen.

Rose grabbed a cup of coffee and sat down at the table opposite her. "I had dinner with Hank and his daughter."

"So, I heard," Lily said, smiling at her. "Willow happened to see you."

"I saw what?" asked Willow, stepping into the room and heading for the coffee pot.

"Hank and Rose together," said Lily.

Willow carried her cup of coffee over to join them and took a seat. "You sure looked happy. I figure Brian and the rest of the team don't need me mentioning it."

"Speaking of Brian," said Rose. "I saw you, Lily, walking with him early in the morning."

Lily's cheeks flushed a pretty pink. "He and I like to walk together for a few minutes before he continues with his run. He's very nice."

"And handsome," prompted Willow.

"Whatever, you two seem great together," said Rose, pleased by the idea. She turned to Willow. "What about you? I know you and Brent are being forced to work together. Is it getting any easier for you?"

"As a matter of fact, it is," said Willow. "Brent's cousin, Trace, has arrived to keep an eye on him. Everyone but Brent is pleased with the idea."

"I've met Trace," said Lily. "He's in stark contrast to Brent—pleasant, easy-going, smart, and humble."

"That pretty much covers it," said Willow.

"I'll be glad to meet him," Rose said. "Maybe he'll be more open to the idea of the inn becoming one of a premium collection. That's what Hank and I will be working on together for the next several days."

"You're doing more than 'playing' together?" teased Lily.

Surprised by Lily's unexpected tease, Rose broke into laughter. "Where'd you get that sass, Lily?"

"It's there," Lily said with satisfaction. "I just haven't used it much."

"We're going to have to watch out for her," said Willow, joining in on the fun.

"You too, missy," said Lily. "Tiffany told me Dan was keeping his eye on you, that he won't let Brent badmouth you. What's that all about?"

Willow tossed her black hair back over her shoulder and shrugged. "I have no idea. He said he'd call, but he hasn't."

"It's a small world here at the hotel. We'd all better be careful," Rose said, half in jest. "The truth is, we've all got jobs to do that are counter to the focus and purpose of our counterparts on the Blaise team. We need to remember that and not let any relationships interfere."

"You're right," said Lily. "My walking with Brian in the morning won't mess up anything to do with the hotel. I promise."

Rose reached over and squeezed her hand. "I'm happy to see you together."

Lily's hand flew to her mouth. "We're not!"

"No, no, I didn't mean it that way," Rose assured her, thinking how some protests spoke of so much more. But she wouldn't follow it up, even to tease. The Desert Flowers needed each other.

CHAPTER TWENTY-EIGHT
LILY

Lily sat in a meeting with Brian, John Rodriguez, Simon Nickerson, the attorney, his assistant, Jessica Hart, and Alec's lawyer, Bennett Williams. Before this Friday meeting, she had met Bennett only briefly. She studied him now. An older man with snow-white hair, dazzling green eyes, and rough-hewn features, he wore jeans, cowboy boots, a white shirt, and a blue blazer. As casual as his appearance might seem, he was, according to Alec, shrewd as a fox.

Now, as a discussion took place about the transfer of duties, Lily listened and carefully took notes on her computer.

When the issue came up about changes in signage, Lily raised her hand. "Remember, the positioning of the hotel has yet to be decided. Is it premature to plan the signage exchange?"

Both Brian and Simon swiveled to face her.

"Ah, yes," Simon said. "I believe that's mentioned in the contract."

Hoping she wasn't ruining anything for Rose, she answered, "I believe it's being worked on in the publicity group."

"Well," said Brian. "Give me time to look into it, and let's move on to the next item on the agenda."

Just when Lily thought her eyelids would close permanently instead of flickering with sleep, Brian called an end to the meeting. Making a final note on her computer, Lily let out a sigh of relief. Bennett and Simon had disagreed about everything, causing the meeting to go on for what seemed many lifetimes.

Brian stood. "Thank you, everyone. Before the next meeting, let me know if you want anything added to the agenda."

Simon and Jessica left in a hurry. John quickly followed, and then Lily was left in the room with Brian and Bennett.

Bennett studied her. "Excellent job of paying attention to detail. Alec told me you're a legal secretary. Anytime you need a job after this is over, look me up. I can always use a little help."

Flushing with pleasure, Lily smiled. "Thank you. I appreciate it."

"Are you planning to stay in the area?" Brian asked.

"I'd like to, but I'm not sure. I have a sister and a niece living in New York. I want to convince them to move out here. It's just an idea at this point."

Bennett smiled. "I hope you can." He turned to Brian. "Glad to see you again. Remember what I said. If you want to get back into lawyering, I'd love to have you. I'm getting ready to let go of the reins. Something to think about."

Brian smiled and nodded. "Thank you, sir. Will do."

After Bennett left, Lily pulled her things together and prepared to leave.

Brian cleared his throat. "Before you go, how about having dinner with me? I'm thinking of someplace casual. Maybe Tico's. I hear their food is great."

"I'd love to," Lily said. Feeling shy, she forced herself to add, "I've enjoyed our early morning walks, Brian."

He smiled as she looked up at him. "Me too. How about six-thirty for dinner?"

"That sounds great." She gave him a little wave as he

walked out.

Left alone in the conference room, Lily squeezed her hands together, scarcely believing her luck. An offer of a job from Bennett and a dinner date with Brian. Life couldn't get better than that.

CHAPTER TWENTY-NINE
WILLOW

On Friday morning, Willow awoke with a sense of excitement. She'd show Trace Armstrong around the hotel this morning and then later, have dinner with friends. She was ready for socializing with others away from the hotel. She'd lost touch with most of her friends from high school, and forming new friendships was important to her.

She decided to walk up to the cabin. The last few days had been unusually warm, and the thought of starting the day in the cooler air of the mountains was enticing. She climbed into her jogging clothes, put on her hiking boots, grabbed a container of water, and headed out, sneaking from the house without anyone seeing her.

As she found the trail and began the climb, she thought of her situation with Brent. He was as irritating now as he had been back in school, though she felt much stronger than she had then. Best to keep things on an even keel, she reminded herself. And now that Trace was there, it would be easier.

She studied the trail ahead of her. A desert shrew scurried by. She'd always been fascinated by the tiny creatures that looked like pointy-faced mice. They were in constant motion, rarely stopping to sleep. Because they had a high metabolism, they constantly had to eat.

A black-tailed jackrabbit bounded out of her way. She smiled, remembering as a child how she'd wished she could hop like them.

She halted and waited while a snake lifted its head and then sidled away from the path in a back and forth motion. She'd seen the black and white markings of a kingsnake, so she wasn't concerned. Rattlesnakes were another matter.

The idea that a desert consisted of only sand and cacti was far from the truth. Trained to keep an eye on the land around her, she saw many signs of life that others might miss. It was this feeling of being part of the landscape that pleased her.

When she reached the cabin, she was ready for a rest. Perspiration from the climb beaded on her brow. She took a sip of water and entered the small adobe building. She checked the interior carefully. While she enjoyed seeing wildlife outside, she didn't like the idea of sharing the inside of the cabin with critters of any kind.

Taking a seat on the wooden bench next to the table, she drew steadying breaths. The exercise was healthy for her. And here in the cabin, she had a moment to think, to draw strength from her surroundings. They'd helped her in the past; they could help her now. After resting for a while, Willow headed back down the mountain trail filled with a new determination to avoid letting Brent's demeaning attitude toward her bother her. She was a smart and accomplished woman.

Later, standing in front of the mirror in her room, Willow double-checked her appearance. She knew while she wasn't beautiful in the same way as Rose, she was attractive. She had a pleasing face, light-brown eyes shadowed by long, natural lashes, dark, straight hair that glistened, and smooth, honey-toned skin. Her figure, of average height, was curved in all the right places. She had the characteristics of both her parents. Better yet, she had their kind, hopeful attitude in facing each day.

Satisfied that the skirt and blouse she was wearing were both professional and attractive, she turned and left the room.

In the kitchen, her mother was alone at the sink washing dishes.

Willow walked over to her and kissed her cheek. "*Buenos dias, Mami.*"

Her mother turned and smiled at her. "And to you, *querida*. You look very nice, so business-like. Enjoy your day."

"You too," Willow said. "I won't be at dinner tonight. I'm meeting friends at Tico's."

"Ah, the other two won't be here either. Seems all of you are settling in."

"You and *Papi* can have a nice quiet meal alone."

Her mother's eyes sparkled. "*Si.*"

They smiled at one another, and then Willow hugged her mother and went outside to the golf cart she now kept at the house for transportation. Alec had made his car available to her and Lily, but so far, she hadn't used it.

At the hotel, Willow was surprised to see a gentleman talking to Brent and Trace in the space she'd been using as her office.

"Ah, here she is now," said Trace, smiling at her.

Brent nodded curtly but said nothing.

"Willow, meet my father, Mitchell Armstrong. He's making a quick visit to the hotel and wanted to meet you." He turned to his father. "This is Willow Sanchez."

"I'm pleased to meet you." His father studied her with a smile that extended to his blue eyes. Tall and distinguished-looking with his handsome features and full head of light-brown hair, he looked an awful lot like his son. "Brent has filled me in on your working together. How's that going?"

Willow took a breath and seized the opportunity to do her job for Alec. "I know some people think all hotels are alike, but I disagree. What Alec Thurston has built here is unique, something we'd hate to see disappear into a collection of hotels that are quite different from the Desert Sage Inn. This is the reason I've agreed to help with the transition. That, and my deep admiration and respect for Alec. I hope you understand that, Mr. Armstrong."

His eyebrows rose with surprise. "Well said, Willow. And please call me, Mitch. If we're going to be working together, we can certainly be on a first-name basis."

"I've tried to explain to her that we know how to run hotels," said Brent. "The Blaise Group is better than anyone else."

"We can always learn from others," Mitch said calmly, though there was a hint of annoyance in his voice. "I came here to see why Alec feels so strongly about using his hotel as the basis for a new collection. Trace said you were going to show him around this morning. May I join you?"

"Absolutely," Willow responded with confidence. She knew how important a simple tour could be to understanding the inn she loved so much.

As the four of them left the room, Willow ignored the scowl on Brent's face. She had just a short time to convince Mitch of Alec's desire, and she was determined to make it count.

She led them from one part of the hotel operation to another. As she'd hoped, all staff members showed pride in their work and gave them a friendly welcome.

Mitch remained quiet between stops but asked questions of various staff members whenever he could. The property sparkled with cleanliness and gave off an aura of comfort, encouraging guests to gather and relax.

Though not one unkind word was spoken, the frowns some

of the staff gave Brent indicated their dislike of him.

"Very interesting," Mitch said when they returned to her office area. "Thank you. Brent and Trace are going to have lunch with me. Would you like to join us?"

"I appreciate the offer, but no thanks," Willow said. "I'm working on a special project with the publicity duo this afternoon."

"I see. Well, perhaps another time. I'm returning to Seattle later today." He held out his hand. "Again, thanks, Willow. I'm sure I'll be seeing you soon.

Willow heaved a sigh of relief after they left her office. If evil looks could kill, Willow would be dead from the way Brent had glared at her when his uncle wasn't looking.

CHAPTER THIRTY
ROSE

After Hank saw Nikki off at the airport, he and Rose worked with Willow in his suite to get Willow's perspective on those features and services at the hotel that would best illustrate the operating style and marketing focus of a whole new collection.

As Willow talked about each part of the hotel's operation, Rose's respect for her grew. First, she understood the hotel business. Second, it was obvious she loved the inn. Seeing it through her eyes made Rose aware of how much more she could learn. It had been fourteen years since she'd worked at the hotel, and a lot had changed since then, especially in the technical areas. Willow, on the other hand, had grown up with technology like most young women her age.

While working with her, Rose jotted down notes on slogans and graphic ideas. Hank did the same.

After Willow told them about giving Mitch Armstrong a tour, Rose half expected him to ask to join the meeting and was pleased when he didn't. She didn't want to discuss and defend half-completed ideas for a campaign that was so important to her.

Willow left them with a promise to say little to anyone else about their work.

"If you don't mind, Hank, I'm going to go back to my room and work on my blog while these new ideas settle in my mind."

"All right, but I'd like to invite you to dinner and back to my house. The temperature in the pool should be perfect for a night swim. How about it?"

She smiled. "Sounds like fun. Where do you want to go for dinner?"

"Someplace a little offbeat. How about Mexican? I'm thinking of Tico's."

"Sounds delicious," said Rose. "What time?"

"Let's go early, say six o'clock. That'll give us enough time to eat and enjoy the rest of the evening."

"Perfect. I'll be ready." She looked up from pulling her paperwork together and smiled as Hank approached her.

"I've wanted to kiss you all day," he said, drawing her into his arms. "I know we agreed to remain professional during our workday, but I can't resist you."

His lips came down on hers, soft, sweet, sure.

Her body melted into his. Having told herself to see where their relationship might go, she was as eager to share kisses as he. Besides, at their age, there was nothing to hold them back from that and much more, aside from the awkwardness of learning what pleased each other.

He stepped away and grinned at her. "Can't wait to have you alone at the house."

"Don't bother to pack a suit. I have plenty of towels," he said, winking at her.

She laughed. "See you later."

That evening, she dressed in a peasant skirt with a bold, floral design and a bright turquoise top she thought would be perfect for the restaurant. She'd looked up Tico's online and seen it was an elegant place with a large patio for outdoor dining. On a warm night like tonight, it was perfect for dinner.

When she left her room and went outside to talk to the

other women, the patio was empty. She turned back and, seeing Juanita, said, "Where is everyone?"

Juanita smiled. "Out. Like I told Willow, you women seem to be settling in."

"They're on dates, too?" Rose asked.

"Dates or with friends, as Willow says."

"Ah. Okay." She checked her watch. She had time before Hank picked her up to see Alec. She walked briskly to his quarters.

Opening the door, she called out to him. "Alec? It's Rose. Can I come in?"

"Sure. I'm in my room."

She walked into his bedroom.

He was lying on a chaise lounge watching television. Seeing her, he clicked off the news program. "You look lovely, Rose. Going out, I see."

"Yes, with Hank. And I'm not the only one. Lily and Willow are away this evening too."

He bobbed his head with a satisfied smile. "I'm glad to see the three of you are becoming comfortable here."

"I think it's important too. Have you talked to Willow recently?"

"Yes," he said. "Sounds like she made an outstanding impression on Mitchell Armstrong. His brother, Duncan, isn't so easy to please."

"Is that why Brent is so difficult?"

"Probably. I understand Mitchell's son, Trace, is quite different."

"I haven't met him yet. But I hear he's a fine young man."

"All sorts of interesting things are beginning to take place," said Alec. "And it's all good."

"How are you feeling?"

He shrugged. "It's a better day than some. I was able to get a little work done today. John came for a visit."

"Oh. Well, I'd better go." She bent and kissed his cheek. "Have a nice evening."

"You too," he said, smiling up at her. "I'm glad things are working out between you and Hank."

"We'll see," she said. She wasn't about to tell him she almost hadn't packed a swimsuit for the visit to Hank's house.

As she left Alec's wing of the house, she heard a car drive up to the front circle. She went into the kitchen, grabbed her purse and other things, and went to the front door to open it.

Hank's lips spread into a grin when he saw her. "You look beautiful, Rose."

She swished her skirt back and forth, suddenly self-conscious. "Thanks. I thought this was suitable."

"More than suitable," Hank said, kissing her. "More like a home run ... er ...hit out of the ballpark." He groaned. "Sorry. Can't help myself."

She rolled her eyes and laughed. "You're bad, but I'll take it as a sincere compliment."

He took her elbow. "Let's go. I'm hungry."

She glanced at him. "Are you planning to rush through dinner so we can go back to your house?"

He laughed at her teasing. "Not exactly."

Still chuckling, he helped her into his SUV.

The restaurant was as attractive as the pictures online.

Rose stepped inside the main entrance and stared at the stark, white-stucco walls of the interior offset by bright-colored posters advertising different Mexican locations. Dark wooden beams crossed the ceiling, and brick-colored Mexican tile covered the floors. The sound of Mariachi music played in the background. She already felt like dancing.

The hostess led them to a table at the far end of the large, extended patio that hugged two sides of the building.

"Ah, a private little nook," Rose said, eager to spend more time learning about the man who'd already stolen her heart. Looking at him now from across the rose-colored tablecloth, she thought he was the nicest man she'd met in a long, long time. Aside from that, the chemistry between them was scintillating, to put it mildly. Just watching him talk to the waiter, she sensed he'd always be kind to her.

She accepted the large menu from the waiter and felt her mouth water. The aromas from the sizzling fajitas being served at a nearby table were enticing. She couldn't remember when she'd last been out to a Mexican restaurant. She glanced around, making mental notes for how to describe the restaurant to her bloggers.

"Is this going to be a margarita night?" the waiter asked with a beguiling smile.

Rose and Hank looked at one another and grinned.

"I'd love one," said Rose. "A Texas one."

"Sure, why not? I'll have the same then switch to beer later," said Hank.

"This is charming," said Rose after the waiter left. "And the food smells delicious. Do you have any interest in starting off with guacamole?"

"Sounds delicious." He laughed. "I'm easy. A real foodie type."

"I noticed Nikki giving you the evil eye when you ordered your steak."

He smiled. "Yes. My girls try to take care of me."

"That's sweet," Rose said, wondering what it would've been like to have a loving family like his.

Their drinks came.

Hank lifted his margarita glass. "Here's to getting to know

each other better." He gave her an impish grin. "Much better."

Pleased by the sexy look he was giving her, Rose tapped her glass carefully against his. "To us."

After sipping his drink, Hank reached across the table and took her hand in his strong fingers. "Rose, you make me feel like a kid again. I'm so glad we met."

"Me, too." Rose felt heat stream to her cheeks and decided she didn't care if he saw how vulnerable he made her feel. Scary as it was, she liked what was happening between them.

"Well, look who's here!" came a voice behind them.

Rose whipped around to find Dan, Tiffany, Trace, Sarah, and Willow walking to a nearby table.

"Well, it looks like a Desert Sage Inn party," she responded smoothly though her pulse had quickened with alarm. She'd hoped she and Hank could quietly see where their relationship was going.

Hank stood and shook hands with the men while the girls gave each other quick hugs.

"Let's pull our tables together," said Sarah, "and make it a real party."

As they were rearranging the tables with the waiter's help, Brian and Lily appeared.

"Come join the group," Rose called.

They added two additional chairs for them.

Rose hugged Lily. "Didn't know we'd all be together. Hope you don't mind."

"No, it's fine," Lily said, but Rose had already seen the look of dismay on Lily's face when they'd first arrived.

"Glad this working group could be together," Brian said, leaving no doubt in anyone's mind that that was how he wanted to deal with the situation. He made sure everyone knew everyone else and took over as the spokesman of the group.

Margaritas were ordered and delivered to the table, and a real party atmosphere emerged.

Rose took the time to study the others. Trace was a pleasant surprise, even more handsome than his cousin and much, much nicer. Sarah was a lively addition to the group. Tiffany was placed next to Trace on one side, Willow and Dan on the other side. Across the table, Lily and Brian sat together. She noted Willow's attention to Trace.

After much indecision, Rose ordered the *Pollo en Mole* like Willow. Prepared with dried chiles, cumin, black pepper, garlic, chocolate, and nuts, the dish looked inviting.

"It's delicious," said Willow. "My mother's is excellent, but I like it here too."

"Your mother is a cook?" Trace said.

"Both of my parents work for Alec Thurston. He loves my mother's cooking," Willow responded.

"That's great," said Trace. "I live alone and have decided I want to learn to cook. Maybe she could show me some of her special dishes. Especially if I'm going to be spending some time here."

"What about Brent?" Rose asked him.

Trace paused before he spoke. "He'll still be around. But my father and uncle decided I should be here too." He looked as if he wanted to say more but stopped talking.

Rose and Hank exchanged meaningful glances. It was clear Trace had a problem with Brent too.

"Tell me about the Desert Flowers thing," Trace said. "I heard that's what Alec Thurston calls you."

Rose grinned at the surprise on Hank's face. "Yes. Lily, Willow, and I are Alec's Desert Flowers. You know, like that program that used to be on television, Charley's Angels."

Trace studied her, turned to look at Willow, and glanced at Lily, his lips curving into a broad smile. "Cool. Very cool. But don't tell my uncle. He'll give you and Alec a hard time about it."

"Like father, like son?" Willow said, cocking an eyebrow at him.

Trace nodded and shrugged. "Believe me, I don't like it either. But don't underestimate them." He put a napkin to his mouth as if wishing he could take the words back.

"No worries," said Brian. "Right now, we all need to work together."

"Agreed," said Hank. "Right, team?"

Rose chuckled as she nodded along with the others.

"More margaritas," cried Dan, and a waiter hurried over to the table.

Sitting with the group at the table, Rose recalled get-togethers like this in the past with staff members of the hotel. Alec had always encouraged friendship among his staff. Glancing at the people around her, she guessed a lot more than friendship was being developed.

Her meal came, and Rose dug into the chicken dish with enthusiasm. She was glad her dinner with Hank had turned into a party. It was such a festive place, and the food was delicious.

It was close to ten when the party broke up.

Hank led Rose to his car and turned to face her.

"Come to my house for a while. It's a pleasant evening. A perfect night for a swim." He drew her close and kissed her.

She loved the feel of his lips on hers and decided a nighttime swim was an excellent idea.

CHAPTER THIRTY-ONE
LILY

Lily left the party with Brian wondering how the evening was going to end. Once they'd come upon the others from the hotel, he became more distant, as if he had to prove it was only a business arrangement. She'd hoped for so much more.

"Great to see everyone, huh?" he said as he led her to his car. "Good for business."

"I suppose so. We all have to work together," Lily said.

Brian smiled at her. "It's nice to make new friends. It can get lonely working on projects like this."

"It's always good to get away from the hotel, whether it's taking morning walks or doing something like this," she said.

He gave her hand a squeeze. "I'm glad you see it that way."

When they reached his car, he stood by and then helped her into the passenger seat. "Guess we'd better make it a short night," he said, sliding behind the wheel. "I've got an early meeting with a plumber in the morning."

"Do you need me to take notes?" she asked.

He shook his head. "No, but thanks. He's going to give us a written report of his findings."

"Oh. Okay." Lily knew she sounded disappointed, but she was feeling like a complete dope. She'd thought Brian might be interested in her as a woman, not a friend because he was lonely.

CHAPTER THIRTY-TWO
WILLOW

Willow and Sarah left the group and went to her car. She'd planned to join Dan, Tiffany, and Trace by herself, but at the last minute, she called Sarah to see if she wanted to come. Sarah was thrilled with the invitation, and Willow felt better about not arriving alone.

Now that she'd spent time with Trace, Willow wanted to spend more time with him. Tiffany, she noted, had the same idea.

Willow sighed as she put the car in gear and watched Tiffany get into Dan's car with Trace.

Sarah noticed. "Trace is something, isn't he? But, then, so is Dan."

Willow nodded but didn't say anything. Dan hadn't seemed interested in her during dinner, and he hadn't yet called her. On the contrary, Trace had been pleasant to her all evening.

When they got to Sarah's house, Sarah said, "Come on inside. My parents are watching Henry, and I want them to meet you."

Flattered, Willow pushed away depressing thoughts. "Thanks. I will. Rose mentioned how much she liked your father."

"He's sad that Alec is ill. And you'll like my mother. My parents are amazing. They're terrific with Henry."

Sarah's house was in a comfortable neighborhood—nothing too fancy but attractive just the same. It was the kind of neighborhood Willow liked, full of families with kids.

Sarah opened the front door and called out softly, "Mom? Dad?"

Her parents came to the front hall, holding fingers to their lips.

"Shhh, He's finally asleep," her mother said. "Too much excitement playing with Grandpa."

Sarah grinned. "Thanks. I'd like you to meet Willow Sanchez, a new friend of mine. She's working at the hotel for Alec, doing special projects. Willow, my mother, Elena Goodrich, and my father, George."

Willow smiled at the attractive older couple, shook their hands, and said, "Pleased to meet you."

"I feel as if we know you," said Elena. "Alec told us all about you. He talked to us about helping with a scholarship for you to go to Cornell. It turned out that with your hard work, you got a scholarship on your own. Very nice, Willow."

"Since graduating, what have you been doing?" George asked.

Willow smiled and nodded. "I've been teaching some, but now that I'm back at the inn, I realize how much I've missed the operations end of the business."

"We're heartsick to know Alec is dying," said Elena, as a sad look crept into her hazel eyes.

"Me, too," Willow said softly, wondering how she could ever explain how much his involvement in her life meant to her.

Sarah checked her watch and turned to her parents. "Thanks so much for giving me an evening out. You'd better go. Dad, you have your golf game in the morning."

He grinned. "Yeah. Somebody new is joining our group. Hank Bowers."

"Oh, he's terrific," said Sarah. "You'll like him. But better watch out. I have a feeling he's a scratch golfer."

"He sure talks sports," Willow said, and they both laughed.

CHAPTER THIRTY-THREE
ROSE

The closer they got to Hank's house, the more Rose's pulse raced. They might talk of a swim in Hank's pool, but she knew the evening might provide a lot more than that. She decided to leave it up to chance. She was already more comfortable with Hank than other men she'd dated in the past.

This time, instead of pulling up in front of the house, he opened the garage door remotely. "We'll go in the back way. More privacy," he said, pulling into the garage and turning off the engine of his car. He grinned at her. "I've thought of being alone with you like this all through dinner."

"Yes, but it was good for the group to be together, don't you think?"

"Sure, but this, being here with you, is the best kind of evening I can think of." He got out of the car and waited while she joined him.

Coming in through the back door gave her a different perspective of the house. The living room, dining area, and kitchen were all compact but comfortable. Beyond them were the three bedrooms in a peaceful and quiet wing.

"Ready for a swim?" Hank said, his lips curving.

"You go ahead," she said to Hank. "I'll join you in a minute."

"Okay," he said agreeably. "I'll leave a towel in the bedroom for you."

"Thanks," she said, grateful for his understanding.

Once she saw that he was in the pool, she headed for the bedroom to get out of her clothes. He'd laid a large beach towel on top of the bed. In the dim light, she took off her skirt and blouse and slipped out of her underwear. Drawing a deep breath, she pulled on the bikini she wore for sunbathing and wrapped the towel around herself.

As she slid the glass door open and stepped outside, she felt like a teen going to her first prom, wondering if her date would like the dress she was wearing. Silently laughing at such a thought, she walked to the edge of the pool, dropped her towel, and jumped in.

She came to the surface gasping and began swimming to get warm. As she glided toward him, Hank watched her, staying in place even as she did a smooth turn for another lap of the pool.

When she finally returned to him, he grinned. "You're a beautiful swimmer."

"Thanks. It's something I try to do as often as I can. My condo has a great community pool."

"I'm glad we have this one to ourselves," said Hank, reaching for her.

Though the water was clear, the rippling of the water from the gentle breeze made it impossible to get a clear picture of him in his swim trunks. Still, she admired his broad shoulders, the bulk of him that gave her a sense of strength and protection. Hair scattered across the breadth of his chest and then came together to angle downward.

She nestled up against his chest, happy for the warmth of his body.

He stroked her hair and let out a sigh before bending down to kiss her.

She closed her eyes and allowed herself to enjoy the deep

satisfaction that settled inside her. As they'd both mentioned, it felt so right for them to be together. It wasn't like the frantic, hot love she remembered from her early days with Alec, but an attraction that was both sexual and deeper.

They settled on the steps in the shallow end of the pool. Hank pulled her onto his lap and caressed her with his broad hands, moving from her back to her front and then tracing her lower curves.

She wrapped her arms around him, getting used to the feel of him. He was in good shape, not too thin nor too heavy.

He leaned back and studied the sky. "There's something so refreshing about being in clear air like this."

She nodded and smiled with pleasure. "I feel as if I could reach up and touch a star. Look! There's Orion."

"I see it. My girls and I used to love to lie out at night and gaze at the constellations."

"It sounds like you and they had such a lovely time together while they were growing up," Rose said, unable to hide the wistfulness she felt.

He drew her closer. "I want that same kind of feeling with Leah. It's amazing to spend time with her."

"That's why we have to move carefully with Sam," Rose said. "I don't want our being together to ruin that for you."

"Samantha can be very emotional," said Hank. "But I'm not going to let her change what I feel for you. It's sudden and unexpected, but I'm sincere when I say I've never felt quite this way about anyone before."

Rose reached up and caressed his cheek. "I feel the same. I was all prepared to dislike you, you know."

"You were? Why?"

"Oh, you know the type. Former professional athlete, full of confidence and all the lingo."

He laughed, startling her. "Oh my god! You make it sound

so awful. Am I really that way?"

"Aside from the home runs, getting to first base, and hitting all the balls out of the park, you're not too bad, Hank Bowers."

He hugged her tighter. "I want it to be just like this, me with you enjoying a laugh to brighten the days."

"And the nights?" she asked, unable to resist the temptation.

"That, my dear, is something I can't wait to show you."

He helped her to her feet. "C'mon. It's getting chilly out here."

Standing beside the pool, they stared at one another, smiles on their faces.

A nice view, Rose thought, allowing him to wrap his towel around her and lead her inside.

After dressing, she nestled up against Hank on the couch, and Rose let out a soft sigh of satisfaction. Staring up into his stubbly chin, she wanted to feel his lips on hers to make sure this was real.

As if he sensed her thoughts, he cupped her face in his hands and kissed her long and hard.

The next morning the three women sat on the patio, sipping coffee and chatting. Hank was playing golf with Sarah's father, Brian was meeting a plumber, and Trace and Brent were having a private meeting between the two of them, leaving Willow and the other two women the time they wanted to rest and relax.

"It's so relaxing to be here doing nothing," said Willow. "Last night was fun. Rose, I hope we didn't ruin your date with Hank."

"No, it was great to have everyone together. I'm glad I got to meet Trace. He seems pleasant. Low key."

"He's something else," said Lily, fanning herself with a hand.

"What's with you and Brian?" Rose said to Lily. "He made it clear his socializing was all professional, very much about being friends."

Lily's cheeks grew pink. Her eyes watered. She set down her coffee mug and heaved a big sigh. "I'm such a dud. I thought ... well, you know what I thought ..."

Rose reached across the table and clasped Lily's hand. "You're no dud. You're a lovely young woman."

Lily sniffed. "Thanks! That's sweet of you to say."

"The fact that Brian asked you out to dinner tells me he likes you," said Rose.

Lily sighed again. "You're right. I'm just not good with the dating scene. And for the last several years, I've been too busy or too tired to do much about it."

Rose turned to Willow. "How is it going with Dan?"

Willow blinked in surprise. "Dan? We're not dating. And I'm not sure I want to. He's already proved to me he doesn't care. Maybe it's time to move on."

"With Trace?" Lily asked, giving her a sly smile.

Willow shrugged and then laughed. "Having coffee with you two is dangerous." She got to her feet. "I'm going to get ready for work." She waved and hurried away.

"She's adorable," said Lily. "I'm glad she's one of us."

"Me, too," Rose said. They each were different, but Alec's idea of having the three women join forces was working.

CHAPTER THIRTY-FOUR
ROSE

For the next couple of weeks, Rose and Hank not only worked together, they spent most evenings together. Rose found it pleasant to have someone to talk to about business. More than that, they spoke about their pasts, their dreams, and what they envisioned in life going forward. As she'd felt from the beginning, Rose found Hank was someone she truly liked. Romance with him was surprisingly both sweet and sexy. Against all the warnings she gave herself about moving too fast, she was falling hopelessly, completely in love.

Hank showed her in many ways how much he cared for her, but she was still waiting for him to say the "L" word. Until then, she couldn't be sure of the future, which was privately driving her crazy.

One evening as they were finishing a late dinner at his house, his cell rang.

He sighed and glanced at her. "Who's calling now?" They'd worked late, and they both were tired.

"You'd better check to see who it is," she said. "The Armstrong brothers were going to get back to us on some of the advertising we've put together."

He left her in the kitchen to get his cell from the patio.

As she slipped the last of the dishes into the dishwasher, she heard him talking on the phone. She listened for a moment and frowned. It sounded like trouble.

She wiped her hands on a towel and went to see if it was a problem at work.

The look of devastation on his face sent her pulse sprinting through her. She clasped her hands and waited for him to speak.

"All right," Hank said into the phone. "I'll get a flight out of here as soon as possible and let you know when I arrive. Don't worry about picking me up. I'll call my driver."

"What is it?" Rose asked, feeling a tremor go through her. Hank looked ill.

"It's Samantha. She's had a miscarriage and is scheduled for surgery tomorrow. Rob is a wreck. He wants me to come right away. Sam's been asking for me."

"Oh my God! Of course, you must go. Let me help you search for flights."

Hank rubbed a hand across his face. "If anything happens to her ..."

Rose wrapped an arm around him. "Don't even go there."

He sighed. "You're right. I'll get organized while you check flights."

Rose's research indicated the earliest Hank could leave Palm Springs and be on his way was 6 AM. She went into his bedroom to tell him.

He was sitting on the bed staring into space.

She gave him the news and sat down beside him. "I'm sure she'll be all right. She's in the hands of the best medical people."

"Yes, but I feel terrible about our disagreement."

"About me?" She felt a knot form in her stomach.

"Yeah. I was pretty straightforward with her."

Rose didn't say anything but simply watched the way his eyes moistened. "Do you want me to take you to the airport in the morning?"

"No, I'll arrange to have someone from the hotel pick me up." He managed a weak smile. "I don't want to interrupt your beauty sleep."

"Are you sure? I'd be happy to do it."

He shook his head. "Thanks, but no. It's late. I'd better try to get some sleep. It's going to be a long day tomorrow."

Rose hid her disappointment. She got to her feet. "Okay, I'd better go so you can get some rest." She hoped he'd ask her to stay, but he simply nodded and said, "I'll walk you to your car."

Rose grabbed her purse and other things and headed out with Hank at her side.

When they reached her car, he held the door for her.

She slid into the driver's seat and looked up at him. "Keep in touch, Hank. I'll be thinking of you and Sam and the rest of the family."

"Thanks." He leaned over and gave her a quick kiss on the cheek. "I'll call you as soon as I can after I get there and see the situation for myself."

"Safe travels," she whispered, kissing him back.

He stood in the driveway as she pulled out and lifted his hand in a wave that almost felt like goodbye.

The next morning Rose awoke exhausted. Her mind had played tricks on her all night, telling her that being with Hank would end up hurting her. It was fine while they were working together in the desert, but he was a family man who lived in Atlanta.

She got out of bed, walked to the window, and stared out at the landscape that always gave her a sense of home. Her thoughts whirled. The southwest was the place she loved and where she had connections that would keep her business going. She didn't need a man to provide for her. Besides, she was proud of the business she'd built on her own.

Weary, she made her way to the kitchen.

Juanita was there. "*Buenos dias*, Rose."

"Morning." Rose smiled, walked over to her, and gave Juanita a quick hug. She loved this woman who was always there for everyone, who wore a cheerful smile and had a big heart.

"You are troubled?" Juanita said, staring into Rose's face.

Rose nodded. "I'm wondering if I'm being foolish thinking anything long-term could come from my seeing Hank. After Alec's project is over, I'll be in Las Vegas, and he'll be in Atlanta. I don't see that changing."

Juanita was quiet, then she said, "The heart will find a way. Have faith."

Rose shook her head, wanting to believe, knowing she shouldn't. After being independent for so many years, she had no intention of giving up her freedom. Why had she fallen so quickly for Hank? But she knew the answer. She'd been attracted to him from the moment she'd met him as Papa B.

Rose accepted the cup of coffee Juanita handed her and sat at the kitchen table feeling as if she'd lost sight of her personal plans that served as a protection for her future.

Willow entered the kitchen, greeted her mother with a kiss, grabbed a cup of coffee, and plunked down at the table opposite Rose.

"What a day this is going to be," sighed Willow.

"What's up?" Rose asked.

"Brent, Trace, and I have been given an assignment. We each have to come up with a list of changes we'd make to the hotel."

"Is that going to be difficult for you?" Rose asked. "You're so knowledgeable about operations."

"We also have to analyze the costs of any changes we'd make and how it would affect the various departments." She swept her hair back over her shoulder. "I might as well be doing this for advance course credit."

"It does sound like a lot of work," Rose admitted.

"Yeah, I'll be busy on my own. We have two weeks to do the project."

"As hard as it sounds, I think you'll do a great job." She got up and went back to her room. While Hank was away, she was going to continue working on a secret plan she had of not only naming the new brand of hotels but suggesting what could be done to certain other hotels in the Blaise Group to join the Desert Sage Inn in the new collection. It was a bold move, but she thought it might bring attention to Alec's wishes.

Rose was in the middle of work that afternoon when her cell rang. She checked caller ID. *Hank.* She'd told herself to let the relationship cool, but her rebellious heart pounded with excitement. "Hi, Hank. How are you? How is Sam?"

"I'm fine, a little tired. Sam is recovering from a small tear in the uterus due to the surgery. The doctor promises it will heal on its own, but you know Sam. It's become a big thing."

"I'm glad it's not worse," said Rose, sensing his exhaustion.

"I've talked to the people at Blaise and told them I'd be here for a while. Duncan Armstrong wants to meet with me at the end of the week here in Atlanta."

"Is the meeting something I should attend?" Rose asked.

"No. I told Duncan I'd handle this. But, thanks. Makes sense. You're settled out there."

"Yes, I suppose that's one way to put it. You're there, and I'm here." Her words felt like a punch to her middle. She cradled her stomach, her fingers cold already. It was just as she'd thought. Away from the glamour of the desert, they were just two people who'd gotten together because they were lonely. And now the real business of handling the project was going to be done as strong adversaries.

"I've got to go," Hank said. "I'll call when I can. I'm in charge of Leah while Sam rests and Rob gets back to work."

"Say hi to everyone for me," she said. "And let me know how the meeting goes."

"Okay. We'll talk later about the campaign I've created for them." The call ended with a note of finality.

Crushed by the suspicion that this was how the future would be—her fighting for a piece of the action as well as credit for the work she'd done—she plunked down on the bed and drew deep breaths. She couldn't let the situation get out of control the way it had with a previous competitor on a hotel project in Las Vegas. Then, he'd seized control, left her out of meetings, and all but ruined her career. That's why she'd formed the blog as an independent business to protect her future. Now, she wondered if it was happening all over again.

Disheartened by the turn of events, Rose got into a swimsuit, grabbed a beach towel, and headed out to the pool. A workout was exactly what she needed to let off the steam that was building inside her. In the past, other men in business had tried to elbow her out of projects. She'd had to work twice as hard to get the notice they'd tried to take away from her. Hank might be a nice guy, but he'd find out just how seriously she took her work.

She jumped into the pool and began to move in smooth, steady strokes, her arms slicing through the water with ease. She'd forgotten how relaxing this felt, how easy it was to push back her worries when she exercised like this.

"Looking good," came a voice above her.

She slowed and glanced up into Alec's smiling face. Pleased

to see him, she stopped and climbed out of the pool. "Hi, it's great to see you outdoors."

"Yes, it's a better day for me, and you know how much I like these early evening hours."

"I remember," she said, smiling. "Want a little company? I could use some."

"Is everything all right?" he asked, slowly making his way to one of the chairs at the table under the protection of an umbrella.

"Not really. But I'm going to work on a new idea, a secret plan of mine." She grabbed her towel and wrapped it around her waist before joining him at the table.

As she explained what she was doing, Juanita brought out two glasses of iced tea and placed them on the table. "Can I bring you snacks?"

Alec looked to Rose. "Do you want anything?"

"No, thanks. This is lovely." She lifted her glass of tea and took a sip, allowing the cool liquid to slide down her throat in grateful swallows.

After Juanita left them, Alec studied Rose. "I like that you're so creative, Rose, especially when I know you've been hurt in the past. You have good instincts and a great mind. Remember that."

Rose couldn't hold back a sigh. "I don't know about my instincts. But I want to make this work for you, Alec. Hank is away on family business, and I'm going to take this time to build contacts here for both my research for you and my use on my blog. I like it here."

"It's a very likable place to live. Having the ability to get away in the summer heat is a real plus, but even so, the desert is still livable in the heat as long as you allow nature to do her thing. And the misters help too."

"You've been content to live here," Rose observed.

"Yes, I couldn't leave. I wanted to be close to them, you know?"

Rose knew he was talking about his wife and baby and nodded. She reached over and wrapped a hand around his. "Are you going to leave us directions as to how you want things done when you ..."

"Die?" he interjected.

"Yes." The thought made her sad, but she knew he'd want things done his way.

"I'm not going to die just yet, but as time passes, I will get even worse." He gave her a half-hearted smile. "I'm glad you agreed to help me out. It makes me feel comforted just thinking of it."

"All three of us are happy to do it. You've been kind to us in the past. Even when things didn't work out, I always knew I could count on you as a friend."

"One thing I want to make sure of is that Pedro and Juanita are well taken care of. They're very special to me. And so is their daughter."

"I like Willow a lot," Rose said. "Lily, too."

"All good women." He smiled. "My Desert Flowers. I suppose many people would think it was condescending or sexist of me to call you that. I mean it, though, in the best of ways, for more reasons than anyone else would know. But to answer your questions, I've left instructions for you, Rose, to oversee everything after I'm gone."

She felt the sting of tears and simply nodded.

They talked a bit longer about some of the happenings in town. Though he could no longer take part, Alec kept his eye on activities in the area as usual.

When Rose saw that he was growing tired, she helped him onto a chaise lounge, made sure he was comfortable, and went inside.

CHAPTER THIRTY-FIVE
WILLOW

Willow rose early one morning, wanting time alone in the hotel to help her evaluate changes she'd like to see. She loved the hotel, always had since her parents had started working there. But that didn't mean changes wouldn't be welcome. Besides, this extra project was something she wanted to do for Alec. When she was done with her assessment, she intended to run the report by him. He might be dying, but Alec was still very aware of his hotel and what was happening there.

She quietly dressed, gathered her things, and snuck out of the house. She'd grab her morning coffee at the hotel. She climbed onto one of the golf carts they kept parked outside the garage and headed off.

The sky was shedding its dark cloak and was beginning to embrace the rising sun. Around her, birds were chirping in the trees, their songs a greeting to the day. Creatures on the ground were rousing. The cool air would soon turn warm, but, at the moment, Willow liked the feel of it against her skin.

At the hotel, she parked the golf cart in her assigned spot in the employees' parking lot and walked around to the front of the hotel. That's where she'd begin to assess the building itself.

She admired how the wide entrance welcomed guests to the hotel lobby, reached through a central courtyard with a statue everyone loved with its welcoming gesture. Large clay pots filled with colorful flowers added to the striking scene.

Inside the lobby, the floors shone from polish and long-term care. The décor was tasteful as always. She studied the arrangement of space and jotted down notes in the leather-bound notebook she'd carried with her.

She walked over to a corner of the lobby where a table held an arrangement of coffee and other beverages and helped herself to a cup of coffee. Taking grateful sips of the hot liquid, she studied her surroundings, observing the groupings of furniture placed for intimate conversations, separated by planters and decorative screens. The recessed ceiling and track lighting provided an ambiance of comfort and luxury. Anything she noted in this area would be minor, but she still wanted to view it from a guest's point of view.

From there, she moved through Saguaro, the family restaurant, which was open from 7 AM to 10 PM every day. She waved to a few of the servers setting up a breakfast buffet and then went into the kitchen, which was a beehive of activity as the chef and her staff put finishing touches on serving trays and chafing dishes for display.

She moved quietly, like a shadow, from one public area in the hotel to another, checking the business center, the shops, and the large patio outside. She'd study the private staff areas another day. For now, she wanted to see the pools, tennis courts, and, of course, their well-known golf clubhouse. She could've taken the golf cart, but she found walking the property gave her a different perspective, allowing her to observe and carefully photograph more details and areas where improvements might be warranted.

At the golf club, she ran into Brent and Trace. They looked surprised to see her.

"What are you doing here?" Brent asked. "I didn't know you played golf."

"Now and then, I do," she responded. "Not when it's so busy."

"We have an 'in' here at the club," said Brent, giving her a wink. "A discount too." He held up a golf club. "Isn't this wedge a beauty?"

Trace studied her quietly. "Maybe we can play together sometime."

She smiled. "Maybe. I'll leave you to your fun." To avoid any more conversation, Willow turned and left. She'd seen the brief look of dislike on the clerk's face when Brent spoke and didn't want to be associated with him. She'd hear about his actions later. There was no faster place for spreading news than within the staff of a hotel. So far, she hadn't heard any gossip about Trace except that he was a hot guy. Nice too.

For lunch, she ate in the casual restaurant, Saguaro, trying to see it through a guest's eyes. She made a few notes about the service staff, the menu, and the layout as she finished her meal and waited for her check. As soon as she could, she'd head back to Alec's house to organize and write up her observations.

She looked up, saw Trace, and gave him a little wave.

He walked over to her. "May I join you?" he asked, giving her a smile that made her insides flutter.

"Sure," she responded, trying to tell herself to stop being foolish. They might be working together for a while, but, in truth, other than that, they had little in common.

CHAPTER THIRTY-SIX
LILY

Lily jogged along the path by the golf course lost in thought. When she'd mentioned she hoped to convince her sister to move out here, she hadn't realized how much she wanted that to happen. She exchanged photographs with her sister and talked to Izzy as much as possible, considering the time difference. But it wasn't enough.

She was so intent on her musing she didn't hear Brian come up to her. Seeing him, she let out a little cry of surprise, stopped, and held a hand to her heart. "Oh, my! You scared me!"

He held up both hands and backed away. "Sorry. I didn't mean to."

"No problem. How are you?" she asked. "Is it going to be another busy day?"

"Yes, I've got to be available for several more inspections. All part of the process."

"Do you need me to join you?"

Brian smiled and shook his head. "No, thanks. It's something I have to do alone. You've been working hard. Feel free to take the next couple of days off. We meet again at the end of the week."

"Okay. In that case, I think I'll use the time to look around. I like the idea of perhaps moving here one day."

"Let me know what you discover." He jogged away from her.

She watched him, marveling at how easy he made using a prosthesis look, but then he seemed such a capable guy in so many ways. She realized she was staring at his butt and laughed out loud. Though she didn't want the other women to know, she hadn't given up hope that he'd see her as more than Alec's secretary.

She thought back to her earlier time at the inn and remembered how much she'd loved it. Maybe being here, helping Alec, was all about making changes in her life. Perhaps she'd get up her nerve to tell him she was interested in him.

CHAPTER THIRTY-SEVEN
ROSE

Rose headed out of the house prepared to act like a tourist so she could gather information for both her blog and her secret plan. Besides noting what attractions there were in the valley, she wanted to drive by other hotels for comparison purposes. If she could convince the people at the Blaise Group that there was more money to be made by upgrading the Desert Sage Inn instead of converting it to one of their 'standard' properties, she might even convince them to include one or two other properties. She'd studied their portfolio and thought there were two possibilities.

She drove her car along El Paseo, stopped at Starbucks for coffee, and headed east on Highway 111 through Indian Wells toward La Quinta, one of the areas she wanted to look at. As she traveled, she marveled at the growth that had taken place since she'd last lived here. But then, why not? The valley was a great place to visit in the winter, and more and more people were deciding to become year-round residents to escape a busier lifestyle on the coast or in colder climates.

The La Quinta Resort & Club was always a treat to see. It reminded her a lot of the Desert Sage Inn. She knew the history and reviewed it in her mind. San Francisco businessman Walter H. Morgan bought 1,400 acres of land from the native Cahuilla Indians in the early 1920s and enlisted the well-known architect Gordon Kaufman along with scores of artisan craftsman to turn his vision into reality. The adobe bricks and roof tiles were all made locally, she remembered. She drove down the long, majestic entrance lined with tall greenery and palm trees to the white-stucco buildings with red-tile roofs.

She was greeted by a valet attendant and happily left her car with him, eager to tour the property. She'd arranged to meet someone from their public relations department for coffee in Twenty6, a bistro restaurant with a 1920s art deco flair. On her way there, Rose breathed in the class, the style, the flavor of the hotel. This, she thought, is what they hoped to maintain at the Desert Sage Inn. Seeing this property, she vowed to fight hard for Alec even if it cost her the relationship she had been building with Hank.

The head of public relations for the resort was a pleasant young woman who reminded her of Willow. Friendly, informative, and attractive, she answered Rose's questions, handed her several brochures and sheets of information, and made arrangements for Rose to return for a proper tour of the property and a heavily discounted stay at the resort.

Rose left the restaurant and took some time to look around on her own before returning to the front entrance to retrieve her car. She didn't need a tour of the entire property at this stage. Just being here, seeing it again, she'd gained the inspiration she needed. And later, after the future of the Desert Sage Inn had been decided, she'd take advantage of the offer for an overnight stay so she could do the hotel justice for her blog.

She drove through other hotel properties in the area, including those in Palm Desert, Indian Wells, and Rancho Mirage, hotels like the J. W. Marriott, Hyatt Regency, The Ritz-Carlton, and Westin Mission Hills. She checked out new developments and shopping areas, getting a better idea of what had transpired in the valley in the last fourteen years. She'd read about the growth, of course, but as the saying went, a picture was worth a thousand words.

By the time she returned to Alec's house, she was exhausted. She couldn't wait to get into the pool and relax with a cold drink before dinner. She checked the patio. Lily and Willow were already there. Pleased, she hurried into her room to change.

As she went into her bathroom to retrieve her bathing suit, her phone rang. She lifted it and saw that it was Hank.

"Hello?"

"Hi, Rose. Just wanted you to know that I've had an initial discussion with Duncan Armstrong, and he is definitely opposed to creating a new collection of hotels. Thought you'd want to know so you wouldn't waste time spinning wheels."

"Really," Rose said, her word coated with ice. "I'm working for Alec, not Duncan Armstrong." How could she have been so stupid as to think they were going to work together when the Blaise Group had hired him? She forced pleasantness to her voice. "How is Sam?"

"Better, thanks. Getting lots of rest while I'm here. I'll let you know when I'll be back in California."

"Okay. Tell Sam I'm thinking of her." Because she was upset with Hank didn't mean she wasn't concerned about his daughter.

"I will," said Hank. "Talk to you later."

"Okay. 'Bye," she said, clicking off the call before the conversation went in other directions. It was, she decided, a good thing she'd had time to step back and rethink things. One of the first things a professional learned in business was staying away from personal relationships when working against one another. She should've known better.

Feeling glum, she got into her suit, grabbed a towel, and

went outside to join the other women. She was grateful for their presence.

Lily looked up from the chaise lounge she was lying on and smiled at her. "Come join us. It's a beautiful evening."

"Yes. Do join us," said Willow, who was sitting on a step inside the pool. "I don't know about you, but I'm glad to be here, away from the hotel. I think Brent is spying on me, trying to figure out exactly what I'm doing for my report."

Lily sat up. "Watch out; he has a habit of making it seem as if all your ideas are his. I've read some of the reports he's written."

Rose plopped down in a chair beside Lily and sighed. "That's not all. Others can try to take over. Hank all but told me not to bother pursuing the idea of setting up the Desert Sage Inn as part of a high-end collection."

"What? Why would he say that?" Lily asked.

"It seems Duncan Armstrong doesn't like the idea."

"So, what? Alec does," said Lily. "We just have to convince the Blaise Group it would be worth any investment."

"I'm trying to keep that in mind when I create a list of suggestions for improving the inn," said Willow. "I hope that helps."

"Thanks," said Rose. "I visited La Quinta Resort & Club this morning. It made me realize how alike the two properties are. Not in every way, of course. But they both have that luxurious feel. It would be terrible to destroy that at the Desert Sage Inn."

"What are you going to do?" asked Lily, looking concerned.

"I'm moving forward with my plan without Hank. Furthermore, I've decided to step away from any relationship I had with him. It's better that way."

"Oh, but ..." Lily began.

Rose glared at her, afraid to let out all her feelings.

"Okay," said Willow. "I get it, but, Rose, don't do anything you might regret. I saw how the two of you were together."

Frustrated, unhappy, Rose refrained from snapping at Willow. She didn't think either one of them understood how long it had taken her to build a reputation in the business, how devoted she was to this idea for Alec. She remembered watching the inn go from a small operation into the beautiful resort it was today. Back then, she'd put a lot of effort into helping it grow. The inn was, in some respects, her pride and joy too.

"I'm ready for some margaritas," said Lily, rising. "Everybody in?"

Willow and Rose glanced at one another, smiled, and nodded.

Later, after a swim in the pool and sipping her cool, refreshing drink, Rose studied the other two women and felt a sense of fellowship. "I'm glad you guys aren't out for the evening. It means a lot to me to have you here. Thanks for understanding why I'm so upset."

"We'll always be here for one another," said Lily. "Right?"

The three of them raised their glasses.

"To the Desert Flowers!" said Willow, laughing when Lily tried to click her full glass against hers and almost spilled her drink.

"Guess it's time for dinner," Lily said. "Juanita left the fixings for a taco salad. I'll put it together." She got to her feet and went inside.

Rose turned to Willow. "With your work for the Blaise Group, do you think I can pull off the new idea for the inn? You have a better idea of the numbers needed for something like that."

"We'll have to wait and see what I come up with, but I'm going to keep it in mind when I think about future operations at the hotel." Willow sighed. "I don't know what Brent and Trace are doing, but I'm thinking of coming up with a whole lot more than minor changes."

Rose smiled at her. "As Alec said, you're so capable, Willow. I'm glad we're on the same team." She nodded toward the kitchen where Lily was putting together the salad. "Lily too."

Feeling much better about her plan, Rose studied the sunset in the fading sky. Orange, red, and yellow hues brightened the sky, spreading their colors like streaks of hope.

CHAPTER THIRTY-EIGHT
LILY

Lily sat with the other two women in the kitchen, eating the salad she'd quickly put together as Juanita had instructed her. She liked the friendship she was forming with Willow's mother. As she'd watched the two of them together, Lily wished she'd had a normal relationship with her own mother. The closest she'd come to any kind of a warm family relationship was with her sister. Older than Monica by ten years, Lily had often assumed the role of mother when her own was unable to take care of them due to a drinking problem.

The camaraderie she shared with the other women here at Alec's house meant a lot to her. She was enjoying herself in a way she hadn't for a long time. As she'd thought so often since she'd been in the desert, she'd somehow become trapped in a lifestyle back home that she had no wish to repeat.

"I've started to look at properties in the area," she announced. "I'm thinking of staying here after we complete the work for Alec."

"Funny, Alec and I were talking about how nice it is to live here, except for summer months. But even those can be bearable," said Rose. I think I like the quieter atmosphere here. Las Vegas is Las Vegas. But I can't make plans just yet. Who knows what's going to happen here? Still, I'm trying to build local contacts with the idea of possibly making a move."

"Wow! It would be great if we all stayed," said Lily. "I'm

going to try to talk my sister into moving here with Izzy. I've missed them a lot." She lifted her cell phone. "Here's the latest picture of Izzy. Isn't she the cutest?"

Rose took the phone from her and studied the latest photo Monica had sent. Her features softened with tenderness. "She sure is a doll. Leah is about the same age. Such a precious stage."

Rose sometimes acted tough, but Lily knew how kind, how caring she was. She'd mentioned things about her childhood that Lily knew still hurt her.

A sigh escaped Lily. Families were difficult. Though she might wish she'd had a mother like Juanita, she didn't know what to expect from a father. She'd never known hers. He was a serviceman who definitely was AWOL in their lives.

Willow got up from the table. "Anybody else want coffee?"

Lily raised her hand. She'd had two margaritas and needed that jolt of caffeine. Because of her mother's problem, she seldom allowed herself more than one drink for an entire evening. Even then, she became concerned if she felt any effects of alcohol.

While she and Willow drank coffee, Rose cleared the table and did the dishes. It was that way in the group, Lily thought. Each pitching in where and when necessary.

"Willow, what are you going to do about Brent and Trace?" Lily asked. "They're closely related to the owners of the Blaise Group, and, in many ways, this project of yours is just giving them ideas for free."

"I know I'm taking a chance for sure, but I have enough pride to do a thorough job for them for Alec's sake. Now that I know I want to get back into operations, I might be able to get references from them for the future."

"Smart thinking," said Rose, coming up behind Willow and giving her a pat on the back. "Alec wouldn't ask you to be here if he didn't trust you to do that."

"Yes, that's what my parents tell me," Willow said. "And there's a part of me who wants to show up Brent. He still thinks he's better than anyone else."

"You go, girl!" Lily said, overwhelmed by an urge to hug her.

CHAPTER THIRTY-NINE
ROSE

Rose spent the next few days feverishly working on her special presentation. Hank might be in charge of the project for the Blaise Group, but she was overseeing Alec's plan. Hank had called to tell her he would be back in California at the end of the week. She'd be ready.

In the evenings and at night lying in her bed, she thought of Hank in a very different way, remembering his kisses, how she'd loved to be with him. She didn't know if they could compete in business and then be close in other ways. It would depend on whether Hank respected her work. Two creative people needed to trust one another not to do damage. Suggestions and other offered ideas were fine, but no way could she live with a man like her ex-husband, who quietly tore at her creativity, shredding it to pieces.

When she'd done all that she could do on her own, she called a meeting of the Desert Flowers and asked Alec to join them.

They sat in the living room so Alec could relax in a comfortable chair. Rose spread her paperwork on the coffee table and began speaking.

"I've called you here to help me. Duncan Armstrong has said he isn't interested in Alec's plan to make the Desert Sage Inn part of an upscale collection. I'm determined to make a case for their doing so, regardless of what he's told Hank Bowers."

She glanced at Alec and smiled at his nod of approval.

"Here's what I have so far. I've come up with a name for the group of three hotels I've identified as eligible for the project. Desert Sage Inn and two other west coast properties of the Blaise Group located in Arizona in the Phoenix area. They will be part of the Corona Collection of Fine Hotels."

"Oh, I like that name!" said Lily. "It has a nice ring to it."

"Yes," agreed Alec, leaning forward. "Go on."

"I'm using the report Willow is working on to prepare an estimate of costs to ensure all three properties meet the criteria for such high-end properties. Thankfully, both Arizona properties are fairly new and are attractive. But they will need some enhancements in the guest rooms as well as the public areas. By doing so, I believe they can raise their room rates substantially."

"What size are their hotels?" Lily asked.

"Pretty comparable. One is 120 rooms like ours; the other is 104 rooms."

"What changes are you recommending?" Willow asked.

Rose smiled at her. "I've pretty much taken your list for the Desert Sage Inn and applied it to all three properties. Your figures seem on point, though if you don't mind, I want Alec to take a look at them."

"Not a problem. I'll be glad to do that," Alec said, sounding pleased.

"I also need to come up with the cost of dressing up the outside. Nothing too dramatic, though the landscaping needs improvement with plantings, artwork, and consistent signage throughout the properties."

"What can I do to help the cause?" asked Lily.

"You can research landscape companies in that area, find out where to get the best exterior artwork around, and when the time comes, I need you to help me put together the report.

I'll type up most of it, but the report itself needs dressing up with the insertion of photos, etc."

"I like how you women are working together," said Alec. "It means everything to me."

"We love you, Alec," said Rose, "and I think I'm right in saying we all love the Desert Sage Inn too."

"Absolutely," said Lily as Willow nodded emphatically.

"When is this report due?" Alec asked.

"Yesterday," teased Rose. "Seriously, Hank will be here in a couple of days, but I'm hoping to set up a meeting with both Duncan and Mitchell Armstrong late next week. Duncan is the more difficult of the two. It was he who told Hank they weren't interested."

Alec nodded. "Yes, Mitch Armstrong is a much more reasonable person. Best to deal with him if you can."

"I figure we'll have to present them with several copies of reports so all their people can study it. We'll put them in attractive covers and make as professional a presentation as possible. We need to do it all ourselves because I don't want to take the chance of anyone else seeing it and undermining it before the presentation to the Blaise Group."

"Yes," said Alec. "Treat this with the utmost confidence. Hitting them with a presentation like this will be much more effective than trying to discuss it. Good job, Rose."

"Perfect," said Willow. "I'm really impressed. I'll give you an update tomorrow on what I'm thinking about."

"And I'll help in any way I can," said Lily. "I've already written down the subjects for research. I'll start this afternoon."

"Great," Rose said. "We'll meet at cocktail time to see how things are going." Her vision blurred as she gazed around the room. "I love you all."

###

With a new sense of urgency, Rose went into her bedroom where she'd set up her workstation and began to review Willow's suggestions, double-checking facts and figures. Now that she had a team helping her, she was more determined than ever to prove her case to the Blaise people. And deep inside, she wanted to prove herself to Hank.

She hadn't heard from him for a couple of days, and that made things easier. She honestly didn't know how she'd feel when she saw him again. Doubt had played with her emotions.

The first shadows of evening were encroaching on the sky when someone knocked at her door. She got up to answer it and was surprised to see Alec.

"Hi," she said, opening the door wider. "Do you want to come in?"

"No, I want you to come to the living room for a follow-up meeting." He grinned. "The other women are already there."

Rose followed him to the living room and laughed when she saw a big bottle of champagne was sitting in a bucket of ice in the middle of the coffee table, along with four tulip glasses.

Alec sat. "Thought we'd have a little celebration. Something for The Desert Flowers." He turned to Willow. "Will you do the honors?"

"Of course," she said, getting to her feet and lifting the bottle of champagne from the ice, carefully wiping it with a bar towel sitting next to the bucket. Then, she unwrapped the foil from the top, twisted off the wire cage, and gently pulled the cork out of the bottle, creating a soft pop.

"Well done," said Alec. He sat back while Willow poured small amounts into the glasses and handed them out.

"I love DP," said Rose. Dom Perignon was one of her favorite champagnes.

"Here's to The Desert Flowers saving the Desert Sage Inn,"

said Alec, lifting his glass. "I think we have a real chance of making it happen."

Rose held her glass up. "Hear! Hear!"

Smiling at one another, she and the others took sips together.

Alec cleared his throat. "I hadn't planned on saying anything just yet, but I want you to know if the arrangement goes through for the Desert Sage Inn to be part of a new collection, I've provided a sizeable bonus for each of you. Something to help you get started on a new life, whatever that may be."

Rose was as surprised as the others. "Alec, that's so generous."

"Seeing how you're all pulling together, I wanted you to know about it. Not as an incentive, but as a thank you for this and so much more." His voice grew shaky with emotion.

Rose went over to him and kissed him on the cheek. "It's not necessary, but I appreciate the thought."

"Me, too," said Lily, giving him a quick kiss. Her eyes filled. "I never expected something like this."

Alec gave her a steady look. "I didn't think you would." He turned to Willow. "I'd like to see you do something you were born to do."

She hugged him. "I never needed a fairy godmother. I've always had you."

He laughed. "You can't know how much I've appreciated seeing you grow into the woman you are."

With everyone seated again, Willow poured more champagne into their glasses. Rose sat back and watched her before lifting her glass in a toast, feeling as if she'd found her family.

CHAPTER FORTY
LILY

Lily lay in bed cuddling up to her pillow, deep in thought. She'd come to Palm Desert to help Alec without any expectations beyond staying at his house as he'd suggested, using her vacation time. Now that he'd mentioned a possible bonus, she realized how much she wanted to be able to live in California.

She thought of her sister. Monica had been more like her child than a sister. Lily lived in Phoenix when Monica asked her to come to New York State to help her through a difficult time. Her boyfriend had ditched her when he learned Monica was pregnant. After being settled in a job she wasn't crazy about and breaking up with a man she'd genuinely thought had loved her, Lily had dutifully packed up to go help her. That was four years ago.

Now, with the possibility of a whole new lifestyle, Lily filled with excitement. She'd saved some money, and her condo was in great shape to sell. Perhaps she could do it, with or without Alec's help. The important thing was he'd given her hope for healthy changes in her life. Maybe she could even meet a man she cared about, a man not associated with her work.

Lily rolled over on her back and stared up at the ceiling fan circling slowly above her. The idea that Rose and Willow might move here was another plus. It was crazy how Alec's wishes had brought them together and were making them friends.

With a new sense of contentment, Lily closed her eyes.

The following day, Lily bounded out of bed with thoughts spinning in her head. She quickly dressed for what had become her routine walk and quietly left the house.

The days were becoming hotter, which meant the early morning hours were more precious to her. While birds sang around her, she stretched and headed out, jogging slowly down to the golf course area.

The early light and the coolness of the air wrapped around her like a lightweight gray shawl. Embracing the feeling, she continued to move, her feet pounding the pavement in a steady rhythm. She hadn't met up with Brian for a couple of days and assumed he was meeting with various contractors in the early hours before it became a disruption for the guests.

She remembered how Rose had decided to step back from her relationship with Hank and decided such a move would be wise for her too. Work and play didn't mix for professionals in the same environment. Maybe after the project was over, she'd let Brian know how she felt about him.

Anxious to begin her tasks for Rose, she cut her morning jaunt short and headed back.

In the distance, she could see Brian running in her direction and hurried her steps to the path leading up to Alec's house. Having decided to play it safe, she wanted no distractions to begin her day. He'd told her to take a few days off and didn't need to know what she was doing.

Rose greeted her when she entered the kitchen. "Hi! You're up bright and early."

"I wanted to get a head start on the day before I begin the work you asked me to do." Lily smiled at her. "I like your plan."

"Do you think we have a chance at this?" Rose said, pouring her a cup of coffee and handing it to her.

"Yes," said Lily. "Even if you can't convince them to agree to it, we'll all have a better idea of how to get the best out of the deal for Alec."

"I was surprised by his offer of a bonus," said Rose. "I don't believe he understands our devotion to him."

Lily's eyes stung. "Ours was a different kind of relationship than the one I think you and he had. But he showed me what it was like for two people to care for one another and the proper way to treat others. My childhood was a chaotic mess."

"He's a lovely person," Rose said. She put her arm around Lily. "He'd have to be for you to be with him."

This time Lily couldn't stop her eyes from leaking. As she'd previously thought, Rose might act tough, but she was tender too.

"Have a nice day," Rose said. "I'm going to get started. We'll meet this afternoon."

"Okay. See you then," Lily replied, her mind already focusing on Phoenix, the two hotels Rose wanted to be included in the group, and what they could do to dress up their exteriors. She sat at the kitchen table, made a couple of notes, and went to get ready for the day, filled with a new sense of hope for the future.

CHAPTER FORTY-ONE
WILLOW

Willow sat at her desk in her room and leafed through some of the personnel policies of the hotel. As she'd thought, professional staff were not allowed to take prime morning tee times for the golf course unless it was for business entertainment. Brent and Trace should not have used that early morning slot to play golf.

She sat for a moment, debating whether to include issues like this in her report, and decided to go ahead with it. It was better to have guests paying for it than for staff to use it for a discounted fee.

As she studied the pages, Willow realized how generous Alec was about offering staff the opportunity to stay at the hotel at discounted rates whenever there was room. She decided to go see him.

She knocked on Alec's door, and hearing his reply, she stepped into his living area and found him sitting at a desk.

"Ah, just the person I want to see," he said. "Let's talk about some of the numbers Rose has secured from you. They're good."

"But?"

"But they need a little tweaking." He pulled the glasses off his nose and peered at her. "What did you want to see me for?"

"I've been going through personnel procedures and rules for the inn and see that staff members are allowed to reserve a room for special occasions. How does that work? Have there ever been problems with it?"

Alec smiled. "As a matter of fact, no. It's been a huge help in spreading the reputation of the inn. One stay for a staff member who then realizes what it means to be a guest here is worth a hundred five-star reviews. Word spreads, and that staff member and family buy into the concept of the importance of properly caring for a guest here at the inn."

"That's what I hoped for. I'm going to re-emphasize that in my report to the Blaise Group."

"Pull up a chair and join me. I want to hear what additional recommendations you're going to make," said Alec.

Willow gave him a quick rundown. "Lily is going to help me put together the report, the same as she's doing for Rose."

Alec smiled and nodded. "Now, let's talk about numbers and the budget."

Surprised to find him so alert, so excited, Willow quickly agreed. It was an "up" day for him.

CHAPTER FORTY-TWO
ROSE

Rose's fingers were cold as she clicked off the call with Mitchell Armstrong. He'd agreed to meet with her in eight days. He'd told her that both he and his brother would attend as they planned on visiting the hotel and meeting with Hank during that time.

Now that the meeting had been established, she wondered if she'd been foolish to bite off a big chunk of an idea that might not work.

As luck would have it, Hank picked that time to call.

"Hello, Hank!" she chirped like a bird forced to sing for its supper. She wanted to keep her work secret, and she needed her confidence.

"Hey, just calling to check in. I've worked on some ideas and thought I'd email them to you for input."

"Thanks, but I'm working on the project for Alec and am asking you to hold back on sending me anything until I'm ready."

"Okay. Sounds like we're not on the same team. What's up with that?"

Rose tried to find the right words. "I need to do this project for Alec. There's still plenty of time for us to work jointly on a PR campaign. By the end of next week, I'll know better which direction to take. Sound like a plan?"

"I guess. How's everything else on your end?" asked Hank. "I've missed seeing you."

"Everything here is fine. The weather is delightful. I bet it's beautiful there with all the trees in bloom."

"Yes. It's very pretty."

"How are Sam and the rest of the family?" Rose asked.

"Samantha is pretty much back to normal. Still trying to take it easy for a few more days while I'm here. I'll be heading out to California after the weekend. Nikki is off, and we've planned a couple of outings. She asked me to say hi."

"How nice. Thanks," said Rose.

"Well, I'd better go. I'll wait to email you the stuff I've been working on. Next week, I'll show you in person." He paused. "Like I said, I've missed you, Rose."

"It hasn't been the same since you've been gone," Rose responded honestly, still not sure exactly how she would react to seeing him again. She kept reminding herself to put business ahead of pleasure.

"I'm hoping to spend a lot of time with you, see where this relationship can lead us."

"Me, too," she said, warming to the longing in his voice. She didn't want to judge him too harshly. The next week would help her decide if she wanted to move forward with him.

After they said their goodbyes and ended the call, Rose sat a moment thinking of Hank. She'd fallen hard for him, but after being alone for these past few days, she realized she might've moved too fast into thinking it was something that would or should last. Shaking her head at her insecurities, she turned back to the project.

She'd worked for hours before she realized she'd missed lunch. Getting up and stretching, Rose went out to the kitchen to grab a snack.

Willow was there, munching on an apple.

"How's it going?" Rose asked her.

"Just putting finishing touches on my report to the Blaise

Group. They've moved our presentation date to early next week. Alec helped me work numbers, but I have more information to gather."

"Great. We'll meet here late this afternoon to go over updates for the report I'm preparing."

"It feels like I'm back at school with all this work, but it's going to be fine," said Willow. She felt a grin spread across her face. Alec had told her she was doing an outstanding job. She hoped it was enough to beat Brent and Trace. She hadn't seen Brent at the hotel at all and little of Trace. Sarah had told her Brent was off property and hadn't bothered to tell her.

"A *very* good meeting for you," said Rose, smiling. "I hope I can be there for it."

Willow nodded. "Yes. Alec is requesting that we all be there."

Rose grinned. Willow would attend that meeting feeling well-protected. She knew what it felt like to have that kind of support. Hopefully, by working together, they'd all accomplish what they each wanted.

That afternoon, Rose and the other women gathered with Alec in the living room to discuss new information for Rose's report. After Willow and Alec handed out sheets of updated financials, Lily spoke about the landscaping company the Blaise hotels used in Phoenix. Pretending to represent a different hotel, she'd discussed general quotes on charges for a variety of plantings and the cost of putting in fountains and staging various pieces of art.

"Nothing outrageously expensive, but we need to consider the size of the property and how we envision changing up the entrances to their hotels. While they're pretty now, they can't compare to that of the inn. They gave me the name of various artists in the area whose work they have used at other properties. I've looked up some of their work." She handed out sheets of paper. "Here is some of the artwork shown on websites by artists I like, and here are photos of the Blaise hotels I downloaded from their websites, with highlights of the areas I'd want to enhance. I used to live in Phoenix, so I know them well."

Rose smiled at Lily, unable to hide her surprise. "Thank you for being so thorough. You're very efficient at this."

Lily's face flushed with pleasure. "Thanks. I like doing research. It's amazing what can happen to a property when certain things are done to dress it up."

Rose nodded. "I've researched a sample of their hotels, and it's clear, though they're attractive, they can't begin to meet the standards of the Desert Sage Inn, as far as upscale décor is concerned. They're simply utilitarian. That's why our working together is so important. We don't want to de-class the inn if that makes sense."

"Right," said Willow. "I get the same feeling the way they run their hotels is miles apart from the way we do things here."

"They may think in terms of what it'll cost to change instead of what it may ultimately mean as a bigger source of revenue," said Rose.

Alec cleared his throat. "Listening to the three of you, it's clear how wise I was to have you work together. You're all real hoteliers," he said with a smile.

Rose glanced at the other two women and chuckled. Maybe, just maybe, they could pull off this thing for him.

CHAPTER FORTY-THREE
ROSE

Rose headed to the hotel for her meeting with Hank, filled with trepidation. She'd told herself to keep things on a professional level, but images of them cuddling on the couch or in the swimming pool kept bumping up hard against that thought. She'd fallen for him. Now she had to figure out how they were going to proceed.

More than anything, Rose was determined to show Hank and Duncan Armstrong that they might try to exclude her from meetings, try to stop her from doing what Alec had hired her to do, but she would prevail. Not by retaliating in a nasty way, but with grace and professionalism.

The wind had picked up. As she drove the golf cart through the property, she was glad she'd pulled her hair back into a knot at the base of her head. Still, tiny wisps of hair were fluttering around her face like the wings of the hummingbirds she loved.

She parked the golf cart, grabbed her things, went into the hotel, and walked across the lobby to the elevator. They'd agreed to meet in Hank's room so they'd have privacy to talk. Heart pounding, she pressed the UP button and drew a deep breath.

As the elevator doors opened, she came face to face with Hank. She stepped back in surprise.

"Hank! I thought we were meeting in your suite," she said, almost babbling.

He grinned and wrapped his arms around her. "I couldn't wait to see you again."

She stiffened, then melted in his arms. So much for wondering how she'd feel about seeing him again.

They moved away from the elevator and walked outside to one of the benches on the patio, away from several people relaxing there.

Rose took a seat beside Hank and looked into his steel-gray eyes. They were telling her so much.

"It's good to see you again," she said, letting out a sigh of contentment. Being with him, seeing the look of love in his eyes evaporated the uncertainty that had gripped her.

He took hold of her hand. "I thought about you every day."

"I thought of you too," she said. "But, Hank, my wanting to be with you has to be separate from work because I have a job to do, and I'm going to do it the best way I know how."

His brow furrowed. "I thought we were working together."

"Yes and no. As I mentioned, my boss is Alec. To be honest, I felt you were pushing me away when you went ahead with a meeting with Duncan with no input or participation from me. That's when I realized we were working for different people, and I had better do my job."

His gaze bore into her. "Is there something you're not telling me?"

"I'm working on something private for him. When we're ready to talk about it, you'll be among the first to know. I can't say anything more about it now."

He studied her silently and nodded. "Okay. I trust you, Rose."

Relieved to have established a way to proceed, Rose smiled and relaxed. The true test of their relationship would occur when she popped her surprise report on the Armstrong brothers and others from the Blaise Group. In the meantime, she'd continue to do both her job for Alec and the project with Hank. She couldn't help smiling.

"Let's go up to my suite. I'm anxious to show you what I've been working on." He pulled her to her feet.

Walking calmly beside him, she followed him to the elevator and got on, squeezing into an almost full car. She couldn't resist glancing at him out of the corner of her eye. He placed a protective hand on her waistline and smiled at her.

The elevator door opened, and Rose exited the car with others, her anticipation building. She knew from the looks he gave her that Hank was just as eager as she to be alone.

Hank swiped his room card in the security slot and opened the door to his suite. "C'mon in. I've got some things ready to show you." He indicated the work desk spread with papers.

She set down her purse and notebook and turned as he approached.

"How about a proper hello?" he said softly, drawing her into his strong arms. His lips met hers. Responding to him, Rose felt desire surge through her, settling in her core. It seemed like forever since she'd felt this way. She reached up and wrapped her arms around his neck, holding him close.

When they pulled apart, they stood smiling at one another.

"Just like I remembered," Hank said, reaching out and cupping her face in his hands.

"Maybe even better," she said. Perhaps it was having him gone that made her see him in a fresh way. He was, as she'd first thought, adorable.

"Will you come to my house after work?" said Hank. "I want time with you. We can order food in, or go out, or whatever you want to do for dinner."

"I'd love to, and ordering in sounds perfect." A smile lifted the corners of her lips. She wanted him all to herself.

He grinned at her. "Now, let's get to work. I haven't been

able to do too much while I've been gone, but I wanted to show you what I have. Feel free to make comments. It's got to work for both of us."

Hank led her to the desk and showed her the papers he'd laid out on top of it.

Rose looked at each one carefully. The ads were good. For the Blaise Group. "Let's see what we can do with the wording. It's a little one-sided as it is."

Hank studied her. "If you're still talking about making the inn the basis of a new collection of properties, you might as well stop. Duncan Armstrong was very clear. He said it differently, but he detests the idea."

Rose's stomach knotted. "Thank you for telling me, but I work for Alec, and I have every intention of following through."

"Okay, let's not argue about it," said Hank, rubbing a hand through his thick hair. "Let's work on the material to hand out to guests during the actual transition. No matter which angle we use for our overall advertising campaign, the information cards we give to them should be clear and easily acceptable to both parties."

"Agreed," Rose said smoothly. She still wasn't sure how Hank would react when she presented her plan to the Blaise Group. For now, she wanted to work together well. And tonight? She couldn't wait to see how much he'd missed her.

Rose left the hotel with Hank, not even bothering to go back to Alec's. They were both anxious to get to his house and have the privacy they'd craved all day.

As Hank pulled into the garage, Rose's pulse sprinted. She'd wondered in the past what it would be like to have a lifestyle of working together and then coming home to a personal life with him. Now she'd get a taste of it.

They entered the house, and Rose felt a warm welcome envelop her. The place wasn't glamorous, but it was home to the man with whom she'd fallen in love. That meant everything.

"I'm ready for a swim. How about you?" said Hank.

"That sounds lovely," said Rose, setting down her purse and notebook. "It's a great way for me to relax."

With a playful tug, Hank drew her into his arms and smiled at her. "I've got another way to work off stress. It's a lot more fun."

She laughed, loving it when he played games with his words. For all the times they'd been together, they hadn't gone to bed yet. Rose understood Hank was still letting his wife go while she was making sure she wasn't being foolish to fall for him so quickly.

Now, though, as she observed the yearning in his eyes and felt his arousal, she was ready for it.

He kissed her and then pulled back. "I don't want to push you, but I don't want to wait any longer to show you what I feel. I know I've been holding back, but I want to say it now. I love you. Earlier today, when the elevator door opened and I saw you there, I knew it was for real."

"I've fallen for you too," said Rose. She wasn't ready to say more.

"Come with me," he said, his gaze full of desire.

She took his hand, and they walked to the bedroom together.

Later, lying naked beside him, Rose reached up and stroked his cheek. Making love with him was magical. She'd thought she'd be uncomfortable learning what pleased him.

But laughter had carried them through a few awkward moments. Joy filled her at how natural and comfortable they were with one another. And when he made sure she was satisfied, she felt thoroughly, deliciously fulfilled.

"That's better than swimming anytime," she murmured, bubbling with happiness.

"Better than many things," he responded, turning to face her

Things had happened fast, and she still had to see how he would react to her independent stance at the meeting scheduled with the Blaise Group. If he handled it poorly, it might change everything.

His hands stroked her absently as he continued to give her an intense look. "I love the feel of you," he murmured before placing his lips on hers, making her forget everything else but the man beside her.

When they finally decided it was time to get up, Rose lay in bed watching Hank move with grace to the bathroom. He was in remarkably good shape and comfortable in his own skin for a man called Papa B. Rose followed him into the bathroom. When he invited her into the shower, she eagerly joined him. Soaping each other turned out to be another exercise that was more exciting than swimming.

The next morning, back at Alec's house, Rose's body hummed with the memory of being with Hank the night before. Life, it seemed, had taken a marvelous turn, one full of hope for the future.

She sprang out of bed, ready to face the day with a new zest for living. She was still smiling when she walked into the kitchen.

Lily and Willow grinned at her from where they sat at the

kitchen table.

"Look who's all happy this morning," said Lily, giving her a knowing look. "I can't imagine why."

"It was pretty late when Rose came home, late enough to wonder what was going on," teased Willow.

Rose laughed. "I don't care who knows it. I've fallen for Hank all over again." She helped herself to coffee and joined them at the table.

"How's that going to work when he finds out about your secret project?" Lily said.

"Yeah, is that going to be a problem?" asked Willow. "He might resent what you're doing."

"He might think it's almost as if you're going behind his back," Lily said.

Rose drew a deep breath and let out a nervous puff of air. "I've explained to him that I'm working for Alec, not the Blaise Group. Part of my success with the project will be the element of surprise. Hank doesn't seem the kind of man who'd let our disagreement over how to proceed ruin our relationship. At least I don't think so."

"Time will tell," said Lily. "The report we're putting together is a real zinger, bound to get the attention of the Blaise Group."

"You both are going to be at my presentation today, right?" said Willow.

"Absolutely," said Rose. "I'm going to take pointers from you, so when it's time to do my presentation later this week, I'll know what works best."

"I know it's going to be wonderful," said Lily. "Here's to the Desert Flowers!" She lifted her coffee cup.

Rose and Willow lifted theirs too.

"Here's to us," said Rose, "and to Willow's project this morning."

"Lily helped me put together the report. It looks great," said Willow. "What do you think I should wear?"

The conversation veered into the proper attire for such a meeting. After they'd all agreed on what would be best, it was time for them to get ready.

Rose hurried to Alec's room to see if he was feeling well enough to attend the meeting. When she knocked on the door and opened it, he was already dressed and sitting in a chair in the living area.

"' Morning," Rose said cheerfully. "You're going to join us for Willow's presentation?"

"I wouldn't miss it for anything. I'll stay as long as I can."

"I'm glad. It's important that we all be present and united," said Rose. "I've got to go get ready. See you soon."

Back in her room, Rose hopped into the shower. As the warm water caressed her body, she sighed, wishing Hank was there. He was such a generous lover. She felt as if she was a young girl again, ready for anything that life offered.

She got out, toweled herself off, and, noticing the smile on her face, realized anyone who knew her would sense something wonderful had happened to her. At one time, she might've cared about being so open, so vulnerable. Now, she didn't.

As she dressed, Rose carefully chose clothing that reflected professionalism, not the romantic she was becoming. Lily and Willow would dress as conservatively as she. The Desert Flowers had vowed to represent Alec well.

When she joined the other women in the front hall, she saw with satisfaction that Lily and Willow were wearing skirts with tailored, lightweight jackets like her.

As soon as Alec met up with them, they headed out. Pedro drove them to the hotel in Alec's car, driving slowly so as not to jar Alec in the passenger seat.

Rose caught Pedro glancing in the rearview mirror and knew he was as concerned about Willow's presentation as everyone else. If it went well, respect for Alec would grow. For Willow, too.

At the front of the hotel, John Rodriquez greeted them. "We're all set up in the conference room. Come with me."

"The Armstrong group up to their old tricks by stacking the room?" Alec asked as he accepted Rose's arm.

John nodded. "They've assembled quite a crowd. I heard Duncan say this was the right time for Brent to step up and take control. He seemed excited about it."

Rose turned to Willow. "Pretend you never heard that. You're going to do fine."

Willow nodded and followed John with the rest of them.

When they reached the conference room, conversation stopped as several people turned to look at them. Rose hadn't met either Duncan or Mitchell Armstrong, but she knew right away who was who. Duncan had an intangible air about him that she recognized—one of privilege, confidence, and condescension. She disliked him on sight. Her gaze swung to the older brother. Mitchell's features were much like his brother's and remarkably like his son, Trace's. Taller, thinner, he had laugh lines around his eyes, making his handsome face more open. His expression exhibited genuine interest.

John made sure everyone was introduced to everyone else. The Blaise Group had brought ten people in for the meeting. Rose wondered why so many in their group had made the trip when John sidled up next to her and said quietly, "I'm giving you a heads-up. They're going to move your meeting with them to tomorrow morning."

Rose felt her stomach curl. "But I'm not quite ready."

"You'd better be," said John *sotto voce*. "Duncan is on a roll."

"Oh, dear," Rose managed before taking a seat at the conference table.

The meeting began with a statement by Duncan that as lovely as the Desert Sage Inn was at present, by making it conform to their other hotels, they could raise the occupancy rate.

"Those would be shorter stays, no doubt," said Alec calmly.

"Yes. Get them in beds and out on their heads," said Duncan, in a lousy attempt at humor.

Rose couldn't hold back a shudder. Why would Alec have agreed to sell his hotel to them?

Mitchell then took over. "My brother's sense of humor is questionable. Alec, as you and I have discussed on many occasions, the Blaise Group will do our best to make the hotel run smoothly and wisely." He looked at Brent, Trace, and Willow. " I'd like to hear from Brent and Trace what changes they would make to the hotel. Then, Willow, I'd like to hear from you."

Rose liked the kind, almost-conspiratorial smile Mitchell gave Willow.

When Trace set up equipment for a PowerPoint presentation, she shot Lily a worried glance. They hadn't done one.

Lily shook her head slightly and turned her attention to Brent, who was speaking.

As one slide led to another, Rose became even more discouraged. The changes Brent talked about would ruin the Desert Sage Inn, take it down a notch or two into a commercial property with short stays and little appreciation for what was here.

When Trace ended with a summary of their views, Duncan bounded to his feet. "Great work, gentlemen. I see how dedicated you are to making this hotel one of our own." He turned to his son. "And you, Brent, are the one to see that it's done properly."

Alec and Rose exchanged silent messages that spoke of despair.

"All right, Willow. You're up next," said Mitchell in a calm, cool voice.

Willow got to her feet and faced them. "I'm pleased to provide you with a list of things I would change or enhance at the Desert Sage Inn to make the performance even better." She paused while Lily handed out handsomely bound reports. When everyone at the table had received one, Willow continued. "I've made it as complete and simple as I could. You notice I start with a summary of ideas. The following pages go into detail."

"An odd way to do it," mumbled Duncan.

Willow ignored him and went through the list, giving details.

"I like what I hear. Let's take a look at the financials ... see what we're talking about," said Mitchell.

Rose smiled at Lily, who was taking notes, sitting beside someone from the lawyer's office.

Lily went through each item, pointing out any costs or savings. Willow had mentioned nothing major, but even Rose could see how tweaking a few areas in Housekeeping, changing hours for the pool, raising the cost of some services, lowering them for others all added up to some impressive changes over time.

"We're proud of the hotel as it exists," said Willow. "But even the inn can be tweaked a bit without disruption to guests or major costs for the owners. It's much more than heads in beds."

There was a shocked silence in the room as Willow's words hit home, making Duncan's face turn beet red.

"This from a woman, a Mexican at that?" Duncan murmured.

Rose was close enough to him to hear it, straightened in her chair, and addressed Duncan directly. "Willow Sanchez was born and raised in the United States and, as an American woman, has every right to be in a leadership position," she said, staring him down.

Alec gave her a startled look. "Was there something said we all need to know about?"

"I think Duncan and I have a clear understanding," said Rose again, looking directly at Duncan, unwilling for Willow to hear Duncan's angry slurs.

Mitchell frowned at his brother. "Duncan, do you have something to share?"

Duncan shook his head emphatically. "No, I don't."

"Fine then, we'll proceed. Willow, that was an excellent presentation. It's giving me and others a lot to think about." Mitchell turned to Alec. "I congratulate you on having such a capable young woman working for you. I'm going to suggest that Willow assume leadership of the transition group at this level. Trace and Brent, you will now be under her leadership."

"You can't do that," cried Duncan.

"Actually, I can and I will," said Mitchell. "As the majority owner, I have that right."

Rose silently applauded. There was a tone in Mitchell's voice that would keep anyone, even his brother, from challenging him. Her gaze swung to Alec. He winked at her.

"I'm not saying the changes you suggested are going forward, Willow, but I am sincere in wanting you to take the lead on the team." Mitchell gave her a broad smile. "Your experience at Cornell has been very beneficial."

Willow glanced at Rose and Lily but said nothing. They all knew how tortuous a time it had been.

CHAPTER FORTY-FOUR
WILLOW

Willow sat in a daze. If someone were to ask her what followed her presentation at the meeting, she would be unable to answer. The sense of elation she felt was balanced by the looks of contempt Brent cast her way. *He's just a spoiled baby*, she thought, warning herself to be careful with him going forward.

When the meeting broke up, Brent hurried out of the room.

Trace came over to her. "Great job, Willow. I like what you did." He held the report in his hand. "I'm going to go over it later, so I can help you."

Willow blinked rapidly against the sting of tears. "Thanks. That means a lot to me."

Trace stepped aside as his father approached.

"I was impressed with your report," Mitchell told her. "I like the fact you went face-to-face with two young men from the opposing team and handled yourself so well. It bodes well for a very successful future for you."

"Thank you," she said, wishing she could bottle up all these compliments. The next couple of months were going to be difficult.

Alec came over to them. "I told you I was going to get some help to represent me, Mitch."

Mitchell laughed. "Indeed. And you have done so." He frowned at his brother. "What is Duncan up to now?"

"I believe he's informing Rose that her meeting with the

two of you has been moved up to tomorrow morning," said Alec.

Mitchell nodded. "Ah, yes. She and Hank Bowers are working on PR together." He studied Rose. "That ought to be very interesting."

"Yes, indeed. I'm going to take my team home," said Alec. "Seems we have some work to do."

"Nice to see you, Alec," said Mitchell with a catch in his voice.

"Thanks. I'm going to try to make the meeting tomorrow. Say goodbye to Duncan. By the way, I'm impressed with your son's part of the presentation."

Mitchell smiled. "Trace is a fine young man. I'm proud of him."

Willow glanced over at Trace talking to the young woman who'd been taking notes for the lawyer.

CHAPTER FORTY-FIVE
ROSE

Rose climbed into the car with Lily, Willow, and Alec, feeling as if they'd won a huge battle in the war against the Blaise Group. She was worried, though, because another struggle lay ahead. By moving her meeting with the group to tomorrow morning, the Blaise Group had taken away three days of preparing for it.

When she got back to Alec's house, she changed into jeans and a shirt and called Hank.

"How'd the meeting go this morning?" he asked after greeting her.

"Better than we'd hoped. Willow has been put in charge over Brent and Trace Armstrong."

"Wow! That should be interesting," said Hank. "Trace is all right, but Brent is a hothead who's difficult to control."

"Exactly," said Rose. "I guess you heard our publicity meeting has been moved up to tomorrow morning."

"Yes. It's not a problem for me. How about you?"

"I'm staying at Alec's house to work on his project," she said, not willing to give away any details.

"What is this project you keep talking about?" said Hank. "Don't you think I should see it? That seems only fair, considering we're supposedly working together."

"This is different from the work we're doing. This is my work for Alec. That's all I'm at liberty to say about it for the moment," said Rose. If Hank knew the details, he might try to shoot them down. Though Duncan didn't like the idea and had made sure Hank was aware of it, she was committed to doing everything she could to change their minds.

"How about joining me for dinner tonight?" He lowered his voice. "Last night was ... great."

She felt herself blushing like a schoolgirl. "Wish I could. But I'll be working."

"Hmmm. Sounds ominous."

"I don't think it should be," she said with a cheery note she'd had to force.

"Okay, we'll make up for lost time tomorrow. See you then,"

Rose clicked off the call and reminded herself that all's fair in love and war, and she both loved Hank and wasn't afraid to stand up for Alec's wishes.

Willow and Lily worked with Rose throughout the day and into the evening hours finalizing the report, printing it off, and assembling it. The end result was impressive.

When they'd placed the last of the reports in a stack on the dining room table, Rose turned to the other women. "If I'm successful, it will all be due to your help. Thank you so much."

"You're welcome. I don't know about anyone else, but I'm ready for a glass of wine and a nice dinner," said Lily. "Juanita has put together some Mexican treats for us. All we have to do is heat them up."

"Sounds great. I'm going to have a cold beer," said Willow.

"Go ahead and find a comfortable place to sit. I'll heat the oven and bring your drinks to you." She couldn't do enough for them.

Carrying their drinks and a beer for herself, Rose returned to them, handed out the glasses, and plopped down on one of the couches in the living room. As she sat with Lily and Willow, her heart filled with gratitude. It now seemed as if she'd known them forever.

"I think we've covered everything very well," she said. "If any tricky questions come up, both of you will be there to help support me. I can't tell you how confident that makes me feel. Five weeks ago, we hadn't even met."

"I had no idea when I came here two other women would be helping Alec," said Lily. "I'm happy it's turned out this well."

"Yes," said Willow. "Alec didn't give me any details either."

"The fact that he brought you here, Willow, tells a story of its own. The role reversal of the teacher and the pupil," said Rose. "He really respects you."

"You did such a great job at the meeting this morning," said Lily. "But beware of Brent. Like you've always known, he's not a nice guy."

Rose shook her head. "His father is no better. It sounds like Alec and Mitchell are the ones who worked out an agreement, but still, I wonder how anyone can expect to deal with Duncan."

"I know John doesn't like working with Duncan," said Lily. "How about Hank? Has he mentioned any problems with him?"

"Oddly enough, he hasn't," said Rose. "But then I know of only one meeting he had with Duncan. And Hank is dedicated to doing outstanding work for a client as much as I am."

The next day, Rose woke early, put on a swimsuit, grabbed a towel, and headed outside. Though the air was chilly, the pool was heated, and she needed to stretch her limbs and loosen the muscles that had tightened with tension.

She dove into the pool and came up gasping, then struck out through the water. Her body heated as she swam one lap and then another, trying to calm her thoughts. Rose hated when nighttime ideas buried her confidence. She worked to get a better frame of mind. She knew she had an excellent report. Indeed, she had a right to make a case for Alec. Why was she so worried? But she knew the answer. In her relationship with Hank, she wanted no secrets between them. She tried to tell herself this project was different. It was, but it didn't sit right with her.

After swimming several laps, she got out of the pool and headed into the bedroom to call Hank. After she punched in his number, she waited for him to pick up. Finally, his voice mail message came on. Disappointed, she ended the call without bothering to leave a message. Time would take care of everything.

Later, Rose stood with Lily and Willow in the front hallway, waiting for Alec.

After minutes had gone by, Juanita came rushing out of Alec's quarters. "Alec said to tell you to go on without him. He's not up to joining you."

Rose swallowed hard and hid her disappointment. "Tell him we'll do our best for him, and we hope he's feeling better." She exchanged worried glances with Lily and Willow, then followed them out to the car. Hopefully, the rest of the day would be better.

Once again, John greeted their arrival and led them to the conference room where Willow had had such success. Lily followed her, carrying a box of their reports.

The same crew sat in place when they entered the room.

Hank rose from his chair and went to Lily. "What is this?"

He turned and looked at Rose.

"My project," she said more casually than she felt.

Willow and Lily handed them out and then took a seat beside her.

"Hank didn't tell me about any report," said Duncan, shooting an angry look at him.

"It's all part of the discussions we were going to have later this week," said Rose.

Mitchell leafed through the report. "After glancing through this, it doesn't make sense to talk about any publicity campaigns you and Hank have worked on until we discuss this."

"Yes. I agree," said Rose. "My client, Alec, is unable to join us, but he has instructed me to present this to you." She didn't dare look at Hank.

"It's not how we planned it," said Duncan. "Why should we take the time to listen to it? I already told Hank I wasn't interested in doing anything special with the Desert Sage Inn."

"But when we signed a contract with Alec, we agreed to be open-minded about such an idea," countered Mitchell. "We told him we'd need proof that it was worth serious consideration." He held up the report. "I say this needs our attention." He turned to Hank. "I'm sorry, but we'll delay your report until we've had time to consider this."

Hank bobbed his head in agreement but cast a troubled glance at Rose.

"Okay, Rose. Take it away," said Mitchell. "I'm anxious to hear what you have to say."

Rose stood. "It's no surprise how Alec, his team, and his staff feel about the Desert Sage Inn being a cut above most hotels. It has a proven track record as a small, upscale property worthy of attention. In wanting to preserve its standing and reputation, I've put together a report detailing how by keeping it this way and adding two additional properties of your own, you already have the foundation for what I'm calling The Corona Collection of Fine Hotels. It's a perfect opportunity for The Blaise Hotel Group to expand into a niche arena, one that can easily be achieved."

"The Corona Collection does have a nice ring to it," said Duncan. "I hadn't thought it through, but I wouldn't mind owning hotels like that."

"Let me explain what would be needed," Rose continued. "If you turn to page sixteen, you'll see I've listed the work that would need to be done to your two hotels in Arizona to meet the standards of the Desert Sage Inn. The following page shows the financials and the ROI of doing so."

"The return on investment is important because even at the best of times, there are always fluctuations in the hospitality business," said Mitchell. He stood and looked around the table. "May I suggest that we all study this and meet back here at a later time with any questions we might have. This report is very complete, and it'll take time for us to understand it. And of course, our lawyers will want to look at it too. Any objections?"

Rose noticed Hank's displeasure, but he didn't speak.

With no one objecting, he continued. "All right. I'll let everyone know when we'll meet again. Then we can decide how we want to proceed."

Rose let out a sigh of relief. The report had spoken for itself. Later, it might be a different story, but for today she was off the hook. To everyone but Hank.

She turned to speak to him, but he was leaving the room with Duncan.

CHAPTER FORTY-SIX
ROSE

Rose joined the others in the car back to Alec's house, disappointed she hadn't been able to speak to Hank. During Mitchell's announcement about postponing his presentation, Hank hadn't seemed angry, just disappointed.

Back at the house, she changed into comfortable clothes and went out to the patio to join Willow and Lily. They had dressed for a swim. Rose knew it would take more than that to make her feel better. She plunked down in a chair at the table and faced them.

"Why the glum face?" said Lily. "You did great."

Willow studied her. "It's Hank, huh?"

Rose nodded. "I tried to call him early this morning to tell him about the proposal, but he didn't answer. I'm sure he's disappointed he didn't hear it from me first. I can't say I blame him, but I've warned him several times that I was working for Alec."

"From a professional point of view, how do you feel about the meeting?" Lily asked.

Rose's lips curved. "It went great. Exactly how I'd hoped."

"Well, then, don't beat yourself up. That's why it's best not to date anyone you're working with." Lily shook her head. "It'll all work out. I've seen the way Hank looks at you."

"There's no doubt about the way he feels," agreed Willow.

"What should I do?"

"Nothing," said Lily. "Just wait and see how things unfold."

Rose went back into the house feeling better about things. Lily was right. She'd just done her job.

As she was fixing herself a cup of coffee, her cell rang. *Hank.* She clicked on the call.

"Hi. I was hoping to talk to you after the meeting."

"I had to leave. Duncan was furious with me for not telling him about your plan ahead of time. He feels I let him down."

Dismay filled her. "Oh, no! I didn't want anything like that to happen. I tried calling you this morning, but you didn't pick up. I'm sorry if I made it more difficult for you. I know you and Duncan had decided not to pursue the angle of making the inn part of a new collection, but that is what I was hired to do for Alec—create some protection for the inn. I had to pursue it."

"At Duncan's request, I'm leaving for Arizona this afternoon. I'll be gone all week."

"Oh, but I'd hoped to meet you." Rose couldn't keep the disappointment from her voice.

"Can't. My flight's booked," said Hank. "I'll see you early next week at the meeting. Take care."

Long after the call had ended, Rose held onto the phone, torn between being upset and totally pissed off. Hank and Duncan had no right trying to direct what work she should do.

Struggling with her emotions, she returned to the patio, hoping her friends could help her. Lily was sitting there alone.

"What's up?"

"Hank called. Duncan was furious at him for not giving him a heads-up on my project. Now, he wants Hank to go to Arizona for the rest of the week. I have a suspicion it might be for him to undermine my project." Rose plopped down in a chair and sighed. "I put him in a bad spot, but he knew I was working for Alec."

"His being away will give you both time to settle this. And if I know you, you'll be just fine."

Rose smiled at her. "How'd you get to be so smart?"

Lily laughed. "I've had plenty of experience with disappointment. Don't worry, Rose. It'll all work out. Now that we all have some time on our hands, how would you like to help me look for possible places to live? I've decided to move here. I'm just praying I can get my sister to agree to come here too."

"I'd love to look at places with you," she said. "I'm thinking of moving my business here. I'm going to be meeting with various people in the community to see what connections I can make for my consulting business as well as my blog."

Smiling with delight, Lily clapped her hands. "It would be so much fun if you moved here too. Let's get started right now."

"First, let's go to lunch, all three of us. After all our hard work, we deserve a little fun. Where's Willow?"

Rose got up and headed into the house. Willow was in the kitchen talking to her mother.

"Sorry to interrupt. Willow, can you join Lily and me for lunch? We're going to celebrate my presentation."

Willow made a face and shook her head. "Sorry, I can't. Mitchell has called a meeting with Brent, Trace, and me. I heard you talking to Lily. What's up?"

Rose filled her in. "So, it looks like we all might be in Palm Desert longer than we'd thought. Nice, huh?"

Willow smiled. "Yes. And, Rose, don't worry about Hank. He'll come through for you."

"I wish," said Rose.

"He will; I just know it."

Rose studied her. "Is that the sixth sense you once told me about?"

Willow chuckled. "Maybe. Sometimes I'm just right about things."

Still smiling, Rose headed to her room. No matter what happened, she was feeling more and more at home in the desert.

For the next few days, Rose concentrated on the positive things happening in her life. She and Lily had looked at various places for Lily to live, and Rose realized that if she decided on making the move to Palm Desert, she'd have plenty of choices for herself. Better yet, she'd had a satisfying conversation with Alec, who was ecstatic about everything she'd done for him.

As days went by without hearing from Hank, memories of being with him crept into her mind, filling her with longing. How many times had they told one another how right their relationship felt? She tried to tell herself that if he'd decided to step away from their relationship, it was for the best. But each time she thought of it, her heart ached.

As the week drew to a close, Rose was surprised by a phone call from Nikki.

"Hi, how are you?" she automatically responded to Nikki's greeting.

"Fine, thanks," Nikki said in a straightforward way that caught her attention. "I happen to be in town, and I'm wondering if you could meet me for lunch. In fact, I'm staying at Dad's house while he's away. Can you meet me here? I've ordered some food from Tico's to be delivered around noon."

"That sounds nice. Thanks for thinking of me," Rose replied, curious to know why Nikki had returned to Palm Desert so soon. She was due to go on vacation with a friend. Maybe her plans had changed.

"Okay, see you then. You know where the house is," said Nikki.

"Yes, I do," said Rose, checking her watch. "I'll see you shortly."

As she freshened up, she thought of the dinner she'd shared with Hank and Nikki. She'd had an enjoyable time and felt she'd made a sweet connection to Nikki. Unlike her sister, Sam, Nikki was open and kind. It would be lovely to see her again.

When she pulled up to the front of Hank's house, she drew a deep breath. It hurt seeing the place again, not knowing if she'd share more times here with Hank. Telling herself to be strong, she got out of the car, walked through the open front gate, and knocked on the door.

The door swung open, and Sam stood at the threshold.

Startled, Rose took a step back. "Where's Nikki? I'm supposed to meet her here."

"Nikki and I tricked you. I wanted to meet with you, but we weren't sure you'd agree to it after the way I acted toward you. I had her call you from Atlanta." She stepped back from the door. "Won't you please come in? We need to talk."

Still surprised by all that was happening, Rose walked inside and drew a deep breath as memory hit her hard.

Sam took hold of her hand and led her to the couch in the living room. "Please sit. There's something I have to say to you."

Rose studied the flush of color on Sam's cheeks, lowered herself onto the couch, and faced her, aware of how awkward Sam felt.

"I got a call from Dad earlier this week. He sounded miserable. Apparently, there's been some sort of disagreement at work between the two of you. I didn't let him explain all the details, details I don't need to know. But I did tell him that if he walked away from you, I'd never forgive myself for once being the cause of friction between you when I opposed the relationship. Nikki and I have talked. We agree we've never seen Dad happier. It's as if you've given him a whole new life, one that he deserves. I think he's ... fearful."

"What do you mean?"

"Loving someone, allowing yourself to be vulnerable is scary. He loves you. You love him too, don't you?"

With her throat thickened with tears, Rose couldn't squeeze out a reply. She nodded.

Sam wrapped an arm around her. "It pained me to realize that, but it's true. Rose, I hope you'll forgive me. I want you to be there for Dad and Leah. They already love you. I hope in time you'll accept me."

Rose heard the sincerity in her voice, saw the anguish on Sam's face, and couldn't hold back the cry within her. As tears streamed down Rose's cheeks, Sam's arms stayed around her.

When Rose finally got control of herself, she lifted her face. "Thank you, Sam. Your support means everything to me."

"I've told him I'm coming to Arizona tomorrow to stay with him for the weekend. We'll have you go tonight instead. Knowing him as well as I do, I have no reason to believe he won't be thrilled to see you."

Rose hesitated, thinking of the pros and cons, and then nodded. "I'll do it."

Sam let out a long sigh. "I needed to hear that. Lily helped me book a flight for you this evening."

"Lily? She's in on it too?"

"Both Lily and Willow," said Sam. "You've got quite a *team*." She rolled her eyes. "Gawd! I sound like Dad."

Rose laughed. "It sounds good, believe me."

"Until it's time to get ready, won't you join me for lunch?"
Rose smiled. "I'd be honored." She held out her arms.
Sam went into them without hesitation.

"I can see why Dad loves you..." Sam said, at the same time as Rose said, "Your father has every right to be proud of you."
They pulled away and smiled at one another.

Later, as they ate lunch, Sam confided she might be newly pregnant again, but she wasn't mentioning it to anyone else until she was sure she was healthy, especially since the doctor had told her to wait before trying again. They exchanged anecdotes on times spent with Hank, and then Rose talked about building her business and how she'd come to start the blog.

The hours flew by as they made an effort to know one another. And later, when it was time for Rose to leave to prepare for her trip, the two of them hugged again.

"Good luck with everything," Sam said, standing on the curb, watching Rose pull away.

Excitement filled Rose as she made her way back to Alec's house. It would be wonderful to see Hank again, and with Sam's and Nikki's blessings, she felt as if everything was all right again.

Lily and Willow greeted her.

"Better get ready for your trip. You don't have too much time left. We need to get you to the airport early to make sure you get through security," said Lily.

"We booked you a first-class seat," said Willow. "This is a big deal."

"It was so sweet of Hank's daughter to play matchmaker,"

said Lily following Rose into her room.

"Wasn't she the one who was so rude?" asked Willow, joining them.

Rose nodded and sat on the bed and let out a sigh. "Both of his daughters want this to work with their father and me."

"Okay, let's see about your wardrobe," said Lily. "We want you to look especially beautiful." She placed Rose's suitcase on top of the bed and began looking through the closet.

At the sound of the doorbell, Willow said, "I'll get it. Mom is gone." She hurried out of the room.

"This one," said Lily, holding up the sleeveless turquoise dress that was Rose's favorite. "That's what you should wear tonight for dinner."

"I like it too," came a deep voice from the doorway.

Lily gasped.

Rose swiveled around to find Hank standing there, his gaze fixed on her.

"Why aren't you in Arizona?" Rose asked, stunned by his appearance.

"Where are you going?" he responded, looking at the suitcase.

Lily dropped the dress on the bed, hurried out of the room, and closed the door behind her.

Rose gaped at Hank, still trying to realize he was actually here with her. "I thought Sam was coming to see you in Arizona."

"I made arrangements for Rob to join her there," said Hank. "Where were you going?"

"To be with you in Arizona," she responded.

Hank chuckled and then reached for her.

In his arms, laughter, the kind born of pure happiness, rolled out of her. Hank joined in, his bass voice ringing low.

When they stepped apart, Rose said, "What a crazy mix-up! But I'm so glad you're here."

His gaze reached inside her. "What we had between us was too special to let anything come between us. Work is work. But love is love, and that's most important of all. I love you, Rose, and I want us to be together. Now and always."

Rose's heart stopped and then leaped to catch up. "Are you asking me to marry you?"

"Yes, I am. But there's just one problem. I left the ring in Arizona. It was too late to go back for it after I left in a rush to catch my flight. Can you wait a couple of days?"

Rose broke into more laughter. "This is even crazier, but I promise to wait."

He drew her into his arms again and held her close. "I love you more than you know. Leah would have me say, I love you to the moon and back. But, Rose, it's so much more than that. Without you, I'm nothing, just a spot in the universe."

Rose reached up and caressed his face. "You're everything to me."

"I love you, Rose, my Desert Rose," he whispered in her ear before his lips met hers.

After a weekend of proving to one another how right their decision was, they waited at Hank's house for Sam and Rob to join them. When Sam heard about the missing ring, she insisted she and Rob deliver the ring in person. Hank then called Nikki, and she agreed to fly in for a few days with Leah so the whole family could be together for the celebration.

That evening, with everyone having fun together, the house came alive. Rose stood outside and watched the family playing in the pool, fulfilled in a way that was brand new to her. Not only would she have Hank in her life, but she'd also have an entire family. Overwhelmed by the love she felt for all of them, she felt tears blur her vision. It took her a moment to realize Hank was kneeling in front of her.

"Rose, will you marry me? We all love you so much." He held open a small, black velvet box.

She stared at the large round diamond surrounded by smaller ones and clasped a hand to her mouth. It was the most beautiful ring she'd ever seen, not because of its size, but because it meant so much.

"Well?"

"Yes. Of course, I'll marry you. I love you, Hank." She looked at the family gathered around them. "I love you all!"

"Welcome to the *team*," said Sam.

Rose was still laughing as Hank stood and swept her up into his arms.

Thank you for reading *The Desert Flowers – Rose*. If you enjoyed this book, please help other readers discover it by leaving a review on Amazon, Goodreads, BookBub, or your favorite site. It's such a nice thing to do.

Enjoy an excerpt from my book, *The Desert Flowers – Lily*, Book 2 of the Desert Sage Inn Series.

CHAPTER ONE
LILY

In the early morning light on this March day in Palm Desert, California, Lily Weaver jogged in nice, easy steps on the path beside the Desert Sage Inn golf course. Her life, which had seemed so settled, had recently gone through a dramatic shift. Alec Thurston, her former employer and lover, was dying and had asked her to leave her job in New York and come to his home in California to help with the sale of the inn and its transition to the buyers, The Blaise Hotel Group. Here, she'd formed friendships with Rose Macklin and Willow Sanchez, two other women he'd asked to help him as well. Alec called them the Desert Flowers. They had separate jobs to help Alec, a man they each dearly loved.

Rose was working with a consultant for the Blaise Group to ensure that all social media and other PR going forward did nothing to destroy the panache of the upscale inn Alec had worked so hard to create.

Willow was working opposite the two young men in the hotel company's ownership family who were vying for the position of managing the inn after the sale went through.

She herself, as someone who had once been Alec's assistant, was on hand to take careful notes of meetings and to oversee and control the paperwork involved while the hotel company did property inspections, market research, and other due diligence activities. She worked alongside Brian Walden, another consultant hired by the Blaise Group to head their transition team.

As she followed the path by the golf course, she admired both the greens and the desert landscape. Some thought the bland colors of the desert were boring. She loved seeing sandy, rocky areas accented by green cacti and a variety of desert flowers. It made each color seem special. Hummingbirds were in abundance, their tiny bodies airborne by the constant fluttering of their wings, allowing them to hover about the bright flowers among the growth. In the distance, snow-capped mountains glistened in the sun, adding color to the purple-gray hue of their textured surfaces.

Hearing footsteps behind her, she turned to see Brian approaching. They sometimes met in the morning as they were jogging. At one time she'd entertained hopes of his being more than a co-worker. On their one so-called date, they'd ended up meeting a whole group working at the Desert Sage Inn, and he'd made it clear that this gathering was all business. Since then, she'd kept her distance. But despite telling herself not to dream foolishly, those secret hopes still lingered.

As he moved toward her, she observed his thick brown hair, handsome, athletic body and the ease at which he handled his prosthetic lower left leg. Brian was the sort of man she hoped to marry someday —kind, thoughtful, and smart.

"Morning!" Brian said, coming to a stop beside her. "How's it going? I haven't seen you in a while. Keeping busy with Alec?"

"Actually, I've been waiting for you to call a meeting. As lovely as it is to be here, I like to feel as if I'm doing my job."

"Ah, well, things have been put on hold while details are

being worked on for the conversion of Desert Sage Inn to be the lead property in the new Corona Collection. I've missed those meetings myself." He smiled at her.

Her heart rate kicked up. That smile was lethal. Telling herself to be professional, she said, "I'm thinking of taking up Bennett Williams' offer for me to apply for a job in his law office. Part-time, of course, until the sale of the inn takes place. I'd still help with that and any other projects Alec might have for me."

"So, you've really decided to move here?" Brian said, his hazel eyes drilling into her.

"Yes," she said. "I've already put my condo in New York State up for sale. I still have to convince my sister to move here, but the rest is underway."

"I'm scouting around for places to live here on at least a part-time basis. At the moment, Austin is still home."

She gazed up at him thinking Texas suited a big guy like him. She could even imagine him in a Stetson.

"I'd better go," Brian said. "Don't worry, I'll let you know when the next big meeting takes place. And if you need any help getting that job with Bennett Williams, call me. He owes me."

"Thanks." She lifted her hand to say goodbye as he jogged away. His steel blade made a distinctive sound as it hit the pavement in syncopation with his other foot. She sighed. The man was dreamy.

Lily watched him for a moment and then headed back to Alec's house where she and the other Flowers were living. Life here was so pleasant. Her childhood had been tough with an absentee father and an alcoholic mother who was distant, even cruel, a lot of the time. She'd been forced to be strong and self-sufficient even when she had the care of her sister, ten years younger and the daughter of a different father. A teacher had given her some guidance, but pride had kept her from asking for more help, which is why as an adult she'd sometimes found it difficult to maintain relationships. Now, at forty-two, she was hoping to find the love she'd missed so much in her life. Alec had been the one to introduce her to a calm, secure, loving lifestyle. She longed to have that again.

She sighed and picked up speed. Enough of fairy tales about finding a prince. It was time to get real.

Back at the house, Lily freshened up and then went to talk to Alec. At one time, she'd hoped he'd ask her to marry him. But Alec had been honest when they started dating, telling her marriage was not part of it. She should've known he'd stay true to his word. He was that kind of man. But their relationship was a gift. He'd taught her to open her heart to love, to find respite from the chaos that had always surrounded her. Prior to that, she'd been cautious about letting a man into her life. God knew, she didn't have the example of a wise woman to follow. She'd never known her own father, and the men her mother had hung out with were unreliable creeps she'd never accept.

As she walked toward Alec's wing of the house, sadness filled her at the thought of him dying. She considered it a real honor that he'd trusted her, along with Rose and Willow, to help him get his hotel safely sold before he died. The Desert Flowers act was like that television show with the man and his three angels, *Charley's Angels,* on a mission to save the inn. Lily loved being part of it.

At the entrance to his private space, Lily knocked gently at the door and cracked it open.

"Alec?"

"Here," came a voice weakened by the cancer that was

slowly stealing his life.

Lily stepped into the living area to find him reclining on a lounge chair and smiling up at her. "Lily, my dear. How are you?"

Normally a large, rangy man with thick gray hair and startling blue eyes, a Sam Elliott look-alike, Alec's thin body and weakened state tore at Lily's insides.

She pulled a chair up next to his and took hold of his hand. "I've been wanting to talk to you. I'm left doing almost nothing while meetings have been put aside. Rose and Willow are very busy, but not me. I'm used to doing my share of work and am thinking of taking Bennett Williams' offer for me to come work for him on a part-time basis. With my upcoming move here, it might be wise to have work outside of the project for you. How would you feel about that?

Alec's blue-eyed gazed rested on her. "I think if it suits you, it's something you should do. Believe me, Bennett wouldn't ask you to work for him if he wasn't serious about it. He told me he was very impressed with you. And you couldn't find a nicer guy to work with. Not only is he my lawyer, he's a friend. He now has a young partner working with him. Another great guy."

"The transition period you hired us for is three months. But you know I'd be happy to stay for as long as you wish and do anything I can to help you."

"Yes, I know. Three months seemed like such a long time. Now, I'm trying to make it through these last two months before the sale goes through," said Alec. "Any day beyond that is an unexpected gift."

Tears filled Lily's eyes. "I wish this hadn't happened to you."

His lips curved into a crooked smile. "So, do I. But after I get through all this, I'll be with Conchita and the baby. At least, I hope I will."

Lily nodded. It was a well-known story that Alec's wife and baby had died in a house fire for which he'd always blamed himself. That's one reason he had vowed never to marry again. Some people thought it was twisted thinking, but Lily understood his devotion to them. He'd shown her what love could mean, and though she'd asked for and wanted much more from him, she knew deep down it wasn't ever going to happen. After he ended their relationship, he found her a job with a business associate in Phoenix and helped her move on with her life. But he could never erase the love and gratitude she felt for him.

Juanita appeared. "Hi, Lily. Time for your medicine, Alec."

Lily got to her feet and kissed Alec on the cheek. "Have a nice day. I hope to see you tonight." She moved the chair back into place. "See you later. 'Bye, Juanita."

Juanita gave her a smile and turned back to Alec. Juanita Sanchez was a cousin of Alec's wife, Conchita. She and her husband, Pedro, were Willow's parents and had worked for Alec for years. They were lovely people. Juanita and Pedro were exactly the kind of people Lily wished she'd had as parents.

Back in her room, Lily looked at her reflection in the mirror. She was of medium height with curves in all the right places—curves she'd once done her best to hide. Her shoulder-length, blond hair was highlighted by both her hairdresser and the desert sun. Freckles, few enough to be of interest, were sprinkled across her nose. She'd always thought she was drab. But Willow and Rose had helped her change—not only with her wardrobe but in believing in her self-worth.

Taking a deep breath, Lily called Bennett Williams' office and asked to speak to him. Her fingers were cold with nerves, and she almost dropped her phone. She was uncomfortable putting herself out there.

"Well, hello," said Bennett after her call went through. "I'm glad to hear from you. I hope you're calling about a job because I've just learned that one of the women in the office is going on maternity leave."

Lily's breath left her in a puff of surprise. Things didn't usually come that easily to her. "As a matter of fact, that's what I wanted to talk to you about. I've decided to stay in Palm Desert following my work for Alec and will need a job. May I make an appointment to meet with you?"

"Absolutely. Send me your resumé, and I'll have my assistant schedule a time for you to come into the office." He paused. "I'm glad you called Lily. As I mentioned to you earlier, I'm impressed with your work."

"Thank you." Lily ended the call and sat down on her bed, struggling to accept what had just happened. The arrangements had fallen into place so quickly it almost seemed as if it had been preordained. That, or maybe her luck had changed. Either way, she was going to update her resumé and send it along as soon as possible.

Two days later, Lily dressed carefully for her interview with Bennett and his staff. In New York, the law firm for whom she worked had insisted on conservative clothes. Here in the desert, Lily agreed with Rose and Willow that brighter colors were acceptable.

Her black skirt, white-on-white print blouse, and hibiscus-colored soft jacket looked both professional and light-hearted. Studying herself in the mirror, Lily smiled at the changes living here had made to her appearance. The tan on her skin and the lack of stress lines on her face made her appear younger than her age and healthier than she'd ever been.

When Lily walked out to the kitchen to face the inspection Willow and Rose were sure to give her, she felt confident.

"Wow! Look at you!" said Willow, smiling at her.

"You look terrific," Rose immediately agreed. "Good luck with the interview."

Lily smiled. "Thanks. For once, I'm not a nervous wreck. Bennett made it seem as if it were a mere formality. I'm hoping so, anyway."

"He'd be lucky to have you on his staff. How many texts and calls have you received from your old job in New York?" said Rose.

Lily laughed and shook her head. "Too many. They keep promising to raise my salary if I come back. They increase the amount each time they call, but I finally told them I'm staying here no matter what they offer me."

"I'm so glad you are," said Willow. "Sarah is too."

Lily filled with pleasure. While Rose was spending time with Hank Bowers, the consultant the Blaise Group had hired and who was now her fiancé, she, Willow, and Sarah Jensen spent time in the evening together whenever they were all free. Sarah, a part-time assistant manager at the inn, was living at home with her parents and two-year-old son while her husband was serving in the military in Afghanistan. They'd quickly become friends. With this kind of support, Lily felt comfortable about her decision to move here. She hadn't yet chosen a place to live because she needed to sell her condo first. Her sister, Monica, who lived nearby her had promised to make sure the condo was ready for showings. So far, no luck, but Lily felt uncharacteristically optimistic.

Driving through the town, Lily bypassed the usual tourist places on Highway 111, turned onto Cook Street and easily found the law office of Williams and Kincaid. She parked the car and entered the modern building trying to stem the nervousness that threatened to break through her shell of calmness. She took the elevator to the third floor and exited into an attractive reception area. A young man smiled at her from behind a long desk.

"Good morning. May I help you?" he asked.

"I'm here to see Bennett Williams," she answered politely. "Lily Weaver."

He smiled. "Of course. I'll let Mr. Williams know you're here. May I get you something to drink? Water? Coffee?"

"Water would be nice," said Lily. "The weather has turned hot."

"It's going to stay that way for a few days," said the receptionist whose nameplate said *Jonathan Waite*. He left and returned with a small, chilled bottle of water, which he handed to her.

Right then, Bennett appeared in the reception area, filling the room with his presence and his booming, jovial voice. "Ah, Lily. I'm so glad to see you. Come on back to my office. We'll talk there."

Lily followed him down a hallway to a corner office whose windows looked out at a landscaped garden below. The fronds of nearby palm trees danced in the playful breeze. But it was the beautiful fountain sitting in a small pond that caught her attention. The free-form shape, like high desert boulders that had tumbled together, was the kind of thing she'd been researching for the Blaise Group's two hotels in Arizona—the hotels they hoped to bring into the Corona Collection of Fine Hotels.

"Something peaceful about water flowing, especially in a desert setting," said Bennett standing beside her.

"Yes. Very refreshing."

"Have a seat," said Bennett. "I'll chat with you, then I'll ask my partner to join us. Okay with you?"

"Sure," Lily said. Bennett, with his easy-going manner and lack of airs made her feel comfortable. She knew enough from being in a couple of meetings with him, though, to understand he was a stickler for detail, much like her old boss.

"As you probably are already aware, our firm deals with trusts and estates, probate, and civil litigation. We've been in business here for close to forty years. Our company is hands-on, which is why we maintain a small staff of ten. It's a close-knit group."

"I like the sound of that," said Lily. "Some law firms get so big you lose some of that close feeling."

Bennett looked over her resumé. "You've got an impressive background. I took the liberty of going ahead and getting a reference from the law firm you worked with in New York." He smiled. "They'd do anything to get you back."

"I know," said Lily. "But I've decided to stay here. I've put my condo in New York up for sale."

"Great." Bennett discussed what he was looking for, how he saw someone like her fitting into the office, quizzed her on strengths and weaknesses, and asked the normal new-hire questions.

Finally, he leaned back. "I'm more than satisfied. Let me call my partner and have him come meet you. His name is Craig Kincaid."

Lily nodded politely and waited while Bennett called him on the intercom. A low voice said, "Be right there, Ben."

Lily waited quietly for him to appear, imagining him as much of a cowboy as Bennett, whose brown cowboy boots were worn with age and activity. They and the turquoise and silver bolo tie around Bennett's neck against his crisp white shirt gave him an undeniable Southwestern flair.

A knock at the door signaled Craig's arrival. Lily turned to see a young, broad-shouldered man with caramel colored-hair studying her with a green-eyed gaze that made her catch her breath. Struggling to maintain her composure, Lily thought he was one of the most handsome young men she'd ever seen.

He came right over to her and shook her hand. "Pleased to meet you, Lily. I've heard a lot about you and have already reviewed your resumé."

The three of them sat together and talked for a while. Craig asked some of the same questions Bennett had, but she cheerfully answered them.

Finally, Craig rose and turned to her. "I'm satisfied by everything I've heard. I think you're going to make a nice addition to our staff, Lily."

She shook herself mentally. He looked like one of the heroes on the cover of an historical novel, one that showed a man in a kilt. That thought brought a flush of heat to her cheeks.

"Thank you," she finally managed to say. "I'm looking forward to it."

"You may occasionally be asked to help me out, but I have an assistant who's quite capable of taking care of me."

Bennett chuckled. "Loretta Morales is the boss of not only Craig, but the entire office. In fact, I thought you and Loretta should have a chance to talk. Do you mind?"

"Not at all," said Lily.

"Why don't I show you the way? Her office is next to mine." Craig stood and waited while Lily got to her feet.

"Thanks," said Bennett. "After you're through with Loretta, you and I will go to lunch and make final arrangements."

"That sounds nice," said Lily, hoping Bennett hadn't noticed her reaction to Craig.

Leaving the office, she walked beside Craig down a hallway,

studying his easy gait from the corner of her eye.

With her short, comfy body and gray hair pulled back into a bun at the back of her head, Loretta was the image of an old-fashioned grandmother. Her dark eyes sparkled as she got to her feet. Names were exchanged, and Loretta greeted Lily with a quick, firm handshake.

"This woman is the one I can't live without," said Craig, with a teasing smile. "I'd ask her to marry me, but she's already taken."

Loretta's laugh rose from her belly. "No woman would ever put up with your shenanigans. Not me, for sure." Still smiling, she turned to Lily. "This young man has to learn to make up his mind. Every woman in the area is after him, but he still hasn't settled down."

Craig's fair-skinned cheeks turned pink, but he gamely nodded. "I'll know when the right one comes along." He winked at Lily. "Loretta treats me like a son."

Loretta's expression turned serious. "Craig's mother and I were best friends. She died way too young. But I'm here to take over for her."

His face softened with affection. "Yeah, Mom would be pleased. I'll leave you two alone to talk. Then Ben is going to take Lily to lunch."

"Okay," said Loretta. "Sounds like a plan."

As Craig walked into his office, Loretta waved Lily to a chair in front of her desk. "Have a seat, and let's get to know one another a bit. Bennett already had me look over your resumé, but I like to meet people face-to-face, see what they're all about."

"I agree," said Lily. "So far, I like what I see here. How long have you been working in the office?"

"For over twenty years. Ben, Alec Thurston, my husband, Ricardo, and Craig's dad, Ken, play golf together. They became friends back when Bennett was growing his business and my husband was a professional golfer. When Ben knew I was looking for work, he suggested I give his office a try. I've been here ever since. The time's coming, though, when I'll want to retire." She leaned forward. "Tell me a bit about yourself. I hear you're helping Alec out. How's that going?"

"It's a sad time for me. Alec is a friend. I hate the thought of him dying. We dated for a couple of years. I moved to Arizona and then to New York to help out my sister who has a precious three-year-old daughter whom I adore."

"Ah, so you like children?" Loretta said, smiling.

"Very much. I'd still like to try for a child of my own," Lily said, then wondered why on earth she'd say something like this on a job interview. It was just that Loretta made her feel so comfortable.

"I've got three boys, all decent men," said Loretta with obvious pride. "I count Craig as one of them. Ben tells me you've decided to relocate here. May I ask why?"

Lily hesitated, not knowing if this was some sort of trick question. "In the time I've been here, I've been happier than I've been in years. I've learned to enjoy being outdoors, have already made great friends, and I want a better lifestyle." She cleared her throat and recalled the words she'd rehearsed with Rose. "I'm very good at my job and can work anywhere. I choose to do it here."

Loretta nodded. "Smart answer." She got to her feet. "I'm sure we're going to get along just fine. I mostly work for Craig, and you'll be on Ben's team, but it's important for all of us to be able to work together. Welcome to the group."

"Thank you so much," said Lily, feeling as if she'd just joined some kind of exclusive club.

# # #

About the Author

A **USA** *Today* **Best Selling Author**, Judith Keim is a hybrid author who both has a publisher and self-publishes. Ms. Keim writes heart-warming novels about women who face unexpected challenges, meet them with strength, and find love and happiness along the way. Her best-selling books are based, in part, on many of the places she's lived or visited and on the interesting people she's met, creating believable characters and realistic settings her many loyal readers love. Ms. Keim loves to hear from her readers and appreciates their enthusiasm for her stories.

Ms. Keim enjoyed her childhood and young-adult years in Elmira, New York, and now makes her home in Boise, Idaho, with her husband, Peter, and their two domineering dachshunds, Winston and Wally, and other members of her family.

While growing up, she was drawn to the idea of writing stories from a young age. Books were always present, being read, ready to go back to the library, or about to be discovered. All in her family shared information from the books in general conversation, giving them a wealth of knowledge and vivid imaginations.

"I hope you've enjoyed this book. If you have, please help other readers discover it by leaving a review on Amazon, Bookbub, Goodreads, or the site of your choice. And please check out my other books:

The Hartwell Women Series
The Beach House Hotel Series
The Fat Fridays Group
The Salty Key Inn Series
Seashell Cottage Books
The Chandler Hill Inn Series
The Desert Sage Inn Series
Soul Sisters at Cedar Mountain Lodge
The Sanderling Cove Inn Series
The Lilac Lake Inn Series

"ALL THE BOOKS ARE NOW AVAILABLE IN AUDIO on Audible, iTunes, Findaway, Kobo and Google Play! So fun to have these characters come alive!"

Ms. Keim can be reached at **www.judithkeim.com**

And to like her author page on Facebook and keep up with the news, go to: **https://bit.ly/3acs5Qc**

To receive notices about new books, follow her on Book Bub: **http://bit.ly/2pZBDXq**

And here's a link to where you can sign up for her periodic newsletter! **http://bit.ly/2OQsb7s**

She is also on Twitter @judithkeim, LinkedIn, and Goodreads. Come say hello!

Acknowledgements

Thank you to the staff at the Historical Society and Museum of Palm Desert for taking the time to talk to us and make the history of the area come alive.

And, as always, I am eternally grateful to my team of editors, Peter Keim and Lynn Mapp, my book cover designer, Lou Harper, and my narrator for Audible and iTunes, Angela Dawe. They are the people who take what I've written and help turn it into the book I proudly present to you, my readers!

I also thank my coffee group of writers who listen and encourage me to keep on going. Thank you, Peggy, Lynn, Cate, Nikki Jean, and Megan. Love you!

Made in the USA
Middletown, DE
01 June 2024